I0523779

STELLA'S NEXT ACT

KAREN FARRELL

Published in 2025

Text and copyright © Karen Farrell 2025

All rights reserved. No part of this publication may be reproduced in any form or by any means without prior permission of the author/publisher.

All characters and events in this publication are fictitious, any resemblance to real persons, living or dead, or any event past or present are purely coincidental.

This book contains references to assault, mental health, and panic attacks.

Title: Stella's Next Act
Author: Karen Farrell

ISBN: 978-0-6458562-5-5 (pbk)
ISBN: 978-0-6458562-4-8 (ebk)

For anyone chasing a dream — this is for you. May
your journey inspire and empower you, and your
dreams unfold in ways you never imagined.

CHAPTER 1

Sydney, 2000

For Stella Longhurst, every day in her twenties, even in the most unforgiving dregs of winter, felt like the first day of spring. She never checked the weather forecast because it didn't matter what the day might bring; she dove into each day with zeal and devotion, constantly striving for her dream of being an actress – rain, hail, or shine.

She lived as though her life were one continuous, uninterrupted movie, performed with no retakes, drawing on novelist Rose Tremain's advice against treating life as a dress rehearsal. Stella's confidence was unshakeable; she knew her direction and had no need of a compass.

Immediately upon graduating from school, she landed a job as a junior publicist at the Australian TV Network, Channel 7, in Sydney. Their publicity manager had immediately liked Stella's chutzpah. At the time, she had been working towards being a full-time actress, reasoning that until she received her big acting break, at least she'd still be working in the entertainment industry.

By day, she masqueraded as a television executive respected for her savvy in promoting highly rated television shows and the national and international celebrities who populated them. By night, she was a thespian. For nearly a decade, she lived on air and enthusiasm, driven to act while juggling her work as a publicist and her dream of being an actress.

Except for one senior publicist, who scoffed at the idea Stella could be dedicated to a role as a publicist while also pursuing acting, nobody at the network considered it a conflict of interest. No one cared that Stella spent her evenings treading the boards – in fact, her colleagues were often her most loyal fans.

***

Stella flicked a long strand of hair over her shoulder, her perfume trailing through the air as she strode towards the entrance to the Channel 7 car park.

Then, as she crossed a speedhump, her shiny black stiletto caught the hem of her trousers and she stumbled, narrowly avoiding landing flat on her face and dropping her breakfast and a tray of coffees in the other hand.

'Someday,' she muttered as she regained her upright position, directing a baleful glare at the stretch of black bitumen and its innocent white lines. As a junior publicist, she wasn't yet privileged enough to park inside the station's car park; earning that right would take at least another five years.

If she made it that long.

Pink and orange caught her eye as she neared security, and she paused to admire the tulips lining the pathway to the doors. Trailing her fingers over the soft petals, she turned her face to the sun with a contented sigh and closed her eyes, a spidery web of veins tracing the fine skin of her eyelids.

Inhaling deeply, Stella flung her arms open, enjoying the breeze as it rippled under her silk shirt, puffing it outwards. The warm air made wisps of hair flutter and caressed the back of her neck.

She stopped at 7's security. 'Good morning, Bouncer Bruno!' she said cheerfully, pausing in front of the network's longest-serving security guard and flashing him a smile. Bruno had been waving celebrities, on-air presenters, and staff through security for a decade.

'You're looking extremely pleased with yourself,' Bruno said, 'and on the first day of spring, too.'

As always, he ignored Stella's lack of an identification badge; she hadn't worn one since she started working at the network, and he'd never mentioned it. She hated the thing. The combination of plastic and bright red, her least favourite colour, clashed with almost everything in her closet.

'It's the opening night of my play, Bruno,' she said, and handed Bruno a flat white coffee, a treat he'd come to expect from her every Friday. 'I'm so excited I could scream.'

Not that you could tell from looking at her; she might be jumping up and down inside, but she'd never let her emotions take over the face she presented to the world.

'Tonight is the night!' Bruno exclaimed. 'Wow! This play came around quickly.' Laughing, he added, 'I might start calling you Audrey Hepburn soon.'

Stella immediately took a few steps back from the security desk and paused for several heartbeats, assuming centre stage. She slid her cat-eye Ray-Bans halfway down the bridge of her nose, maintaining eye contact with Bruno. Then elegantly shuffled forward, just as Audrey Hepburn's Holly Golightly had, in order to peer through the window of Tiffany's in the dreamy opening scene of *Breakfast at Tiffany's*.

'This evening, I'm giving the world Meg McGrath from *Crimes of the Heart*,' Stella said, pulling her croissant from its paper bag and daintily taking a bite of it, then washing it down with coffee, unabashedly relishing in Bruno likening her to Audrey Hepburn. After a moment, she set her coffee and pastry on the security desk and adjusted imaginary elbow-length black gloves like Holly Golightly's, and fleetingly wished she'd worn her pencil dress that day, which would have fit the character far more convincingly.

'Senior moment,' Bruno said, excited to receive Stella's undivided attention. 'I couldn't remember the damn name of the play.'

Stella grinned as she picked up her coffee and croissant and headed to the foyer for the lifts. 'Hey,' she called over her shoulder, 'don't be a slack arse. Book your tickets and bring your wife to the play!' She blew him a kiss as she stepped into the lift, cramming the rest of the croissant into her mouth, not noticing the slivers of pastry that had fallen onto her shirt.

'We're performing the play at the Apex Theatre,' she shouted, to make sure he heard.

Bruno sprang to his feet and declared, 'The wife and I will be there. Cheers for the coffee!'

Stella hummed absently to herself, sipping her coffee, as she waited for the lift to arrive at the third floor. As she walked into the publicity department, she spotted a bottle of champagne on her desk, and for the first time that day, a flurry of butterflies poked at her stomach. She pulled off the card as she sat down and read,

Go get 'em tonight, kiddo. We know you'll be brilliant in this role and couldn't be prouder.

Love,
Dad and Mum

She switched on the four televisions opposite her desk – there was a dedicated TV for each competitor station – and turned up the volume on the television airing music clips. Grinning, Stella spun her office chair around, her feet hovering off the floor as she silently sang the words to David Bowie's *Heroes*.

For Stella Longhurst, life could only have been better if she were living her life as a full-time actress.

***

Stella's high school drama teacher, Mrs Brown, had believed in her ability, frequently encouraged her to take up a career in the performing arts, and significantly influenced her decision to pursue acting. Mrs Brown had often favoured Stella for the lead role in school productions, casting her as Cecily Cardew in *The Importance of Being Earnest* and Josephine March in *Little Women*. She had the ability. Mrs Brown had told her more than once. That *something* that marked those who could succeed.

Just before Stella graduated, Mrs Brown made a point of pulling her aside. 'Stella,' she said, 'you have natural talent, with aplomb aplenty to succeed. Don't waste your gift. Burn your talent until it's reduced to ash, dear girl.'

On that memorable day, as she took in Mrs Brown's advice and was enveloped in her teacher's generously applied peppery cologne, Stella had been captivated by the blue eyeshadow highlighting her teacher's hooded eyes. Bette Davis' eyes, she'd thought, and wondered if anyone had ever compared her teacher to Diva Davis previously. As a budding actress, Stella constantly observed people – studying their mannerisms, clothes, make-up, gait, and character traits, tucking these observations away for future reference.

Stella had straightened her posture, standing as tall as she could as she prepared to reply to her teacher's directive. Pausing dramatically before speaking, hoping her response might make her favourite teacher proud, she said, 'Mrs Brown, I vow never to be a 70-year-old woman sitting in a rocking chair and wondering if I should have pursued my dream. I will fight until my last breath to realise my dream – to succeed as an actress.'

In that moment, Mrs Brown's pride and approval had been everything.

And then a director and a fellow actor irrevocably changed Stella's life, bringing her cherished acting career to an abrupt halt and sending her into years of endless numbness.

Many years later, all Stella could think was – so much for her promise to Mrs Brown.

CHAPTER 2

Sydney, 2010

On Saturday mornings, budding actors attended classes at Central Casting in Sydney's eastern suburbs. They huddled into a tiny room without knowing in advance which characters they'd play or which random movie scenes they'd perform.

So small was the rehearsal room that the actors fought for a position on the couch next to the director; mostly, they ended up crammed onto the floor with knees pressed to their chests or legs crossed, overlapping one another. The space thrummed with intensity and the competitive energy of so many actors in one place.

It only took one Saturday morning to end Stella's dream of being an actress.

At the time, there was no indication of just how awful the day would become. She started out the day on a good note, performing a scene from *Pulp Fiction* to the praise of Jay Styler, their cantankerous and difficult to impress director. Improvisation could be a brutal exercise in dismantling a student in front of their peers – the ways a student walked, talked, and even breathed were all up for scrutiny. Some weeks, Stella felt acid burning a hole in her stomach for several days leading up to those Saturday morning rehearsals. Jay instilled fear of public humiliation and retribution in his students, and being early in the new millennium, actors had no psychological or mental health safety nets. Many actors who took Jay's class became emotional collateral, suffering from acute anxiety, depression, or self-doubt, due to his stringent demands – demands that many students tolerated until the day they finally broke.

Stella personally believed that Jay was bitter that he'd never broken into the big-league. The extent of his acting career consisted of acting in several low-performing Australian TV shows, and once it became clear that his skills weren't going to cut it, Jay took to directing and teaching acting classes instead. With his acting days behind him, his singular life's purpose transformed into taking his acidity out on young, ambitious actors and actresses, hiding behind the excuse that the acting industry was oversupplied and needed culling of the less talented. Outwardly, Jay declared that it was his job to separate the wheat from the chaff and to discourage less adept or archetypally unattractive actors from pursuing a career in the performing arts. Jay even took joy in humiliating actors he knew were innately talented.

Jay encouraged the actors to massage his feet between scenes, and the truth was that he and his girlfriend Gabriela, 15 years his junior, were lucky not to be sued for psychologically torturing impressionable young actors and actresses.

Each week in class, Jay pushed Stella to test her ability and forced her to play parts she'd never be interested in auditioning for. On this particular Saturday, Jay instructed her to play a housewife selling a cleaning product in a television commercial.

'Look, Jay,' Stella said, mustering up her courage, 'This is not me. It isn't exactly a complex role. Can't you give me a role I might actually have a chance of performing?' Stella clamped her knees together and sat back in her seat before continuing, 'Do we have any scenes from the *Pride and Prejudice* film adaptation with Rosamund Pike as Jane Bennet?'

Jay stared at her for a long moment before saying, 'You're above auditioning for TV commercials?'

'Success as an actor is largely based on the roles you say no to,' Stella said, 'rather than the roles you say yes to.'

Jay snorted. 'You're not that successful yet, Stella. If you ever reach the level of success where you get to choose your own roles, *then* you can raise your casting preferences with me.' He held up a finger to forestall Stella's objection. 'If you want any of that to happen, you need to show me your range as an actress. You can't afford to be precious.'

'I'm not being precious –'

'If your agent puts you up for a dog food commercial,' Jay interrupted, his voice sharp, 'you will do it! You'll audition for soap operas. You'll do whatever you have to if you want to have a chance in hell of making it. Or have you forgotten that Naomi Watts did a commercial about giving up dinner with Tom Cruise for her mum's lamb roast?' He jabbed a finger at Stella's chest and said, 'You are not above anything, Stella. You want to be an actor? You damn well must work for it.'

It was that day, that Saturday morning that Jay ripped into her, that Stella's acting career came to an end. That day, Jay finally pushed Stella too far.

The morning's spirit-lifting success of the *Pulp Fiction* scenes was overlooked by Jay's angry rant. If Stella had known the day was only going to get worse, she might have left early – and saved herself a world of misery.

Instead, she stayed – and found herself in a scene that would have been cringingly intimate with anyone, she was unfortunate enough to be paired with Steve Crosley, a showy guy with a handsomely sized ego and an actor that none of the women liked working opposite. From previous experience, Stella knew that Steve had a habit of clumsily blundering through scenes, his every step shadowed by the overwhelming scent of Le Male aftershave. It didn't seem to register that he had no natural acting ability. As best as she could figure, Stella thought someone must've told Steve to take acting classes to meet women.

For some of the actresses, it was the first time they had been asked to play a prostitute. This particular scene, from an indie film Stella could never remember the name of, was intimate, requiring deep trust and clear communication between the actors. Acting required a silent contract of human decency between artists – don't take a scene out of context and don't take it too far, particularly when the scene in question was a sex scene. Steve Crosley had missed the memo on showing respect for other people.

'Lucky you,' a fellow actress, Susan, whispered to Stella, her tone sympathetic. 'Getting to work with Bruce Willis wannabe today!'

'He'll make a great stuntman if ever his West End thespian career ends,' Stella said, and then added, 'Ugh. He's awful. Maybe if I pretend he's Sean Penn, it might get me through the scene.'

'Sean Penn, really?' Susan laughed. 'He doesn't do it for me. I guess your Sean Penn is my Eric Bana. Anyway, better you than me!'

'Thanks,' Stella muttered, as Susan flounced off to her own group scene in another room. 'That's…so unhelpful.' She flicked through the summary and her lines. As the prostitute, she was to request upfront payment for her services.

The scene started off okay, nothing out of the ordinary. And then, on her knees and midway through unzipping Steve's pants, Stella stopped, looked up at the face looming over her, and in her best urban Brooklyn accent said, 'Yew gotta pay me first, before we do it.'

When they'd rehearsed the scene, the actions to this point had been consented to by both actors, and the scene was meant to immediately end after Stella's words. Turned out, Steve Crosley had other intentions.

With his legs spread wide and pelvis pushed forward, Steve paused for a heartbeat, looking wildly down at Stella. In that moment, he became a betrayer of trust. He took a thick section of her long hair, and as he wrapped it around his hand, layer upon layer, she realised with horror that he was subjecting her to his control – and with her hair around his fist, there was nothing she could do.

Steve-the-defiler bent and clamped his knees around Stella's shoulders, using her hair to pull her head back so hard that her knees lifted off the ground. Her face slammed hard into Steve's pelvis; the smell of cheap washing powder stung her nostrils as he pumped her head backwards and forwards in short, sharp blasts against his jeans. Every time her mouth crashed against his jeans, she could feel his firmness and taste bile at the back of her throat.

Saliva leaked out of Stella's mouth, forming an ejaculation-like streak across the front of Steve's jeans that she glimpsed every time her head came forward and her lips grazed the open zip.

The visual apparently giving him an excuse to go completely off script under the flimsiest of reasons, Steve exclaimed, 'Look at what you made me do, you filthy whore!' As he spoke, he continued to force Stella's mouth against his zip and past to his warm underpants, her spittle an angry white slash against a red that that matched the colour of her face, chest, and neck.

Realising as she struggled against his hand that Jay wasn't going to call 'Cut!', Stella drew her right arm back as far as she could and slapped Steve repeatedly against the small of his back. The moment his grip loosened, she wrestled free and lurched backwards as she stumbled to her feet.

'Arsehole!' she shrieked, dragging the back of her hand across her mouth. She looked at Jay, hoping for an intervention, and instead encountered not a glimpse of support or acknowledgement of what had happened.

'What's your problem?' Steve demanded, dusting his hands together. Stella watched as strands of her hair drifted from his hands to the floor. 'You said to make the scene realistic!'

The beads of sweat on Steve's forehead told Stella that he was culpable on a level he wasn't willing to admit. She knew, looking at his face, that he knew there had been no agreement to perform the scene this way during rehearsals.

For a moment Stella looked around, hoping for support; then, realising nobody was coming to her defence, she managed to yell, 'Fucking pervert!' The walls of the tiny rehearsal room closed in and squeezed against Stella's heaving chest. The more she tried to breathe, the less air seemed to fill her lungs. 'That isn't acting,' she managed to get out. 'You just assaulted me!'

She wanted to run from the room, but her legs wouldn't move, like she was trapped on the marshmallow stairs from *A Nightmare on Elm Street*. She could feel sweat dripping down her back, the clammy wetness of her sweat-soaked underpants; for a moment she thought maybe she'd weed herself. She pressed a hand firmly against her chest, trying to anchor herself in the knowledge that her heart wasn't going to burst free from under her skin, and noted how her kneecaps jangled against the bottom of her thighs. Her legs shook so badly she was surprised she was still upright.

When neither Steve nor Jay said anything, Stella turned to scan her fellow actors; their shocked faces confirmed that she wasn't imagining things; she wasn't overreacting – the incident had actually just happened, and it was very, very wrong.

Her eyes snagged on Susan, who was shaking her head in wide-eyed disgust. 'This is a circus, Jay,' Susan snapped. 'Kick Steve out! He's an animal – we're not on a goddamn porn set!'

Stella's heart thrashed about in her chest, like a fish caught on a hook, fighting for its life; feeling as though she was suffocating. She looked to Jay, hoping for understanding. Instead, she found a cold, unaffected man who looked over the rim of his glasses, his eyebrow raised, and then spoke the words that would irretrievably change Stella's life.

'When you're hot, you're hot,' he said, catching Stella's eyes, 'and when you're not, you're not.'

Jay's words rang so hard in Stella's head that they nearly perforated her eardrums. Those words told her that she should accept what had happened in the name of art. Those words told her that she was untalented and useless as an actress. Those words would haunt her for many years.

'Everyone, leave the room,' Jay barked, and then, seeing Stella shift her weight, added, 'Except Steve and Stella.' In silence, the actors filed out of the room. 'You, too, Susan,' he added. 'Wait in the other room.'

Susan slowly rose from her seat and shuffled out of the room, her eyes meeting Stella's in apology.

Even though the room was empty except for Stella, Steve, and Jay, it felt small enough to Stella to trigger a sense of claustrophobia.

'Take it from the top,' Jay said, looking down at his notes. 'This time, do the scene with the two of you standing at the start.'

Steve started the scene by pressing himself against Stella; she flinched, but was frozen, unable to move or intercede, too shocked to fight back as he blatantly edited the script, replying to her character's request for payment by saying, 'I don't gotta pay anything before we do it.'

Steve placed his hand on the back of Stella's head again, forcing her towards him.

Stella looked to Jay again, hoping the director would intercede – but he continued to turn a blind eye, supposedly in the service of art, to test her acting range. In that moment, realising Jay was willing to condone Steve's abuse to advance his actors, she broke.

Even as words couldn't escape her mouth, Stella charged up her jelly-like legs and mustered her courage to finally move, sprinting out of the room, down the stairs, and out the door of Central Casting.

She regained self-possession so many streets after that she had no idea where she was.

Wheezing as she dragged in breath after breath, she pulled herself upright and spotted a coffee shop on the corner. Stumbling inside, she bolted for the bathroom and locked the door behind her with fumbling, shaking fingers. Leaning back against the door, she sucked in deep breaths, trying to calm her pounding heart. Slowly, the echo of her heart in her ears began to fade as she came back to herself. Or as much of herself as she was anymore.

Slowly, afraid of what she might see, she inched closer to the blotchy mirror above the sink and peered at her reflection. The same blue eyes stared out at her, their usual wide-eyed curiosity dulled. Her lipstick was a garish slash across her face, reminiscent of a clown, her neat brown eyeliner and black mascara smudged and smeared around her eyes. She looked broken, and it terrified her.

Standing there, confronted by a reflection that was both her and not her, her world split between before and after. Stella could feel her dream of being an actress, a dream she'd held since she was eight years old, shattering into pieces too fragmented to piece back together. She'd never in her life experienced that kind of all-encompassing fear.

She thought she might be going insane. Perhaps she was.

CHAPTER 3

Northern New South Wales, June 2022

With her bedroom door shut behind her, Stella started to wriggle out of her jeans. The damn things were so tight it felt like they were glued to her legs, slicked down by sweat and making her feel two sizes larger than she was. She finally peeled them off her, annoyed at how they caught on her ankles, and sank down on the edge of her bed with a relieved sigh. Taking a deep breath, she wrestled her wraparound blouse over her head before discarding it onto the growing pile of clothes on the bed.

The jeans were a setback. An unfortunate one, as the cling-wrap feeling lingered as she tried on each new outfit. No matter what she put on, it felt like it was glued to her skin. Including the cotton dress she'd bought especially for her date, in the likelihood of pre-empting a clothes war.

Already late for her first date with Heath, each costume change only fuelled Stella's frustration, until she started to seriously consider cancelling the date.

There's still enough time to cancel without being rude. I could say I have an excruciating headache, or a relative had a stroke.

Taking a deep breath, Stella picked up her phone.

> Hey Heath, I'm so sorry, my younger sister just called. She urgently needs my help with something. I'm not sure what's happened but it sounds serious. Sorry, I can't make it.

She deleted the text and tried again.

> Hey Heath! OMG, I'm so sorry, I can't make it tonight. I have a heinous headache. I've been holding out to see if I felt better, although I'm concerned loud music will make it worse. Hope we can catch up another time soon.

A second before Stella pressed send on the text, a message from Heath flashed up on her phone.

> I just arrived. Every man and his dog are here. The cover band's great! Let me know when you're here and I'll come out to meet you.

'Shit. Damn it. Shit. Shit. Shit,' Stella said before typing a response to Heath's text.

> Cool. It sounds like it's a superb night in-the-making. I'll be there in 30!

Every pore in Stella's body clamoured for her to cancel, but Heath's enthusiasm propelled her to stop procrastinating and get dressed. After surveying the chaos of her wardrobe spread across her bed, she finally returned to the rust-coloured mini-dress she'd tried on four wardrobe changes before the clammy jeans and decided it would do. Superstition told her that the dress must do; it was inevitable that one ended up wearing the first outfit tried on.

Stella smoothed the front of her hair with a straightener and popped in hoop earrings. *This is utterly abortive*, she thought, staring into her mirror. *And invariably a waste of time.*

Taking a deep breath, she shifted gears, trying not to be defeatist.

Jesus, Stella... She pinched the bridge of her nose between her fingers. *There's no need to take it so seriously! It's only a date! Enjoy the music.*

With that, she escaped her bedroom and went to the kitchen. With a few minutes to spare before jumping in the car, she poured a small glass of wine and settled on the lounge.

On the bookshelf, a photo of herself performing in *Romeo and Juliet* years earlier captured her attention. It transported her back to her acting days, before the incident with Jay and Steve. In the play, the female actors in the production had performed all the male roles, inverting the Elizabethan stage tradition in which all roles would have been performed by men or boys. Stella had played Lord Capulet, Juliet's passionate and strong-willed father, to positive accolades in the *Sydney Morning Herald*'s arts review section.

She'd felt so stupid when she initially portrayed Capulet; about 60 years of age, the character was about as far from herself as she could imagine – an ailing and brusque male, debilitated by age and physical characteristics. The literal interpretation of Capulet – parading about with an exaggerated limp and verging on yelling the part – was clumsy. She was ever grateful to the director for his patience as she navigated the role, guiding her through the difference between showing and feeling emotion.

In the end, her performance of Capulet had earned the respect of her cast and crew and universally positive arts reviews. Her stint as Capulet quickly established her as a credible actress in the acting circles she found herself in, and she began to feel comfortable in the theatre world.

With each new play, the theatre became more her home – a joyful place where dialogue, different perspectives, and characters were dissected, where artists connected, escaped, and brought stories to life.

If she could measure, bottle, and sell the magic of theatre, she might…

Shit! Look at the time!

Stella finished the wine and bolted out the door, late for her first date with Heath.

CHAPTER 4

When Heath invited Stella to The Jezabels concert, she was delighted; she loved the Australian indie rock band.

She'd met him online a few weeks earlier. He met three of Stella's essential criteria: non-smoker, can spell, and tall. They had exchanged just enough messages that she felt comfortable suggesting they progress to a phone conversation – she wanted to hear his voice and feel his energy. Talking on the phone was critical: to make sure a guy who checked out on paper didn't have a voice like Mickey Mouse. As someone trained in voicework, Stella couldn't date someone without an engaging voice.

She had learned this dating rule a few months earlier, when she went on a date with a strapping fellow who could punctuate, spell, and respond to messages without delay, didn't use emojis, and was the actual age stated in his profile in real life: 43. He'd told her about the nervous tic, which she was fine with, but when he opened his mouth the Mickey Mouse voice was the kicker. *Such a waste*, she thought, before reluctantly staying on a date that lasted one-and-a-quarter drinks. Mickey Mouse slapped a wet kiss on Stella's cheek before they parted company, saying, 'I know I'm a bit different.' Stella felt a world of pain for him, yet she swore it would be her last online dating experience.

Then there had been the photographer who worked for a radio station and turned up to their date in a souped-up black Mercedes Benz with lowered wheels. In the driver's seat, he confidently reversed the Merc into a tight parking spot, rap music blaring from the car's speakers. When he jumped out of the car, baggy hip-hop jeans hung down around his coccyx and a large chunk of plaque was wedged between his two front teeth when he smiled.

On parting company, after a hasty coffee date during a work lunch, the photographer had promptly texted Stella.

Yo. Nice to meet ya today. Let's do it again. NSA.

What's NSA?

No strings attached. Sex without talk. I'm up for that.

Stella promptly blocked him.

She loved the idea of dating a first responder, just not one like the firefighter she spent some time chatting with once. He spammed her with so many messages and images of himself in firefighting gear, before they'd even been on a date, signalling alarm bells to Stella.

So, she vowed never to give her number out again to anyone she met online. Instead, she requested their number and set her phone to No Caller ID before initiating contact.

But when she first rang Heath, she didn't bother switching her phone number to a private one. She relaxed her golden rule. Possibly because she forgot, or maybe because she was worn down. Heath was her last shot at the online dating game.

Heath's text – Here's my number, you can ring it, or not – immediately piqued Stella's interest. She could have interpreted the text's sentiment as dismissive or arrogant, but instead, she sensed the online dating game had worn Heath down, too.

The irony wasn't lost on her that their first conversation occurred in a parking lot outside a framing store. Not exactly romantic. She rang him in between chores, nibbling nervously at her bottom lip until he picked up.

'Hi!' she said. 'It's Stella.'

'Hi!'

She leaned back against her car. 'Funny thing, I happen to be standing in front of a framing store, and I seem to remember you're a painter. Think I can pick your brain?"

Heath laughed, the deep sound rolling through the phone.

No Mickey Mouse here, Stella thought, a smile curving her lips.

'Nice way to break the ice,' Heath said. 'Framing is a pretty broad topic. Is it a canvas artwork? Because if it's a contemporary artwork, a canvas floater frame looks great and integrates well with the artwork.'

Integrates? She'd never heard the word integrate applied to framing before. Though, to be fair, despite a successful career in public relations and her work as a freelance writer, Stella's love of words didn't keep her from using words out of context...or mispronouncing them.

'What style of painting is it?' Heath asked. 'Realism, abstract, surrealism? Is it an oil painting?' His interest impressed Stella. 'So as to give me a guide on what type of frame might suit it.'

So, as... Stella paused, taking in Heath's voice. Even after years of not acting, Stella still easily observed the nuances of people's behaviour, the way they spoke, wrote, and presented themselves. She figured, artist Heath, with his deep measured and quietly confident voice, who offered free advice on framing paintings, was probably from the country.

'Choosing a frame can be a bit of a minefield,' Heath continued, bringing Stella's attention back to the present, 'especially if you don't want it to cost an arm and a leg.'

Grinning, she said, 'Good to know. I have to ask, is your whole family creative, or are you the black sheep?'

He laughed again. 'I grew up in a family of creatives. I've got two younger brothers, and our parents encouraged us to express creativity however we wanted.' She could hear the smile in his voice as he continued, 'We didn't have a TV, so we had to entertain ourselves. Drawing, listening to music, playing music... Trips to the local art gallery, sometimes. My parents didn't mind if we ran amuck, shoeless, and messy. We liked to play paint wars in the backyard, and then we'd get hosed down before we were allowed to come back inside.'

'Did you all end up in creative careers?' Stella asked, genuinely interested.

'Well, I picked up a paintbrush when I was two years old and never put it back down,' Heath replied. 'Elias is also a painter, and my youngest brother, Gael, plays saxophone.' A slight pause and then he added, 'I did briefly consider a career playing the drums, but that ship sailed a while back. Anyway,' he said abruptly, 'I'm here talking away about myself. You said you were a publicist?'

'I spent over a decade working in Channel 7's publicity department,' Stella told him. 'For a while I was Head of Publicity whenever my boss was on leave. But… Oh, I don't know. It's just, there's only so long you can work on selling other people's stories, and making them famous, before you start to get tired.'

'So…you're not a publicist anymore?' Confusion laced Heath's tone.

'I've moved more over to events,' she confessed. 'Which means I end up working for some odd companies. Like the Geoscientist Institute, of all things. I'm in the process of finalising plans for their upcoming annual conference, which is the most esteemed event on their calendar.'

'Wow,' Heath said, sounding impressed. 'Did you always know you wanted to work with people?'

'Um…' Stella stared out across the car park. 'Not exactly. I mean, I was an actor. But that was a long time ago,' she added hastily. She didn't really feel like talking about it, and crossed her fingers that Heath wouldn't ask any questions.

'I'd love to hear more,' Heath said, 'but I've actually got to get going. It was so great to hear from you, though – we'll talk soon?'

'Yeah,' Stella said, a smile softening her lips. 'I'd like that.'

***

A few days after their first phone conversation, Heath finally plucked up the courage to text Stella.

Might as well bite the bullet, he told himself, and opened a new text message.

> There are still tickets to see The Jezabels tonight. ☺
> If you want to go?

> Oh, I love The Jezabels! I've seen them play with my sister.

No emojis. Did that mean she wasn't overly enthusiastic about going?

Can I pick you up?

I'll just meet you there. Thanks for offering, though!

***

The Northern Hotel in Byron Bay was alive with men clad in black t-shirts, casual shorts, and jeans; the women's Doc Martens and workers boots were softened by tanned legs, mini-skirts, and singlet tops. The crowd clinked wine glasses and inhaled cans of beer and pre-mixed fizzy cocktails. The night was bursting with potential. An inner-city pub, feet-stuck-to-the-carpet energy danced in the air.

Heath could feel the buzz of his second beer, providing some Dutch courage. He'd only recently dipped his toe back into the dating scene after being single for a while, but he had a good feeling about this date. That said, he was still feeling some nerves, pretending to be interested in the conversation his friends were having, even as his attention was glued to the hotel's entrance.

Geez, I hope she comes up trumps. Realising his fingers were tapping the table, he consciously stilled them, his sea green eyes on the door. *She gets bonus points for spontaneity and coming along tonight… Accepting my invitation at the last minute.* He sucked in a deep breath. *I hope she looks like her photos. Christ, I hate this online dating game.*

'Heathy, stop looking at the door, mate!' Scotty nudged Heath with his elbow, laughing. 'Chill out! You'll be a ball of sweat when she gets here.'

Ping. A message flashed up on Heath's phone:

I'm in line, waiting to get in!

Heath used the pylon beside him as coverage to scan the queue for Stella.
Not her.
Definitely not her.

Nope.
Don't think so.
Hope not.
There!

Without an ounce of guilt, he took advantage of his position to surreptitiously size Stella up while her attention was focused on strapping an entry band to her wrist.

Behind her, the sun was setting, a fiery beacon against a backdrop of a mild amber sky, putting on a spectacular show in Byron Bay.

She's gorgeous.

She looked up at the same time he popped out from behind the pylon. A gentle breeze lifted the bottom of her dress, dragging his eyes downward; the upward quirk of her lips told him she'd seen him notice. The colour of her dress blended perfectly into the sky behind her. If he had a paint brush, he'd paint this moment.

Coming up to her, he felt like he was all legs and arms and excitement, and nervously smoothed his brown, shoulder-length hair. She was beautiful, and it was such a relief to find that she was as spectacular in person as she'd seemed online and on the phone. She didn't need to acknowledge that he also looked like the photos in his profile – the way she walked straight into Heath's open arms to hug him signified her approval.

Heath briefly introduced her to his friends, who engaged in amiable conversation before he hooked his arm into Stella's, moving her through the crowd until he found a corner for them to nestle in, one that was perfect to hide in and watch the band. The hordes of people surrounding them blurred into a mirage of theatrical smoke. For Heath, only Stella existed for the rest of the evening.

Lead singer Hayley Mary and the band smashed the set open with *Prisoner*. They were crowd-pleasers – unashamedly kicking the set off by giving the audience what they wanted to hear.

With space at a premium, Heath was able to inch his way closer to Stella, until their arms pressed against each other. He knew they didn't have to stand *that* close – he knew that she knew that, too – but neither moved to put distance between them. It felt like a magnetic bubble surrounded them, pressing them together with just the right intensity of invitation and fabricated aloofness.

Everyone in the audience suddenly became a piano player as the exuberant anthem *Endless Summer* played.

Glancing down at Stella, Heath noticed her nostrils flare, her body seeming to physically echo the excitement radiating off her. His smile stretching across his face, he mouthed the words to song after song straight at Stella, encouraging her to let loose and enjoy herself.

Beaming, he sang at her – words about summer and waves…

He felt his smile snap across his face. He couldn't believe he was standing there, with this woman, who was so much more than her photos.

Stella was smiling so hard that her cheeks puffed out, making her resemble the cutest chipmunk Heath had ever seen. She didn't seem to care, and that just made her even more attractive.

Heath bobbed his head up and down with infectious energy as he sang. Pre-empting the final chorus, he took out his phone to film the crowd. Unable to help himself, he briefly turned the camera to Stella, sneaking a few seconds of her dancing and singing.

He sang especially loud the words about summer, lovers and painting…

The intensity of their dancing turned up, and Heath was delighted as Stella loudly chanted the rest of the chorus with him, their smiles as wide as they could be.

Singing like exuberant teenagers at the top of their voices, Heath knew they were creating an exceptional memory – and he could tell Stella knew it, too.

It was a faultless first date.

CHAPTER 5

Stella finished the last bite of her tiramisu and smiled at Heath across the table. As she set down her fork, he leaned forward and touched the corner of her mouth with his thumb, then sat back again.

'You just had a bit of cake,' he explained.

Her cheeks flushed. 'Oh,' she said, embarrassed. 'Thanks.' *Oh, God, why am I such a dork?*

He grinned. 'It was a cute look.' He hesitated, and then added, 'Though if I were closer, I don't think I'd have used my thumb...'

Stella's cheeks pinked again, this time echoing the warm feeling low in her abdomen. 'I'll keep that in mind,' she said, boldly meeting his gaze and allowing her eyes to trail down to his thighs, their muscle perfectly accentuated by his jeans.

'So, what is it you're looking for in a relationship, then?' Stella asked.

Heath's laugh rumbled through her.

'What is anyone looking for in a relationship? Really, though, you know, I just want someone who's here with me, you know?'

'What, not a fan of long distance?' she asked curiously.

'No,' he said, and the firmness in his voice surprised Stella. 'Sorry,' he said, 'I'm just a little touchy when it comes to long distance.'

'Bad break-up?' she guessed.

'Not exactly. More like...the longer I'm away from my partner, or she's away from me, the more the relationship ends up struggling. All props to anyone who can make long distance work, but that's just not me.'

They sat quietly for moment before Stella broke the silence. 'Shall we get the bill?'

'Soon,' Heath said after he'd flagged down their waiter, 'You know one thing we haven't talked about in the –' He glanced down at his watch. 'Wow, we've been here three hours. Makes this an even more impressive oversight.'

'You going to tell me, or am I going to have to guess?' Stella said.

'You never told me about your days as an actor!'

Stella flinched. That…was not what she'd been anticipating. 'Um,' she said judiciously. 'It's a while ago now. So…'

'Oh, come on,' Heath teased, 'you must have some amazing stories. Come on, spill the beans.'

'Like I said, it's been a while.'

'I'd love to hear about all the roles you've played. Why'd you give up? Too much pressure?'

'Just leave it alone,' she snapped, withdrawing, and crossing her arms defensively.

He stared at her for a moment, mouth open in surprise. 'Didn't mean to rock the boat,' he said at last. Their waiter reappeared; Stella reached for her purse, but Heath waved her off. 'My treat.'

While he dealt with the bill, Stella called an Uber, their plans to walk to his nearby flat dashed by their awkward exchange. Five minutes away – perfect. She'd be able to hop in about the same time they left the restaurant, avoid any more awkwardness.

Honestly, Stella was frustrated with herself as much as she was irritated by Heath. As she gathered her things, she thought back over the evening – everything had been so perfect, and then in the space of a few minutes, everything had soured. As much as she wanted to blame Heath, seeing as he was the one who'd brought it up, she had to admit to herself, however reluctantly, that he couldn't possibly have known she'd react so poorly.

Sigh.

The more important question, she supposed, was whether she was going to let the evening's end destroy any possibility of moving forward with Heath. From his body language, she got the sense that he'd backed off almost entirely, as though he wasn't sure if any future had gone completely off the rails.

Did that make the next move hers?

And if so… what did she want that move to be?

***

Their second date could have been perfect, Heath mused, standing in the cool night air outside of the restaurant, minutes after somehow colossally putting his foot in his mouth. He glanced sideways at Stella, whose arms were crossed over her chest again. He couldn't read her at all right now. Maybe not to be unexpected given he barely knew her, but at the same time it felt like he'd known her forever.

More than anything else, he couldn't help but chastise himself for pressing Stella, who was in fact still a near stranger, with questions about her acting career when, in retrospect, it was clearly a sore point. He should have seen his questions made Stella uncomfortable.

You live and you learn, he thought glumly, picking at the rim of his jeans and shuffling awkwardly.

Taking a deep breath, Heath said uncomfortably, 'I guess we should call it a night?' He wasn't giving up hope entirely, but…

Stella looked up at him for the first time since they'd come outside. 'I ordered an Uber.' Ah. Hope dashed, then. 'It should be here any minute.'

An Uber hurtled past them at that moment, leaving behind an even more awkward silence. As they watched the car's taillights disappear, Heath belatedly realised neither of them had tried to alert the driver to stop or turn around.

'Was that – was that your Uber?'

Stella made a huffing sound. 'The driver wouldn't have missed us standing here.' A pause. 'Right?'

'Well, at least you know it's not a cunning ploy on my part to get you up to my apartment,' Heath joked awkwardly, and then closed his eyes in horror. 'Sorry.'

'Another Uber is on its way,' Stella said, clearly not seeing his joke as worthy of response. 'Three minutes.'

Heath nodded, too peeved with himself to risk saying anything else that might make the situation worse. He still couldn't figure out where her thoughts were, other than on the damn Uber. Her posture wasn't especially encouraging; she stood stiffly upright, her petite shoulders squared; her chin and neck jutted forward as she looked down at her phone.

To break the silence, or let it be?

Though she was only really starting to admit it, Stella had begun thinking about her acting career again recently. She'd made a habit of consciously burying that chapter of her life, but…

It wasn't Heath's fault, really; there was no way for anyone to know that asking her why she'd stopped acting would trigger a reminder of her first full-blown panic attack.

Despite her annoyance at Heath's probing, Stella knew he hadn't meant to be mean – he'd just accidentally bungled his attempt to get to know her.

The missed Uber had been a sliding door moment – it struck Stella as so astounding that such a seemingly inconsequential moment could change so much. The universe had delivered her a second chance with Heath, and she was determined not to waste it. She knew they'd shared something remarkable on their first date and dared not give the universe the middle finger for its generosity.

Heath had just opened his mouth to say something when Stella blurted out, 'You're about to miss out on getting to know the woman of your dreams.' She stared at him, embarrassed by the bravado of her alcohol-fuelled words, and how loudly she'd said them. She'd never said anything so bold before.

A few silent seconds passed before Heath moved to Stella. He took her hand and said, with quiet confidence, 'Come with me.'

The second Uber arrived. The driver watched them walk inside and drove off.

CHAPTER 6

If it had been a movie, Stella thought later, a Hollywood film director might have introduced a clichéd B-grade sex-on-the-dinner-table scene. Where, with one fell swoop, the male actor's forearm would hastily clear the table of objects before hoisting the female co-star onto his hips, laying her back on the table, and proceeding to have sex for 30 seconds in the missionary position.

It could have reeked of a similar stereotype that Stella couldn't control herself from ripping Heath's shirt off when they hit his apartment – but the feeling was clearly mutual. Despite themselves, in spite of how dinner had ended, there was no ignoring their heady chemistry. Stella couldn't bring herself to regret morphing into the type of screen characters she would outwardly scoff, because secretly, she bought into them – hook, line, and sinker. Playing out the type of characters that directors illuminated again and again in movies to give the audience hope that, perhaps one day, they too could live this same euphoric experience.

Stella found herself in the most exhilarating intimate scene of her life. Being with Heath quelled an emptiness that she hadn't really noticed until it was filled.

What was unusual was that this wasn't a scene she had ever found herself in. She hadn't had a boyfriend in years, and she never had one-night stands.

'You are somethin' else,' Heath whispered, his eyes meeting Stella's in a way that made her feel he was looking *into* her, not at her – his gaze filled with an inexplicable knowing.

'You are so *handsome*,' Stella replied, standing facing Heath, her skin-coloured dress already on the floor, its shoestring strap tangled under one of her boots. There was something in her voice that she hadn't heard before. *Handsome.* In 38 years, she couldn't remember that particular intonation. It was something new in her tone, something that emerged when she referred to Heath as handsome. She'd never referred to men with sentimental terms of endearment, but now... There was a lilting naivety in her voice, and something else that she couldn't quite put her finger on...

Wait.

Did she sound...happy? She registered how unusually confident she felt.

Since giving up her acting career, she hadn't often felt joy.

But now... Heath was looking down at her with intensity, as though drinking her whole, inside and out – and if she had to guess, he very much appreciated the black Yves St Laurent lingerie, which she'd worn principally for him. She couldn't say she minded his tight-fitting jeans, either. His eyes caught at her chest, then moved up to meet her gaze. Her tan boots, which she'd worn because they accentuated her muscular runner's legs, brought her to Heath's chest height.

They stood pelvis to pelvis; goose bumps speckled her arms, all of her tiny hairs standing upright.

'You are a very attractive woman,' Heath said softly, moving strands of Stella's long brown hair away from her face.

Gosh, she loved his voice.

He ran his hand over the top of her hair, gently tilting her head back to reveal her neck, his green eyes holding her blue ones. Stella felt a level of trust between them that usually was only won over years spent together. Like a cat allowing its owner to scratch its tummy as a sure sign of confidence, Stella slowly turned her head, parading her neck, offering it up. Heath brushed his fingers against her skin before gently kissing up and down the front of her throat, scruff on his face gently scratching the side of her face.

Jesus, who is this guy? Stella thought, briefly trying to disguise how shallow her breath was before giving up.

'Are you okay?' Heath asked quietly.

Stella's eyes narrowed and she nodded, silently and spontaneously giving Heath permission to kiss her.

With one hand still tilting her head back and his other hand firmly round her waist, Heath pulled Stella against him and kissed her for a long time.

For Stella, there was a familiarity to the way their mouths moved together, as though they had been kissing for lifetimes.

This moment will be etched in my memory for time eternal, Stella thought. She sighed faintly into Heath's mouth and let him wrap his muscular arms around her back, drawing her forehead against his broad, bare chest. They paused in silence, paying homage to the moment, before moving to Heath's bedroom.

The white candles Heath lit flickered golden light around Stella, casting dancing shadows of her shapely stomach, butt, and legs against the wall.

Heath sat on the edge of the bed, calm but with intense focus, and beckoned for her to stand between his denim-clad legs, her boots allowing her to dominate him in height. He looked up at her, then pressed his thighs against her bare legs as she stepped in between his, holding her so that she couldn't move. Not that she wanted to.

Stella glided her fingertips over the length of Heath's collarbones, shoulders, and chest. *His skin.* It was so smooth – light olive and perfect, without a blemish.

Without saying a word or breaking eye contact, Heath repeated, 'You are somethin' else,' his voice reverential.

After exploring each other's bodies into the early hours, Stella tucked herself against Heath, enjoying their silence, listening to music, enveloped in a cocoon of each other.

CHAPTER 7

As Stella stood in the lounge room the next morning, waiting for Heath to call an Uber, she noticed things she'd been too busy to notice the night before.

The apartment was inviting, the lighting soft. Images of surfing holidays were preserved on large, faded canvases that took pride of place in the lounge room. Framed photos filled shelves. There were photos of family members and a dog, looking adoringly at whoever had taken its picture. Tall piles of books were stacked in piles. A pair of well-worn thongs lay upside down at the front door. His apartment was spotlessly clean but overflowing with paintings and artwork. He liked incense. He was a reader.

Every new bit of information was a revelation that Stella was curious to soak up.

As she pulled an art book from the bookshelf, a photo of Heath with a woman dislodged from behind it. Little hairs on Stella's forearms stood up as Heath walked back into the room.

'Who's this?' Stella asked curiously, studying the photo of Heath and a stunning blonde.

Heath came to peer at the photo over her shoulder. 'Oh, that's my ex, Candice – sorry, I didn't realise that photo was back there!'

'She's pretty,' Stella said. 'Was she the one who soured you on long distance?'

Heath hesitated, just a touch too long, and then said, 'Yeah. She's American, and things just didn't work out.'

'You look so happy in this photo,' Stella commented.

'Short lived.'

Stella registered a hint of nostalgia in Heath's voice and said quickly, 'I'm sorry. I didn't mean to pry.'

Heath smiled at her and dropped a quick kiss on her temple. 'No worries.'

***

Half an hour later, Stella smiled at the café barista as he handed over her dirty chai. She took a sip; it was smooth and piping hot, just as she liked it. Taking up a seat at a table by the window, she read over the event brief her colleague Alison had sent her in preparation for the Geoscientist Institute's upcoming annual conference, which Stella was responsible for overseeing. The Institute might have been one of her odder clients, but it didn't make their event any less worthy of her attention.

Feeling her phone vibrate, she pulled it out of her bag as a text message from Heath flashed up on the screen.

Have a great day 😈

That's attentive, Stella thought. *An early morning text message.* Considering she hadn't left his place all that long ago…good sign.

She noted the emoji with an internal eye roll. The devil emoji was a bit cheeky, but she opted to interpret it as a reference to the once-in-a-lifetime experience she and Heath had had last night.

He is devilish, yes.

While Stella had long been obsessed with the importance of language, she let Heath's use of emojis slide. Somehow, he could get away with routinely using both idioms and emojis. For Stella, when it came to Heath, it seemed different rules applied.

Even as the smell of coffee wafted into Stella's nostrils, she could still smell Heath from the night before. The musky cologne he wore lingered, despite the shower she'd taken…and she loved it.

She caught herself crumpling her lips up to meet her nose, taking short, sharp breaths. She'd snuck a whiff of Heath's cologne when she went to the bathroom; she'd pressed the bottle so close to her nose that it left a trickle of aftershave on her top lip. She'd inhaled Heath then, and did so now.

***

Heath pulled his phone from his pocket and grinned. He loved that Stella had responded immediately to his text.

I had an incredible time last night. Thank you. x

She isn't a game player, Heath thought, pleased. *Gorgeous, intelligent, funny. The total package.*

As he tossed his phone into the car, a smile broke across his face, and he ran towards the water, a surfboard tucked under his arm. He tracked his way to the thin layer of grass, skirting the edge of the pathway to the beach.

He was still stunned he'd redeemed himself last night. He'd been sure he'd ruined things, albeit inadvertently, hitting a raw nerve when he'd quizzed Stella about her acting career.

Yet, somehow, the evening had ended on not only a positive note but an ecstatic one.

Bracing himself, he ventured onto the blistering sand. Spotting a mum struggling in the heat to carry her baby off the beach, he immediately dropped his surfboard to relieve the woman of her bags and beach umbrella. Huddled safely in a tiny patch of shade moments later, the woman was effusive in her thanks and relief.

'It's a scorcher,' Heath commented.

'Isn't it just?' the woman exclaimed. 'The heat crept up so quickly, I hardly had time to get off the beach. Thanks so much for your help.'

'Pleasure!' Heath yelled over his shoulder as he bolted towards the water. If he could say anything about himself, it was that he treated women with respect.

When he was in his early 20s, he'd chastised a male passenger for monopolising a bus seat. A big buffoon of a male, with legs spread double the width of his hips, oblivious and loudly snapping a broadsheet newspaper open and shut, had taken complete ownership of the bus seat. The man had no regard for the woman seated next to him, who sat with her knees pressed tightly together, balanced precariously on the edge of the seat, in danger of falling into the aisle. Heath had said, "Stop monopolising the seat, mate," with just enough threat in his voice for the bloke to take him seriously, close his legs, and shuffle over. Heath was still perplexed that the man had needed to be asked to create room for the woman next to him.

At the water's edge, Heath wrapped a leg rope around his ankle, as he'd done a gazillion times before, and dove into the water as if it was his last day on earth.

He'd always been at home in the ocean. Next to a rainforest, it was his favourite place to spend time. The sea had held a special place in his heart since before he could even swim. It was the place where his ashes would be spread, he imagined, surrounded by a circle of fellow surfing friends.

Waves lapped at his bronzed six-pack as he paddled out to take his position in the line-up. If he'd been so inclined, he could have been a wetsuit model, which might make him conceited, but he wasn't one to focus on how good his long, lean, and exquisitely chiselled body looked. He was in excellent shape for 45 – and not an air of conceit about him.

Heath paddled past the breaking waves and lay on his back on his surfboard, soaking up the sun. The coolness of the water made the sun's heat more bearable.

Recent memories of Stella flashed through Heath's mind, as though he was turning the pages of an animated flipbook, each page displaying a new recollection of her.

Stella dancing in his bedroom, her candlelight shadow projected on the wall. Stella walking towards him when they first met at The Jezabels concert. Stella sitting on top of him on his bed, staring adoringly down at him.

The whole evening in some ways felt surreal, because how could he have screwed up so royally and yet had the evening turn out so well?

Even as he pondered the question, he could see Stella above him, a cheeky wry smile on her face as she looked down at where he lay on his surfboard.

The whole of Heath's back rested contentedly against his surfboard. He was so happy floating in a sea of memories of Stella that he didn't care that he might not even catch a wave.

She really is somethin' else.

CHAPTER 8

The annual Geoscientist Conference had finally arrived. As part of the events team from the Geoscientist Institute, Stella had been busily preparing for 450 delegates to arrive at the Sydney Convention and Exhibition Centre. The Geoscientist Institute, the peak body representing scientists in Australia, had run the event for five consecutive years.

'People are exceedingly needy at events,' Stella told Alison, a novice but enthusiastic events junior.

Passion and drive had made Alison stand out among the many young university graduates who'd applied for the event assistant position. Stella had been on the interview panel and vouched for Alison, instinctively knowing that she had the right mix of organisational and communication skills and attention to detail to make a great events person.

Obviously listening to Stella with only half an ear, Alison frenetically arranged the custom printed lanyards in alphabetical order for the delegates – who were due to stream into the Sydney Convention Centre in 30 minutes.

'Be prepared,' Stella advised, 'for any of the event attendees to morph into a dependent child during the conference. You'll need to always hold their hand. Point them in the direction of the toilet, which no doubt they'll be standing right in front of, ensure their obscure dietary requests are met, and assist with a multitude of wardrobe malfunctions.'

'Got it.' Alison nodded enthusiastically, shuffling from one foot to the other as she continued to arrange and then rearrange the lanyards.

'Did you bring flat shoes to wear?' Stella asked, catching sight of Alison's high heels.

'Yes,' Alison said, anxiety bleeding into her voice. 'I packed a pair of runners and some ballet flats. They're in the wardrobe room with my dress for the dinner tonight.'

'As beautiful as they are, swap the Tony Bianco shoes you're wearing for flats,' Stella said. 'And activate the fit app on your phone to count your steps. I'll shout you a bottle of champagne if you take more steps than me.' She paused and then added, 'You won't.'

Alison looked appreciatively at Stella, who was using a handheld label maker to stamp staff names onto work phones and computers, so they didn't get mixed up. Stella knew she worked with dispassionate speed; the motions, which she'd made endless times, were by now automatic.

April, a confident and perfectly coiffed junior event organiser, whizzed up to the reception desk to double-check the morning coffee order.

'Large dirty chai for Stella, soy latte for Alison, double espresso for Vanessa, skinny flat white for Tim and Bron,' April reeled off. 'What about Oliver? Does anyone know what time bossman Oliver is arriving?'

Nobody responded. Stella rolled her eyes, then hid a grin as she realised the rest of the team had done the same, their shoulders rising and falling with indifference perfectly in sync.

'Okay!' April said, 'So, adding to the coffee order, a triple shot of we've got no fucks to give for Oliver,' and darted off.

At that moment, Oliver entered the building, sauntering towards the event registration desk, wearing oversized Louis Vuitton sunglasses, Alexander McQueen jeans, and a yellow floral-print Gucci jacket. Oliver had made it clear that he didn't like being photographed, and yet always wore garishly loud outfits and assumed centre stage at corporate events.

Alison's back notably stiffened as she saw Oliver walk towards them, carrying his lunch for the day, a Ziploc bag half-filled with chopped carrot sticks and cherry tomatoes.

Oliver intentionally avoided eye contact when he said, 'Day five in the job. I'm presuming you were on time, Alison?'

'Um…' Alison was clearly flustered. 'Yes, I arrived just before 6 am. There was quite a lot of traffic but I managed –'

Oliver cut Alison off to greet Thomas Carnegie, the first delegate to arrive at the conference.

'Thomas!' Oliver exclaimed, drawing out the 'o.' 'It's so wonderful that you could make the conference.' Exaggerating the number of conference attendees, he said, 'We have nearly 500 people attending this year. The technical program is so impressive.'

'Hi, Thomas, you're nice and early,' Stella said, then commented under her breath, 'As in *way* too early.'

Reaching past Alison in his haste to locate Thomas' lanyard, Oliver deadpanned to her, each syllable in Thomas' name accentuated: 'Thom-as Car-ne-gie needs a lanyard!'

Alison, who somehow managed to trip over herself without even moving, grabbed a lanyard and handed it to Thomas, along with a conference map and program. The event map, which had taken Stella four hours to create in its colour-coded precision, was marked by bright, obvious arrows indicating where the keynote presentations, speakers, and workshops were taking place.

Thomas put the lanyard on back to front and barely looked at his map before blustering, 'Where is the opening speaker presenting? I can't see this on the map.'

Stella mumbled under her breath, 'Should've made the directions in 72 point,' as Alison collected her thoughts to answer Thomas' question.

'You wouldn't think that it would be such a difficult question.' Oliver smirked at Alison before she could open her mouth, slung his bag down on the reception desk, and took Thomas by the elbow to escort him to the Plenary room. 'Thomas, the keynote speaker, Julie Bolton, is the Principal Research Scientist at CSIRO Mineral Resources. She is going to blow you away,'

'And we're off to the races!' Stella declared, too loudly. Oliver stopped outside the Plenary room to shoot a piercing look at her.

***

Thirty minutes later, all staff were stationed at the reception desk, welcoming hundreds of excited delegates as they streamed through the door.

Stella was in the middle of doing a quick rundown with emcee and former ABC Radio presenter James Turton when a message from Heath flashed up on her phone.

Hey gorgeous, hope your day has started well. Flat out like a lizard painting here.

A selfie popped up of Heath wearing a white singlet and cargo shorts with paint splashed across them. His brown hair was highlighted with light streaks from hours of surfing, and splotches of paint dotted his week-old beard, looking every bit the artist cliché.

Knowing she shouldn't have her personal phone turned on during the event, she couldn't stop herself from pinging a quick text straight back to Heath:

You make painting look like easy work.

As she pressed send, she smiled at the thought that only a few months ago she'd regarded emojis as trite, the lowest form of communication, whereas now she saw their merit as foreplay.

He's hot, Stella thought as she said to James, 'We've got a hot to get through. Oops, I mean a lot!' She managed a laugh, feeling her cheeks flush. 'We have a lot to get through. Let's go backstage and get you mic'd up.'

Doing her best to give James her undivided attention, Stella walked and reeled off the correct pronunciation of the presenters' names. Even as she was speaking, a movie of the mind-blowing scene she and Heath had had only hours ago played in her mind. There was little she could do to stop the images popping up.

'So, James, while we might be dealing with boffin-types, don't mistake this audience for being boring.'

An image of Heath lying on his back, naked on the lounge.

James commented, 'So, the audience will handle a joke or two?'

The movie in Stella's head kept playing.

Their eyes lock. There is an inexplicable telepathy between them; they speak to each other without saying a word, knowing what the other craves. Heath runs his fingers down the side of Stella's ribs, over the curve of her hips. 'God, you're beautiful,' he says in a gravelly voice.

'Stella?'

James' voice jolted Stella back to the business of the day. 'Pardon? Oh!' She shook her head. 'Sorry about that! They're a good audience. They'll appreciate a joke. Feel free to give the audience a bit of a roasting. They're scientists, not scientologists. They have a good sense of humour.'

Hundreds of butterflies quiver in Stella's stomach as Heath sits up momentarily, wrapping his arms around her, before laying back down again, his arms flung wide and open in complete submission.

'Excellent,' James said, oblivious to the world inside Stella's head. 'I've done my research on geoscientists. I've got a few jokes up my sleeve. The panel topic, *How to Increase Diversity in Geoscience Programs*, should stir up some strong debate.'

'*Do whatever you want to me...*' Heath flashes her a movie star smile.

'Stella?' James almost yelled.

She stared blankly at James for two or three seconds, saying nothing as she tried to recall what he'd just said, before finally saying, 'Of all the STEM disciplines, the geosciences rank among the lowest in ethnic and racial diversity.'

She was amazed that she'd managed such an articulate response when, really, all she could think about was the next movie she'd make with Heath.

***

At 3 pm, Stella caught Alison checking her watch to note how many steps she had taken for the day so far as she hovered near Stella, waiting for an opportune moment to give her boss some lunch and interrupt the back-to-back interviews Stella had been conducting with geoscientists.

'Thanks for your time,' Stella said to Ben, her eighth interviewee for the day. 'We'll edit the interview and top and tail it with introductory and closing logos, then shoot it off to you for consent. Nothing will go live on our website until you've approved the interview.'

Just then, the Spanish videographer, who'd been struggling with English all day, chimed in. 'Um, Ben, please could you repeat and spell jour name and jour job again. Sorry. Gracias.'

Aware they were in danger of falling behind schedule, Stella said, 'Diego, you should've asked Ben to repeat his name at the top of the interview if you needed it.' She stifled a sigh. 'Never mind, we'll work it out in the edit.'

As Ben repeated his credentials to camera, Alison seized the opportunity to shove a sandwich under Stella's nose.

'Only three interviews to go,' Alison said enthusiastically.

'Four. I still need to interview the Young Ambassador; we added her to the schedule.' Stella wolfed down a large bite of the sandwich. 'I'll have a ten-minute break and interview Rosie next. Can you pull her out of whatever presentation she's in and bring her over? She also needs to do a tech run-through of her speech for tonight.'

Alison started to head off then spun on her foot to walk backwards, calling out to Stella, 'I've done a reconnaissance of the ballroom – everything looks great. The flowers look incredible on the table.'

Stella gave Alison a thumbs up, downed the rest of her sandwich, and took herself off to the furthest corner of the conference centre. She put her work phone on silent, kicked her shoes off, and massaged her feet as she read over the questions for the following interview, which centred on changes to the earth since it was formed. After some consideration, she decided to cut the questions short for the final interviews, in order to keep to schedule. She needed time to dart to the hotel, change into a cocktail dress, and make it back to the conference for pre-dinner drinks by 5 pm.

Hurry up and make it tomorrow already.

***

At 5 pm sharp at the Convention Centre, Stella stood to the side and surveyed the room. A wildly extravagant amount of pre-dinner drinks and canapés were being consumed by delegates, who exchanged lively pleasantries and industry gossip between sips of champagne and beer.

The formal wear transformed the men and women, who excitedly postured and preened themselves as they moved among their colleagues. Even diminutive Allan Miller, a respected geoscientist who had worked in the industry for 30 years, looked taller in his tuxedo.

The evening's black-tie networking dinner was really just an opportunity for the delegates to get drunk. Nobody ever exchanged business cards at conference social events, although they sometimes did exchange hotel room numbers.

Oliver, wearing an arrestingly bright fuchsia jacket, was already on his second glass of champagne. By the third drink, Stella knew he'd perform his usual routine of trying to entice the staff into a group motivational huddle, some of whom would refuse in embarrassed protest. Respect was hard to win, even for one day a year, particularly when it was undeserved.

Stella stopped to speak to April, who was directing sponsors to the cordoned-off VIP area.

'Wow, you look incredible, girl!' Stella said and then, without missing a beat, continued, 'Have the photographer and Diego arrived?'

'Yep, they're both in the ballroom, capturing vision and photos of the room before it's filled. Oh, and guess who else just arrived?' April scoffed.

'You're not serious,' Stella said with a groan. 'Surely, he hasn't invited Alfonzo again. It'll stuff up the seating.'

April made a face. 'Yep. Nope, he's here. And Oliver's already speed drinking with him.'

'Tell Alison that Alfonzo is Oliver's husband. Ask her to rearrange the VIP table to boot someone off so they can sit together. Also, warn Alison that those two will get smashed. Tell her not to let a drop of alcohol pass her lips but to encourage delegates to ply themselves with as much booze as they want.'

'Alison's double-checking the table settings. I'll go and speak to her now.' April patted Stella's hand. 'Keep breathing, Stella. You gave me that piece of advice at my first conference.'

Throughout the rest of the evening, Stella earned every step she took on her Apple watch. She split her time racing between schmoozing event sponsors, keeping the emcee and presenters to schedule, interviewing the award winners, managing media and photo opportunities, and overseeing social media activity.

With the industry award winner announced, the formal proceedings of the evening came to an end. Stella escorted Dan

Hardy, the newly minted and exceedingly proud winner of the Geoscientist of the Year Award, to the media board, where he was strategically positioned in front of a marketing banner with the Geoscientist Institute logo emblazoned across its top.

'Congratulations on the award, Dan,' Stella said. 'You must be thrilled. Let's do a short interview about what it means for you to win this award while you're having your photo taken.'

'Sure, Stella. I'm amped; let's do it!'

'Please repeat the question I ask back to me,' Stella said, 'as my voice won't be heard in the video. We'll use text to represent my questions.'

'OK, got it,' Dan said.

The interview wrapped once Stella was satisfied that she had several quotes from Dan that she could use for publicity. She then updated a media release she'd written earlier, adding the award winners in their respective categories, and disseminated it to media. Exclusive interviews with the Geoscientist of the Year, Professional of the Year, and Emerging Professional were placed with select media outlets.

It's almost a wrap, Stella thought, letting out a long sigh as Mandy Jenkins, Director of Geominerals and the Platinum sponsor for the event, sidled up and slurred,

'This is a magnificent event. Congrats!'

Stella acknowledged her comment with a nod and then directed Mandy to the toilet when she asked. She immediately stumbled off in the wrong direction.

The technical crew waited patiently for Stella to wrap them for the night, which she did with a round of free drinks. Then she directed the team to commence bumping out the event as the last delegates straggled out the door.

A glance at her watch confirmed that she'd taken 32,000 steps for the day. With that number of steps, she was convinced that Alison owed her a bottle of champagne.

***

Once back in her room at the Mantra Hotel, Stella unzipped her black dress, grateful to escape the thin film of sweat coating the fabric, and draped it over the hotel chair. A few hours earlier, the dress had been starchier than a white business shirt; now it felt like old trousers, worn out and slippery under the bottom.

She turned her phone on silent, poured a tall glass of white wine, took a long sip, and slumped back on the bed. A current pulsed from the bottom of her swollen feet to the crown of her head. Sometimes she wondered if her throat closed over like this not from overuse but rather as a psychosomatic response to not saying what she truly thought. Spiritual guide Louise Hay would have had a field day with her.

Stella batted her eyes back open the instant they closed and tried to avoid reliving the humiliating encounter with Oliver that had occurred only an hour earlier.

Some people shouldn't drink.

Vanessa, the junior event assistant assigned to shadow Diego to ensure his videography work was acceptable, had left the event early to go drinking with two young male scientists. Stella was aware that Vanessa was having issues in her personal life and let the incident slide. She'd deal with Vanessa's unprofessionalism later.

Stella knew that Oliver was right – as the junior team manager, the responsibility lay with her to ensure that the junior staff fulfilled their respective roles and obligations. Still, the way Oliver had spoken to her in front of colleagues and members was indefensible.

'*Who* was stupid enough to hire a videographer so inept that he forgot to charge his battery and stuffed up getting footage of the winner!?' As Oliver had barked out the words, he leaned forward, close enough that she inhaled a shot of whiskey.

He's progressed to hard liquor. I have no chance.

Uncomfortably close, she could see that Oliver's red eyes matched the tiny veins coursing across his face and neck. As a result of Oliver's uninvited invasion into her personal space and verbal lashing triggering a panic attack, she had jumped back from him, unable to speak, and gasped in deep breaths of air, praying her trembling hands would go unnoticed.

The downlights were unforgiving, highlighting Oliver's thinning hair. His signature short black slick was stuck together in wisps of hair by the sticky alcohol sweating from his scalp.

Stella knew there was no point in reminding Oliver they'd been lucky to secure Diego's services at short notice, given that the Institute's regular videographer had called in sick at the last minute. Instead, she took a great deal of pleasure in noticing his fuchsia jacket matched his bright pink nose.

Oliver continued, 'We'll debrief this shit show next week when we're all back in the office,' and then staggered off, Alfonzo tripping behind him.

Jordon and several Institute members had witnessed Oliver's uncalled-for reprimand of Stella. The level of compassion in Alison's eyes almost reduced Stella to tears; several Institute members within earshot of the conversation made sure to acknowledge how much they had enjoyed the conference.

In that humiliating moment, their support meant the world to Stella.

***

Stella blinked her eyes open again, peeled herself up from the bed, and finished the glass of wine. Pouring another, she reactivated her messages to receive a flurry of texts from Heath.

> **Hey baby doll, I've organised the perfect frame for your painting. I'll collect the painting from you and drop it down to the framers.**

Another text revealed that Heath had arranged a surprise getaway to a rainforest retreat at Tamborine Mountain, their first weekend away marking a milestone in their young relationship.

Bursting with excitement, Stella immediately responded.

> **Hey, honey. Thanks for organising the frame. I appreciate it so much! <3 A weekend getaway!? How wonderful.**

Overwhelmed by her feelings for Heath, Stella switched her phone to silent to gather her thoughts.

The last time she'd had her heart broken was when she was acting.

CHAPTER 9

Stella noticed that Heath was unusually fidgety; he tucked his t-shirt into his jeans a second time as they walked up the pathway to her family home for dinner. It had been several years since Stella last introduced a boyfriend to her mother, and she had played down how excited her mum would be for fear of making Heath more nervous.

'Don't be nervous,' she told him encouragingly. 'My mum can be over the top, but she's a doll. She'll love you.'

Before Heath had time to respond, Pam Longhurst flung open the door.

Settling her hands against Stella's cheeks, Pam squeezed softly as she kissed the top of her daughter's forehead four times.

'Hello, you two!' Pam beamed and scooted up to Heath, hugging him tightly and then releasing him to pat the outside of his shoulders.

'Hi, Mrs Longhurst,' Heath said, smiling.

'Mrs Longhurst.' Pam laughed. 'Oh, gosh, that's respectful but entirely unnecessary. Call me Pam.'

'Pam,' Heath agreed. 'It's lovely to meet you.'

'It's wonderful to meet you! Stella has told me a lot about you – all five-star reviews – no need for concern!' Pam entered the house, motioning for them to follow. 'Come in, come in! Oh, no need for that,' she said as Heath started to remove his shoes.

They followed Pam's gold and leopard print kaftan into the lounge room, where they were greeted by lavish trays of hors d'oeuvres.

Pam gestured for Heath to make himself comfortable. She poured a glass of wine and held it out. 'Wine? There's beer too if you'd prefer,' she burbled. 'You certainly are a handsome devil.'

Blushing, Stella avoided eye contact with Heath as she took the glass from her mother and handed it to him. She squeezed Heath's hand and flashed him a smile as Pam continued to chatter away.

'I hear you're an artist,' Pam said, crossing one leg over the other and leaning against the back of the couch. 'A family trait, or are you the lone wolf?'

'I'm a painter,' Heath said. He sipped his wine and continued, 'My whole family is pretty creative – my middle brother is a painter, too, and our younger brother is a musician. I feel pretty fortunate to make a living out of being an artist.'

'We love creative types in this family!' Pam exclaimed, her face lighting up. 'I'm an actress – it's a talent I handed down to two of my daughters.'

Shifting in her seat, Stella resisted reminding her mother that she hadn't acted in decades.

'So, where are you from?'

'Have you heard of Alstonville?' Heath asked. 'It's a hinterland town in northern New South Wales. A bloody gem of a place, where I had a wonderfully misspent youth on a small farm.'

'Oh, lovely,' Pam said. 'You must have got up to some scrapes, you and your brothers. What a difference it can make to have boys rather than girls!' With a wink at Heath, she added, 'My girls, of course, never got up to any trouble.' A smile crossed her face. 'My other daughter, Alinta, is a singer.'

'Where *is* Alinta?' Stella asked.

'Alinta!' Pam shouted. 'ALINTA! Your sister is here! Come downstairs, honey.'

As her mother moved to the stereo to put a Neil Diamond album on, humming to herself, Stella couldn't help but notice the way Pam's fingers brushed lovingly – but briefly – over the photo of Madison that sat on the mantelpiece. Stella missed her big sister, and knew her mother did, too.

Her attention was distracted as her mini-me appeared at the top of the stairs, wearing a ten-thousand-dollar, braces-corrected smile that reached from ear to ear. Alinta let out a squeal of excitement when she saw Stella and bolted down the stairs two at a time.

Stella popped to her feet and flung her arms around her sister, whispering in her ear, 'Mum's in excitement overdrive.' The sisters exchanged a knowing look.

'Hey! Nice to meet you!' Alinta batted Heath's hand away and gave him a hug instead before plopping down on the lounge next to him.

'You're the baby sister of the family?'

'Yep. That's me. And I've milked the can-do-no-wrong child stereotype my entire life for all it's worth,' Alinta poked her tongue out at Stella then poked Heath's ribs.

'Want me to tell you some stories about my sister? I have many.'

'I've got all night,' Heath responded.

'Oh!' Pam said, delighted. 'He's good looking and funny, too!' She turned up the music and turned back towards the group.

'Stella is the shittiest driver known to mankind,' Alinta burst out as Pam busied herself topping up everyone's drinks. 'Never willingly get in a car with Stella unless you want to risk your life!'

'You said you had dirt on your sister,' Heath said, straight-faced. 'Tell me something I don't know.'

Alinta narrowed her eyes at him. 'She failed her driver's licence twice.'

'I knew that, too.'

Stella grabbed her sister in a bear hug and squashed her into the lounge, clamping her hand over Alinta's mouth.

'She's a bloody first-class klutz!' Alinta said, her voice muffled. 'But of course, you know this because you would have seen her trip over herself!'

'Alright, stop teasing each other,' Pam said, laughing. With a smile at Heath, she added, 'It's so nice to have both of my girls home.'

Stella released her sister and snuggled back down on the couch next to Heath.

'You know she was an actor, right?' Alinta said.

'Yep, I sure do,' Heath said, shaping an imaginary tick in the air.

'Wow.' Alinta considered this information. 'You *must* be very special if Stella's spoken to you about her acting career and brought you to Sydney overnight to meet us.' Alinta raised her eyebrows at Stella.

'Alinta…' Stella said warningly.

Alinta flashed her a mischievous smile and blurted out, 'But I bet you didn't know she was not only a hugely talented actress but gave up and sold herself short of a successful acting career.'

Tension crackled in the air until Pam clapped her hands together and said, 'Let's eat!'

***

After dinner, Stella joined her mother in the kitchen, automatically taking up her old role of washing the dishes for her mother to put them away.

'Can you believe we still have the same dinner set that your father and I got when we were married all those years ago?' Pam commented, admiring the cream dinner set. 'And only two plates broken by you over the years, my dear. Miraculous!'

Gazing wistfully out the window, Stella found herself absently washing the same plate several times.

'It's so old that it's come full circle and back into fashion.' Her hands stilled as she watched her mother stack plates into the cupboard, just as she'd done a thousand times before.

Stella returned her gaze to the garden outside the kitchen window while her mother collected more dishes from the dining room. The same thick eucalyptus tree from her childhood still bore the scars of the Longhurst sisters' initials, inscribed into the neck of the tree so many years ago.

'I remember when you three girls vandalised that beautiful tree.' Stella turned to see her mother gazing at her, a gentle smile on her face. Without waiting for a response, Pam added, 'It was the only time I remember your father being angry with Madison. He was furious at her for encouraging you girls to deface nature.'

Stella shared a laugh with her mother and started washing a new batch of dishes.

'I loved listening to you and Madison running lines from your shows.' A sad smile flickered across her face. 'Or auditioning at the kitchen sink.'

'We squeezed in every opportunity to rehearse together,' Stella replied. 'There were many acting awards dreamed about at this sink!'

Setting down the dish in her hands, Stella moved to the fridge, poured herself a glass of water, and leaned against the kitchen cupboard.

'Mum...'

'Hmmm?' Pam looked up at her, dishcloth in hand. When Stella didn't answer, Pam made a huffing noise, took off her apron, and flipped it onto the kitchen bench as she turned around to give Stella her full attention.

'Oh, for heaven's sake. I know something's on your mind. What is it?'

'My old acting teacher Ray Stevens emailed me,' Stella blurted out. 'There's an audition coming up for *A Streetcar Named Desire*. The one that's going to the West End.'

The way Pam buckled forward into herself, Stella momentarily thought her mother might faint. Lowering her voice to a whisper, she continued, 'I'm beside myself with excitement, you know, but terrified! It will bring up so much that I ...'

'There is nothing to be terrified about,' Pam said encouragingly. 'What role is it?'

Stella bit her lip and met her mother's eyes. 'Blanche DuBois.'

Pam's hands flew up to cover her mouth, muffling her shriek of excitement. 'Nothing would make me happier than seeing you act again,' she said once she'd composed herself. 'There's been such a void in our family since your father and Madison died, and as dearly as Alinta and I love you, neither of us can fill the gaps in your life that they left behind. But I think – and have thought, for years – that acting would make you come alive again.'

'I don't know if I can do it,' Stella confessed. 'I mean, I want to, so much, but I just...don't know. I haven't done anything in a decade.'

'You have! The community theatre auditions you did last year count for something.'

'This is an audition for the West End – not the local amateur theatre group! Anyway, I didn't get any of the parts I auditioned for last year.'

'The roles just weren't meant for you! Think of those auditions as practice – as a warm-up for a *real* audition.'

'I don't think I can to it.'

'I do,' Pam said resolutely. 'I know you can.'

'Are you sure you're not just living vicariously through me, Mum?' Stella asked after a moment. 'Because you wanted to be an actress?'

'That ship sailed a long time ago.' Pam took Stella's hand and squeezed. 'But you still have a shot at it. Ray Stevens believes in you. Madison, Alinta and I believe in you. As does your father, rest his soul.'

'I'll think about it,' Stella promised. 'Besides, the call's gone out to agents for Australian actresses to audition. I don't even have an agent.'

'What did Ray say about the audition?'

'He knows the director and might be able to get me an audition. If I want one… It's a long shot at best.'

Pam paused for a moment, looking intently at Stella.

'Think of Madison. Think of how excited she'd be for you. She never had a chance to pursue her acting career, but you do. Do it for Madison, if not for yourself.

Stella flinched at the mention of her sister.

'Anyway, Mum, look – I've only told Alinta and Gina. Nobody else knows. I'm not telling anyone until I make up my mind and know I have the courage to go ahead with the audition.'

'Does Heath know?' Pam asked, and then continued, 'Gosh he's lovely, isn't he?'

'He is lovely,' Stella agreed, 'but I can't…' Her voice trailed off.

'Speaking about these things can be a jinx,' Pam said immediately, nodding. 'That's alright, darling. Tell him when you land the role.'

'It's not that simple,' Stella protested. '*If* I land the role, it'll require me to…'

She stopped short of revealing why she quit acting. She felt it was kinder not to tell her mother about the assault; her mother was already dealing with the deaths of her husband to cancer followed by her eldest daughter a year later. Instead, Stella let her mother believe she'd stopped acting because Madison had died. It was too late to burden her mother with an admission that the *Streetcar* audition had the potential to trigger her, bringing the assault she'd tried so hard to forget back into focus.

'You two are thick as thieves,' Heath said, cutting her off as he entered the kitchen. 'What's all the chatter about? You girls gossiping away in here? Could've sworn I heard my name.'

Stella managed a smile when he winked at her.

'Oh, nothing, we're just catching up about Stella's work,' Pam said.

'I'm busting to go to the bathroom,' Stella said abruptly. 'Don't let Mum make you wash up!' she called over her shoulder as she left the kitchen. 'You're a guest!'

***

Stella topped up her wine and tucked her feet beneath her, leaning against the back of the couch. 'It's good to see you.'

Alinta smiled. 'Good to see you, and nice to meet Heath! He's a catch.'

Stella smiled and said, 'He is that! I just hope he thinks of me the same way.'

'What does that mean?' Alinta asked, brow furrowing. 'Are you guys having problems or something?'

'No, not anything like that, really at all.' Stella let out a frustrated sigh. 'It's just…he's got this ex, um, Candice.'

'Ah.' Alinta nodded. 'Is she a little too familiar, or something?'

'I'm not sure. I haven't even met her.'

'Did he tell you about her?'

'There was a photo of them in his flat, and when I asked, he told me about her. He said they were together for a short while, but he didn't say when. Because she was a make-up artist and had lived abroad and they tried long distance, but it just didn't work out.'

'Okay,' Alinta said slowly. 'I mean, displaying a picture with you and your ex when you're dating someone new is a little weird, but otherwise I'm not seeing the problem? Or did she move back and start trying to make inroads?'

'The photo wasn't exactly on display,' Stella admitted. 'More like it had fallen at some point and he'd never noticed.'

'Right. That's better, then, not worse. Why is there a problem?'

Stella sighed again, feeling silly. She couldn't help but wonder what it was about Candice, and her presence in Heath's life, that made her so uneasy. 'They're still in touch. I've seen her name pop up occasionally on his phone. He certainly doesn't try to hide their friendship, which is a good thing. It's just, I don't think they ever really stopped chatting even after they broke up. Heath says it's totally platonic, and I believe him, but I can't help thinking if I were her, how reluctant I'd be to let him go and how hopeful I would be to one day rekindle the relationship.'

'Is this about Candice, or is this about the fact that a show in London would require you to leave, and do long distance with Heath, who's already decided that long distance doesn't work?'

Stella narrowed her eyes at her sister. 'Are you moonlighting as a therapist now, little sis?'

'Only for charity cases,' Alinta said, putting her nose in the air. 'You wouldn't be able to afford me.'

Stella burst into laughter, Alinta joining her seconds later, and both were still doubled over when Pam and Heath walked past as Pam took him on a tour of the Longhurst home.

***

Heath had been excited when Stella told him she wanted to introduce him to her family. He saw it as a demonstration of how she felt about him – you didn't share a partner with family unless things were getting serious, and he liked that their relationship was headed in that direction.

Now that he'd met the Longhurst women and seen how lovely they were, he tried not to take it personally that Stella had previously rejected her mother's requests to meet him. Maybe it had felt too soon to Stella; it was hard to know for certain. Regardless, he was delighted to be here now, thoroughly enjoying himself as Pam gave him a tour of the Longhurst home.

As they moved through the house, he noted how affectionately she regarded each of her daughters, how much she admired their talents. He suspected that the tour had been proposed just for her to showcase some of the girls' photos – pictures from their various plays, for instance, adorned the main hallway.

'This photo takes pride of place for obvious reasons,' Pam said, pausing at one photo in particular and gently reaching out to touch the frame.

'I see Stella,' Heath commented, 'and I'm guessing that that's Madison next to her. What's the significance?'

Pam's usually light voice shifted into a more serious register when she answered. 'Of course… You wouldn't know.' She cleared her throat. 'This was from *Taming of the Shrew*. Stella and Madison played Kate and Bianca, respectively. They were both marvellous in their roles, but Stella truly shone in this performance. Kate is an extremely challenging role to play, you know?' Pam tapped triumphantly on the photo's glass casing. 'Stella won a few acting awards back in the day, not that she'd tell you that.'

Pam moved further down the hallway and opened the door to Stella's childhood bedroom, its walls lined with large nostalgic black and white framed photographs of Greta Garbo, Helen Mirren, and Meryl Streep, along with dog-eared posters of *Taxi Driver* featuring a young Jodie Foster and Jessica Lange starring as the troubled 1930 actress Frances Farmer in *Frances*. Also featured in the time-warped bedroom was a giant poster of English actor and playwright Steven Berkoff from his play *One Man*.

'Our Stella spent a lot of time performing in the mirror in this room.' Pam laughed and pointed to the full-length mirror in Stella's modest bedroom. 'She was always performing.' She winked at Heath and they continued the tour.

Pam stopped briefly outside of the closed door to Madison's room. 'I haven't been able to go into this room since the car accident,' she said quietly. 'It was a decade ago now, but I can't bear it.'

'I'm so sorry for your loss.'

'Time doesn't heal grief.' Pam stared at her daughter's door. 'Contrary to what people say, I've found that it only gets worse.'

Knowing it was such a deeply personal subject, and honoured that Pam was opening up to him about the family's tragic loss, Heath waited a moment out of respect and then said cautiously, 'I can't imagine what it would be like to lose one of my brothers.'

Pam sniffed delicately and looked sideways at him, letting him see her still-raw grief. Tears streamed down Pam's face as she said, 'When Madison died, Stella's hair fell out in clumps. Her body stopped working how it's meant to, and I couldn't do anything to help her. She shut down completely… Lost her confidence.'

Heath stroked the side of Pam's arm and said softly, 'It must've been devastating to…' His voice trailed off.

'They both desperately wanted to be actresses,' Pam said. 'When Madison died, Stella's dream died with her. In some ways, I think Madison's death impacted Stella more than her father dying. It was unbelievable that Madison died so soon after Fred…'

After a while, Heath commented, 'Stella rarely speaks about her sister. I know it isn't because she doesn't love her.'

'She can't. Madison's death killed Stella, too, in many ways.'

CHAPTER 10

Stella and Heath took artful photos of one another because they adored each other.

Their photos were ethereal, and Stella told him that she wanted him to paint one photo in particular, its sepia tone making it look as though it had been taken in a Parisian hotel in the 1930s.

Crumpled white cotton sheets fall in long drapes off the bed. Pale pink velvet pillows are scattered around the floor and bed and a painting of an aqua seascape sits above the bedhead. A delicate vase hangs from the roof, whimsical English ivy spilling down its sides. Stella's legs are in the air, her knees slightly bent with toes stretching upwards towards the ceiling. A hint of Stella's breast hugs her ribcage. Heath's hand presses delicately on Stella's legs. The light in the full-length mirror catches the shape of Heath's muscles across his broad shoulders. He peers around the side of Stella's legs, looking straight at her. It's an exquisitely graceful and elegant scene – otherworldly and sensual.

'This photo deserves to be painted,' Stella said again. Heath murmured his agreement. 'I know it wouldn't exactly be appropriate for anyone to see it but us, and of course no one would ever appreciate it, but…' She sighed. 'I can just see it, life-sized, regally framed – a frame you'll have picked out, of course – just celebrated for its beauty.' With a smile, she turned slightly and nuzzled her nose against Heath's neck. 'I guess I'll have to be satisfied knowing it'll always be in my phone.'

More than that – to Heath, that photo became an emblem of their relationship, of the love they had yet to confess to each other, something to be occasionally messaged between them as a love note without words.

Heath was queuing at the supermarket when the Paris hotel room photo popped up on his phone. As he glanced down at it, he admitted it to himself at last:

Jesus, I'm falling in love with her.

It had only been a few months since he'd started dating Stella, but their infectious energy had received a silent nod of approval from their respective friend groups, for which he was grateful.

Heath had invited Stella to an art exhibition, which the most important people in his life also attended. Though he rarely wore a suit jacket, the exhibition – a significant charity fundraiser featuring several of Heath's paintings and works by other artists – was important enough for him to throw one over a shirt. As Stella had told him more than once, he was the guy who could slap on a shirt and jeans and look like a million bucks.

'You look beautiful, baby girl,' Heath said when he opened the door to find Stella wearing a black dress with heels to match.

'For a hippy painter, you scrub up okay,' Stella said, following Heath's eyes as they traced over every inch of her body.

At the exhibition, Heath wrapped his arm around Stella's waist. From her smile, he could tell she enjoyed his gentle familiarity, that she saw he was listening intently as she spoke, telling her she had his full attention.

Heath kept a careful eye on Stella as they moved around the exhibition, introducing her to new people and artists every few steps. After what felt like the tenth new person in as many minutes, he reached for Stella's hand and gave it a little squeeze. 'How are you going?' he asked, eyes intent on her face. 'I feel like I've thrown you to the wolves tonight.'

'I'm enjoying myself,' Stella said with a smile; she was so skilled at burying her nerves when she met new people; she deserved an Academy Award. 'Your colleagues are great.'

'They're telling me I'm a lucky man.' He grinned and pulled her close to whisper in her ear, 'How did I get so lucky?'

He knew he was a fine catch, even if he was usually modest about it. The quiet confidence he carried came from a *what you see is what you get* approach to life. That, and being a self-made man. He'd carved out an illustrious career as an award-winning painter with a reputation for creating exquisite works, and he was proud of who he was and what he'd accomplished.

'Did you ever think you'd be here?' Stella asked. Heath frowned, confused, and she clarified, 'I mean with painting. When you first started out, did you think you'd be this successful?'

He studied the painting in front of them, trying to think of a way to respond that didn't sound arrogant. Finally, he said, 'Well, when I graduated from uni with my bachelor's, I already had requests to produce artwork from several companies and a private gallery. So that gave me a major start. And, not to sound smug, but my paintings have featured in TV shows and art and lifestyle magazines. I guess I've been lucky.'

Stella tugged him slightly to move on to the next piece of art. 'What's the most interesting commission you've ever had?'

Heath laughed. 'There was this singer, oh man! I was ferried to her home out in the sticks via a helicopter, and the whole place was just big, and opulent, and just the whole nine yards. Took me a while to complete the project, but I got a bird's eye view while I was there of how the very rich and famous live.' He shook his head. 'Not really my cup of tea, but it's an arena I play in when I have to – I just always try to take it with a grain of salt. A bit like these exhibitions. I love doing charity fundraisers but generally, I find exhibitions and events painful.'

Stella nodded and then said, 'You and me both. Let's do a runner out the back door!'

Heath laughed, 'Soon! … But not just yet. There are a few special people I want you to meet.'

A woman sporting a stylish grey-white bob, purple reading glasses and a cream linen suit held court at the centre of a group of people. Whenever she animatedly swooped her arm into the air, the sequin bracelet she wore splotched colourful dots against the white gallery wall. Heath could tell from the smile on Stella's face that she'd guessed that the woman was his mother.

Squeezing Stella's hand, Heath tugged her through the crowd behind him until they joined the small group at the opposite end of the gallery. He sneaked up behind his middle brother Elias, who was about to take a bite of quiche, caught him in a headlock, and ruffled his hair.

'You only came for the food, you glutton. Leave some for the other guests!'

'You dickhead, Heath!' Elias exclaimed. 'You nearly made me drop the quiche.' Elias jutted his hand forward to shake Stella's. 'Are you sure you know what you're doing hanging out with this bloke? I'm Elias.' A grin flashed across his face as he added, 'Also a painter, and a better painter than my brother.'

Janie swooped in to stand in front of the trio, introducing herself to Stella while Heath waved at a potential art buyer. 'Hello, darling!' Janie said, recapturing Heath's attention. She patted his chest several times, pleased to see him. 'The exhibition is wonderful. Congratulations, darling.'

Heath let himself get drawn into a conversation with Elias, but kept one ear on his mother's conversation with Stella.

'I hope the art snobs aren't boring you too much,' Janie said, her hushed words still reaching Heath's ears. 'It's amazing how seriously artists take themselves.'

'It's really lovely to meet you, Janie,' Stella said with a smile. 'I'd noticed that everyone's opinion is the most important one in the room.' She plucked a glass of champagne from a passing waiter's tray and gulped a mouthful, quickly wiping the corner of her mouth where it had spilled.

Janie laughed. 'I think artists sometimes forget that no matter how many degrees or formal education they have, anyone's opinion is just that – an opinion.'

Stella took another sip of champagne and quipped, 'Artists do speak a rarefied language at times!'

Lifting her arms in an open gesture towards Heath, Janie continued, 'Anyway, we do love artists. There are some very special ones in the world.'

'Agreed!' Stella said a little too enthusiastically.

Heath glanced at her and winked as she blushed.

'He isn't in the least pretentious,' Stella said as Heath moved in to place a hand on each of the womens' shoulders.

He kissed his mum on the cheek, saying, 'Stop singing my praises, Mum. You're embarrassing me.'

As Stella was distracted by Elias, Janie turned to her son and said, 'She's as beautiful as you said, Heath. And charming. And I see you've already got a red dot on one of your paintings. It's good to see one of your works sell for such a worthwhile cause.'

'It means a lot to me, and Stella, that this fundraiser is for cancer research,' Heath said quietly. 'It makes me somehow feel like I'm contributing in some small way to her father, even though I didn't know him. Fuck cancer, hey, Mum.'

'Yes, darling,' Janie responded quietly. 'Sadly, cancer doesn't discriminate. I'll always be grateful that we still have your father after his cancer scare a few years ago.'

'When does Dad get back from his fishing trip? I'll bring Stella over to meet him.'

'He's back next week,' Janie smiled and nodded knowingly. 'It must be getting serious if you're wanting to introduce her to Pa. I'm happy for you, darling.'

Just then, the emcee chinked a champagne glass to bring the crowded room to silence for the formal part of the evening.

As soon as the speeches and acknowledgements were over, Heath moved Stella through the crowd and found the women who had organised the exhibition. They offered congratulations on a successful event, said goodbye to Heath's family, and then escaped, keen to get back to his place and be alone together.

Back at Heath's apartment, Stella took her shoes off and flopped down on the lounge, clearly exhausted. She'd told Heath earlier how draining it was having such a long commute to work each week for a job and boss she despised.

Heath lit a few candles and turned on the Friday Night Special playlist they'd created. He sat on the floor and motioned for Stella to rub his neck and shoulders, which were stiff from working all week. She pulled herself up from the couch, sat with her legs around Heath, and took his shoulders in her hands. It was nearly midnight, but her touch made him come alive.

Stella and Heath created a beautiful love bubble in his ramshackle, tiny two-bedroom bachelor pad. That weekend, their intimacy was constant and moved to another level.

Heath knew he and Stella were a rare combination of two people who instinctively knew what the other needed physically, emotionally, and intellectually.

***

On Sunday afternoon, after two days of being glued to each other, Stella and Heath lay at the opposite ends of the lounge with their legs entwined. One of Heath's long legs stretched across the middle of Stella's body, and his foot gently rested on her chest. They were in full swing, play-acting the characters they occasionally rolled out to entertain themselves.

Heath played Mr Hyde Park, an arrogant and stiff yet hilarious Englishman. Stella played Claude, a beautiful and sophisticated French woman, the type of lady who'd only wear silk knickers and never fart.

They fell in and out of character, laughing at the ludicrous stereotypes they depicted. An astute observer, Heath had an uncanny ability for razor-sharp impersonations, delighting Stella whenever he effortlessly dropped into the deadpan Mr Hyde Park and his excellent comic timing. He felt so confident in her company and secretly loved it when she said he could have been an actor.

Heath brought characters to life purely to entertain Stella. Her second favourite character was Alessandro, a suave metro Italian who never swore, wore too much cologne, and always ordered for Stella at restaurants. Then there was Russell, a lazy pie-eating, beer-swilling bogan football player who represented any man who'd ever been rude to a woman.

Stella loved that they could break into different characters so easily, on long drives, at the beach, or over the phone. This spontaneous side of Heath felt open to her alone, something that nobody else got to see.

As they lay on the lounge, Heath's foot still gently resting on Stella's chest, he asked, 'Why don't you start acting again? I know you'd love to.'

There was a long pause, as Stella's heart began to race, before she removed his foot and sat upright, collecting her thoughts.

'I bet you were a good actress,' he said carefully.

Stella stared into the middle distance before finally saying, 'My old acting teacher, Ray Stevens, thinks so. He often emails or messages me to ask when I'll get back to the stage.'

'Ray Stevens believes in your talent, then.' He paused, watching her, and then asked, 'Do you think you were a good actress?'

'Was I *good*?' Stella repeated, her voice contemplative.

Inherently, she knew she was a talented actress. But it was always awkward answering this question, especially since she'd almost never discussed her acting career since the horrific experience that caused her to give it up.

She pondered Heath's question a second time and then tried to downplay her response, hoping to satisfy his curiosity without going into more detail. 'Was I *good*? ... I guess I was okay.'

'You're being modest,' Heath said. 'Your mother couldn't tell me quickly enough that you won four acting awards and had a couple of professional agents. You must've been better than okay!'

'I suppose I was good,' Stella said after a long pause. 'I did a lot of theatre. I loved acting but never got a significant break.'

She could almost sense him trying to decide whether to press her for more information, knowing she had unfinished business as an actress.

'I'm sorry this makes you feel uncomfortable,' he said gently. 'I guess I'm curious about why you aren't willing to give acting another try if you loved it so much. There's no time like the present, and it isn't too late to go back to it.'

Stella paused again before continuing, 'Look, it's a long story, Heath, and I don't want to get into it right now. Suffice to say, what happened in my acting career broke me in every conceivable way, and I'd rather not relive it.'

Heath leaned over and kissed her on the cheek. As he pulled away, there was something about his expression that made Stella think there was something more he wanted to say, but instead he shook his head, hoisted himself off the couch, and plodded off to the kitchen.

He'd been right, though; she had won awards, like Best Actress for *Time Inside*.

The two-hander play had toured to different states in Australia, and Stella's parents had told her so many times they were the proudest they'd ever been sitting in the audience watching her receive the award. Her co-star, a 70-year-old man, had won Best Actor for his performance as the menacing elder to whom her character was sent to do community service as punishment for petty theft.

As quickly as this proud moment arose, it turned to distress at the memory of Jay Styler and that minuscule rehearsal room. Jay's criticism and failure to admonish Steve Crosley had had more lasting impact than Crosley actually pushing her face into his crotch that day.

Stella had read that anxiety takes hold of its host in extraordinary ways. Though she usually felt entirely at ease speaking to large audiences, since Jay Styler had wreaked havoc on her life, she had discovered how quickly she became distressed or claustrophobic in confined spaces. An intimate dinner or work meeting in a small room, particularly if she was the centre of attention, could immediately transport her back to the trauma she'd experienced that day.

From her research, Stella had learned that avoidance behaviour only fuelled anxiety – the energy it took to evade certain situations causing stress itself – yet she would purposely schedule appointments at the same time as work meetings, to escape the glare of people on her. When it was her turn to do a weekly work-in-progress update in front of colleagues, her palms would sweat, and her ears would ring as the moment came closer to when everyone's attention would be on her. She would twist her fingers under the table and try to stop her eyes from bulging, making her look like a deer in headlights. Sometimes her mouth would make a weird jerky movement at the thought of making words come from it. A mere two-to-five minutes of speaking publicly before long-term colleagues might send her into a ruminating spin for days beforehand. Sometimes when she felt pressured to be on show, she'd be transported back to the rehearsal room she'd run away from... To the day when she learned to run away from her fears instead of facing them.

For an actress once filled with fervour and confidence, it was embarrassingly crippling.

***

Heath returned from the kitchen and placed two cups of coffee on the dining room table. 'Where have you gone, baby girl?' he asked. 'You're a million miles away.'

Stella turned to him with a smile. She loved it when he called her baby girl, that he could get away with it. The gentle way that his voice dropped to an intimate tone, as though there was something slightly sacred about the pet name.

My God, you're a solid human.

'What were you thinking about?'

'I was thinking,' Stella said slowly, 'about the time I won an acting award for *Time Inside*. It's one of my happiest memories. I also remembered –' She stopped short of finishing her sentence.

'What?' Heath asked. 'What did you remember?'

She hesitated, and then said, 'It's criminal that the #MeToo movement didn't exist when I was acting. A spotlight must be shone on both men and women who abuse young performers, the Harvey Weinstein-types of the world. There are plenty of cowboy and cowgirl directors and producers who destroy young actors' careers. I speak from personal experience.'

The tears welling in her eyes seemed to tell Heath that she'd discussed the acting topic enough for one day.

'That's horrendous,' he said at last. 'Look, you don't have to go into detail about it. Now, or ever, if you don't want to. I know you have unfinished business with your acting career, but I'm not going to push you on it if you don't want me to.'

She looked up at him, amazed as always just how easily he could read her, and so much more accurately than any clairvoyant. Though she appreciated that he was willing to back off, the truth was, Ray's email to tell her that a production of *A Streetcar Named Desire* needed an understudy had prompted daydreams about reigniting her acting career. And the understudy role was for a character she'd performed years earlier, as a student.

She'd abandoned her dreams a decade ago, but this? To perform this role again? It would absolutely be her dream come true – mainly as the play was being performed in London, and she'd always dreamed of living and acting in London.

If only she could get past her destructive insecurity to enquire about the role.

CHAPTER 11

Loud music reverberated through Heath's ute on the hour-long trip to Tamborine Mountain, the lush green canopy of the Scenic Rim providing a gorgeous 360-degree panoramic backdrop.

Stella sat like the Queen of Sheba with her legs crossed in a lotus pose in the passenger seat, gazing out the window with her face turned upwards, long hair trailing in the wind. She sang the chorus to Powderfinger's *Passenger* at the top of her lungs, accompanied by Heath on drums, smacking the heel of his hand on the steering wheel.

He could have been a drummer, Stella thought. *He has music in his bones.*

She reached across the centre console to rest her hand on Heath's thigh, a gesture that hinted at the claim she was beginning to feel. She was more affectionate and softer with Heath than anyone she'd met. Her hand had begun to fall naturally into this position; she'd caught it in the same position a few weeks earlier at a Vance Joy concert. Dressed in theatre attire for the seated theatre-style performance, they had huddled in close to watch the band churn through three hours of popular hits plus a smattering of new tracks, with Stella's hand repeatedly finding its way back to the warmth of Heath's leg between bouts of applause.

The ute gathered pace up the mountain, winding in and out of curves in a rhythmic swirl.

Heath turned the music down to point at the passing scenery. Stella smiled; with his love of nature, he might have been born under a eucalyptus tree. She eyed him appreciatively; his green flannelette was unbuttoned and rolled midway to his elbow, revealing a thick, bronzed forearm and offering a rugged farmer aesthetic.

'It's a lush playground out there,' he said enthusiastically. 'Sections of the Gondwana Rainforest are World Heritage areas – and too right.' He guided the ute around a particularly sharp curve and glanced sideways at her, a smile lighting up his face. 'Let's walk through one of the national parks tomorrow and find us a waterfall.'

An invisible layer of charged energy vacillated between them; as the tips of Stella's fingers pressed into Heath's thigh, she wished she could bottle the grounding feeling she got any time she was touching him.

He reached over, cupped Stella's cheek, and gave her a wink.

She unfolded her legs, freeing them from lotus position to rest her feet on the dash, moved by how a simple wink could display such a deep knowing of affection. She caught Heath looking to the road and then back at her, squaring his eyes momentarily at her – she knew he was waiting for a reaction. She had a habit of joking around to break an occasion's intensity; he understood her thoughts and feelings like no other, to such a degree it was humbling.

'You look so happy right now, Heath,' Stella said laughingly. 'I'm so happy for you.' Her words intentionally mimicked the type of shmaltzy thing people tended to say when they approved of a friend's newfound relationship happiness.

'You're so lucky to have found me, baby,' Heath deadpanned in response.

Stella took a few deep breaths to collect herself and said, 'I can't work out if you're better suited to the ocean or the mountains.'

'I guess it depends on the time of year,' he said thoughtfully, 'but I'd happily live both by the ocean and in the mountains. The ultimate would be to have surf at my doorstep with mountain ranges as a backdrop.'

'It's definitely the ocean for me,' Stella said, 'but wherever it is, the house must have lots of books. And music constantly playing.' She stopped herself from further elaborating on her dream home, worried that maybe their relationship wasn't yet to the point of discussing where to live. 'Gosh, this view is beautiful,' she said abruptly. 'Mother Nature in all her glory.'

'The female form is present everywhere in nature,' Heath commented. 'Women give birth to life, and Mother Nature is constantly producing new life. In fact, the word 'nature' is Latin for birth or pre-natal.'

'How apt,' Stella said. 'I hope we find a waterfall tomorrow.'

'We'll find one, Stelz. We just might not be able to swim in it because of the wildlife.'

She cranked the volume on the stereo as they chimed in with Powderfinger's *Waiting for the Sun* at the top of their lungs, singing over the sound of the ute roaring up the mountain.

*****

Hidden among the trees, the private treehouse at Martha's Rainforest Retreat was the perfect setting for their first romantic getaway, just as Heath had hoped.

A recently lit fire was already warming the room when they arrived; a bottle of champagne sat chilling in the fridge. French linen robes hung next to the spa above white slippers, and fine chocolates formed a heart on the black kitchen benchtop.

The cabin's five-metre-high glass windows led to an outdoor balcony overlooking a spectacular subtropical rainforest, home to a menagerie of birdlife, mammals, and reptiles. It met with Heath's approval, but he watched Stella carefully as she took in their surroundings, looking for her endorsement of their home for the next two nights.

'This is all I'd need for a home,' he said. He was usually critical of colour schemes, but so beautiful was the room's design that it had won him over. 'It just needs an art studio.'

He sculpted a house in his mind's eye. A home he shared with Stella, its walls lined with art, with stacks of books littered about and music rattling the window frames.

'This place is spectacular,' Stella said. 'Whoever selected the décor has a great eye. I'm so excited to be spending the weekend here!' She paused and brushed light fingertips across his chest, bringing him back to the present moment. 'What are you thinking about?'

'You. I'm always thinking about you.'

He considered telling her about his wish for them to live together but was distracted by the look in Stella's eyes. Her dilated pupils were an invitation for intimacy, one he'd become very familiar with. It only took a few seconds for them to step up into the bedroom to explore each other's bodies.

He cupped Stella's face in his hand and angled her mouth upwards to meet his lips. He sealed his upper and lower lips around her mouth, pausing for a few seconds to just feel her whole mouth inside of his.

The calm before the storm, he thought as he released her mouth.

Stella undid the top two buttons of his shirt and tugged at the collar, her eyes flirting with his. As he pulled the shirt up over his head and threw it to the ground, he saw Stella inhale a musky whiff of underarm sweat mixed with deodorant drifted over her; he knew from previous experience that she liked the way he smelled.

She brushed her lips across his and turned to press their cheeks together, taking in his smell and the warmth of their bodies against one another.

He unbuttoned Stella's cardigan to run feather-light fingers over her belly. Goosebumps appeared on her arms and legs. He rested his hand on the soft part of her belly and stretched his fingers as wide as they could go, pressing the tips of his fingers into her skin. 'I love your curves,' he whispered in her ear, and then moved his hands to shape her ribcage.

Wedging his fingers into the band of Stella's skirt, he turned her towards him and pulled her close, their bellies and breath syncing in rhythmic anticipation; he unzipped her skirt, flicking it down her thighs to the ground.

Stella exaggeratedly stepped out of the skirt, pausing briefly to reveal her naked self to Heath, before gracefully repeating the movement with her other leg. Her confidence with him was unmatched.

'You are stunning,' Heath said, settling his hands on either side of Stella's hips to turn her around and guide her face down onto the bed. 'Stay there, I'll grab some oil.'

The warm afternoon sun shone through the glass, the dappled light shifting across the bed and highlighting Stella's olive skin and the chestnut strands in her dark hair. Droplets of oil spilled across the top of Stella's shoulders, down her spine, and over her plump butt.

Heath leaned into her. 'Do you want a massage?' She didn't need to answer him; he knew she did.

Staring at Stella, lying face down on the bed, Heath knew she would be imagining his expression, the way his eyes glistened with a level of interest that suggested he was seeing her naked for the first time.

He adored how she trusted him. She was his masterpiece, and much of her body would receive a generous brushstroke of oil from his fingertips over the next hour. Her shoulders, back, arms, legs, buttocks, and feet had his undivided attention. He slid long fingers all over her body, massaging her into a surreal, hazy spell.

He turned her over to expose her naked front body and massaged the front of Stella's body with inquiring strokes, knowing instinctively where to touch and knead, his fingers invigorating and relaxing her simultaneously. It was therapeutic and sensual in equal measure, with muffled sighs announcing her enjoyment.

During the following hour he pleasured her, after which she lay motionless for several minutes, swimming in a haze of bliss. Heath watched as she softened into a pool of jelly. The room was thickly quiet, the birds had stopped singing.

'This is what nirvana feels like,' Stella murmured at length. 'Mmm…heaven.'

A takeaway pizza and glass of red wine by the open fire sealed the night as the perfect start to their weekend away.

CHAPTER 12

A light knock on the cabin door at 8 am signified that a breakfast basket had been delivered.

Heath, who was already up and brewing coffee, collected the basket. It was charming, Stella thought, the way the basket casually dangled from his forearm, the white bathrobe billowing behind him as he glided across the room to set it down on the table with the aplomb of an experienced butler. A man of his towering size rarely emanated such aplomb, making her admire his grace.

'Your breakfast is here, dearest.'

The clipped English accent announced that Heath had invited Mr Hyde Park to the cabin for breakfast.

Stella lowered her voice, swallowed her vowels, and spoke with precision as Claude, a sophisticated Parisian who would never squeeze a pimple in front of her partner.

'How utterly kind of you to collect our breakfast basket, Monsieur Park. Dites-moi, what lies beneath the napkin in the basket?'

Mr Hyde Park whipped the cloth napkin from the basket with flair and discarded it on the floor.

'Why! There is a veritable feast here, ma chère mademoiselle. The kitchen has made an impressive attempt to cater to our every need.'

'Faaabulous!' Claude warbled. 'S'il vous plaît, Monsieur Park, list all the items, merci.'

'Well, well… There are croissants, cinnamon and sultana swirls, muesli with freshly whipped yogurt, hard-boiled eggs, and toast, plus an assortment of jams and honey. Did I mention toast?'

'Oui! Such a feast!' Claude exclaimed. 'Just what we need to build our stamina for the walk.'

'Mademoiselle Claude... I should have also mentioned there are crumpets and waffles. I wonder what the peasants are doing for breakfast.'

Mr Park tuned the stereo to the jazz channel, poured coffee, and set the table. Claude threw a dress on and met Mr Park at the table for breakfast.

The two sampled the many breakfast options, never skipping a beat in the guises of Mr Hyde Park and Claude. Their endless banter ranged from a discussion about which jazz musician they were listening to - to which bushwalk trail they'd take for the day - to whether they'd visit a vineyard later or go paragliding instead.

***

Of the different hiking trails, they chose a modest trail to explore the natural eucalypt forest surroundings, with towering gums as their guide.

Stella took the lead, setting a quick pace towards the rainforest's bedrock. Heath knew she enjoyed testing his fitness levels; she hadn't exposed a competitive side yet, but he suspected that when she did, her competitiveness would match his.

'You've set a cracking speed, Stelz,' Heath called after her. 'Be careful you don't roll an ankle.'

'You have one job,' she teased. 'Keep up with me.'

Challenge accepted.

Despite legs so much longer than hers, he only just managed to keep up, though he stopped occasionally to capture candids of her among the magnificent rainforest canopy, sneaking photos as she darted along the trail.

He liked how her energy picked up in certain circumstances, how she could wring the life out of any situation and turn challenges into adventure.

His focus shifted from scanning the ground for potential hazards to the back of Stella's head, her ponytail bobbing up and down as she skipped across rocks and branches on the trail. They could be 70, 30, or teenagers; their compatibility was matched by boundless energy, common interests, an equal intimate appetite and a thirst for knowledge and conversation.

The sound of rushing water, so quiet at first, rapidly increased towards what was sure to become a deafening pitch.

'Waterfall!' Stella called over her shoulder, so loudly that native birds scarpered in the opposite direction. She burst out of the trees and stopped to stare out at a sparkling, rushing flow of water.

Heath paused to capture the perfect snapshot of Stella standing at the edge of the waterfall and enjoying the scenery before catching up and coming to stand beside her. 'What a beauty.'

'The waterfall or me?' Stella quipped.

They stood shoulder to shoulder for a long time, enjoying the scenery, hoping to spot a platypus in the water.

***

Saturday morning flew by, and as afternoon drew near, Heath and Stella found themselves torn between going paragliding or to a vineyard.

'Rock, paper, scissors,' they chimed in chorus.

'Paper wins!' Heath boasted.

The next round – 'Scissors wins!' Stella yelled.

'Paper wins!' Heath shouted after the third round, his fist pumping the air before he performed a loud drum roll on the dining room table. 'We're going paragliding, Stelz! The wind is perfect for flying today; we can visit a vineyard tomorrow.'

A dare-devil solo skydiver and a deep-sea diver lived underneath Heath's calm and collected exterior. For Stella's part, her nerves and lack of paragliding experience, were buoyed by Heath's enthusiasm.

'We've got a good wind,' Heath said. 'It's blowing in exactly the direction we need. You'll be on cloud nine in the sky!'

The things one gets oneself into… Stella thought.

The first thing Stella noticed, standing on the Tamborine Mountain launch site overlooking the breathtaking valley, were the many trees between herself and the landing area. She paid earnest attention as the safety officer, Mick, robotically reeled off information to the group of expectant paragliders about wind strength, bomb-out areas, sink cycles, turbulence, shadows, and more than she cared to know about the perils of potentially hitting a tree.

Mick spoke efficiently and matter-of-factly with a broad Australian accent, the hint of boredom in his voice unnerving her. It should have been comforting that Mick had supervised countless launches, although the way he casually roll-called other first-time paragliders' mishaps did border on gauche. The plaster cast pinning Mick's right arm across his chest, which he occasionally stroked affectionately, added a level of drama that he appeared to revel in.

''Scuze the busted arm, won't you,' Mick said. 'All you virgin paragliders can rest in the comfort that I broke my arm coming off my motorbike, not falling out of the sky.' He paused for a few awkward moments, waiting for the group to join in laughing with him. 'Righto, then,' he said, once a few weak chuckles had sounded. 'Let's do a quiz on the equipment.' Pointing to the wing, he looked at one of the women and said, 'Jane, what's this thingy called?'

'Um, it's the parachute.'

'Oops! Wrong answer, Janey. You might need to call on the help of Tarzan with an answer like that.' Mick laughed again at his own joke and proceeded to beat the good side of his chest with his unbroken arm, making a Tarzan call to rival Johnny Weissmuller.

'Jesus Christ,' Stella mumbled to Heath. 'Our fate is in the hands of this imbecile.'

'There's no such thing as a parachute in paragliding,' Mick continued. 'I think what you meant to answer, Janey, was wing.' He turned to Richard, a middle-aged, well-spoken man. 'Dick – I mean Richard, apologies. What do you call this thingamabob?' Mick narrowed a knowing squint at Richard as he indicated the thingamabob in question.

'I believe you'll find it's a compass, Mick.'

'Well done, Dicky! You shoot all the way to the top of the class.' Mick winced and readjusted his cast before saying, 'Look, all you lot need to know is that paragliders fly on the same basic principles of flight that aeroplanes do. To keep the nylon wing pressurised, we use ram-air technology. When air enters the large opening in the front of the wing, it gets trapped and forms a pressurised shape.

That's basically it. Do what your tandem flight instructor tells you to do, and you'll be fine. Oh, and please don't vomit or wee on your instructor!'

Stella's gaze remained fixed on Mick, her eyebrows raised so high that she could feel her hairline forced back on her head.

This man doesn't have a scintilla of obligation about him. I'm about to die from smashing into a tree and this man's only concern is pee.

Knowing there was little room for error in paragliding, Stella wondered if she should plant her butt down on the sloping hill and remain a spectator for the day.

Farcical thought. There's no way you'll disappoint Heath – put on your big girl pants and get on with it, Stella. Today you become a paraglider.

With the help of her instructor, Stella slung the harness onto her back and connected the leg and chest straps, paying particular attention to ensuring the A and D lines weren't tangled, as instructed.

Heath tapped Stella on the shoulder. 'Are you ready?'

'I've never been readier.' She wondered if he could see the different truth in her eyes.

'You can pull out if you're nervous. Don't feel you need to do this for me. Baby, don't do this if you don't want to.'

'I've spent a lifetime forcing myself into situations that make me nervous,' Stella said reassuringly. 'I'll be okay. but thanks for checking in.'

'Seriously?' Heath frowned. 'You need to be honest with me. If you don't feel comfortable, sit this out. The last thing I want is for you to force yourself into a situation you're uncomfortable with.'

'Well, I have been falling off things and over things my entire life,' Stella told him with an awkward little laugh. 'I'm so clumsy. If anyone's prone to crashing, it would be me.'

Heath was quick to respond. 'You'll love the feeling of being free as a bird once you leave terra firma.' His reassurances bolstered Stella's nerves as he continued, 'The best advice I can give you is to let your body become one with the craft and the instructor. Ride the vessel and let it ride you. It's like riding a Vespa; you become one with the object. You told me you've ridden plenty of motor scooters travelling in Asia; just relax into the experience.'

'Riding a Vespa at 20 kilometres feels a lot different than tempting death by flinging myself into a tree at high speed,' Stella muttered. 'But, yes, I'll meld, fuse, and compound myself into the craft. I can work with that metaphor, Heath.'

Heath took a step back down the steep hill, threw his arms into the air to balance, and released a close-mouthed laugh before bursting out, 'Who else would say, "Compound myself into the craft!?"' He grinned at her. 'You do have a way with words… I'd like to compound myself into you.'

'*I* have a way with words,' Stella said pertly. 'This, from the man who quotes idioms as though they are gospel and trots out low-budget movies lines like, "*Riiide* the vessel and let it ride you."'

The group of awaiting paragliders split off into smaller groups with their instructors, positioning themselves for their turn to glide off the mountain.

Their harnesses and helmets bumped against one another as Heath skipped back up the hill to take Stella into a ginormous bear hug and slowly whisper, 'I. Adore. You.'

A northerly breeze fanned the goosebumps trailing up the side of Stella's neck, where Heath's breath lifted off her skin. She softened her whole body against the warmth of his, their helmets bumping together. 'I adore you, too.' Caught off guard by the emotion in her voice, so close to saying *love* but knowing it wasn't the right time, she predictably shifted to lighten the moment. 'Should I be worried that you're professing your undying admiration for me because you're about to fly off into the distance and never come back?'

'You don't know the half of how I feel, Stella,' he said earnestly, holding her hands in his. 'You know, I –'

Mick took an exaggerated swig from a super-sized can of Red Bull, and proclaimed with sudden importance, 'It's no time for fornication, love birds. Gliders need to be on their game.'

Stella was first to jump off the mountain with the pilot, shooting Heath a determined look as they took flight. As they soared above the ground, she quietly recited a mantra from her acting days.

No matter which character she played, whenever Stella was in the wings and about to go on stage to perform, she would psyche herself up by repeating, 'Confident, cool, composed Capulet.' The meditative mantra had always served as a psychological security blanket whenever she needed to push past her comfort zone, whether those were work presentations or social settings where she might feel awkward. She would cast any panic aside, employ the mantra, and draw on her acting ability to become the most animated storyteller in the room, completely zapping her energy yet maintaining her reputation as a raconteur extraordinaire.

Ever since she could remember, Stella had made a career out of rescuing others from dying a death of social awkwardness – including colleagues, friends, family, partners, and total strangers. It had never been a conscious decision to make it her responsibility to resuscitate a floundering conversation – to practically trip over herself at parties to fill a void in a discussion – or to save an awkward scene of partygoers hiding behind muffled coughs and quick successive sips of their drinks. Introverts couldn't be expected to talk when drinking or eating, so drink and eat they would.

It was just what Stella did, probably because she'd fought introversion since the fateful last day she acted, when everything had changed.

Observing people's vulnerability pained her. Nothing could stop her from rescuing someone from their own awkwardness.

Sometimes Stella would rescue a person simply by pretending that their social awkwardness didn't exist.

CHAPTER 13

Stella tucked her knees to her chest, rolled onto her side, and wrestled the sheets over her head. A perfect weekend at a rainforest retreat and an upcoming short week weren't exactly rousing her enthusiasm for work. The 90-minute daily commute from Terranora in northern NSW to her office in Brisbane was almost as insufferable as working with Oliver.

Ping!

She didn't need to check her phone to know that the text was from her mother.

> How was the romantic weekend getaway?

Rolling onto her other side, Stella held a pillow against her head, counted to 30, and said, 'ping' at the exact moment her mother's second text arrived.

> What are you doing about the audition, Stella? Lucille Ball was 40 when she got her big break with *I Love Lucy.* It isn't too late to follow your dreams!

Still in bed with one eye glued shut, Stella reached for her phone.

> The weekend was great. I actually feel happy.

> Rushing to get out the door to work. I'll ring you later.

Stella flicked through several social media feeds, each post receiving a second of her attention, before scanning ABC News for the day's headlines.

Three minutes later: *ping!*

> I haven't spoken to you in days, Stella. Yes, ring me later.

> Drive carefully on the highway.

Ping!

> You didn't answer me about the audition. I noticed that.

Except for her father, Stella's mother had always been her biggest fan and loved reading parts her daughter performed in, although she sometimes took her involvement too far.

*****

When Stella had played Ginny in Alan Ayckbourn's *Relatively Speaking* at the Apex Theatre in Sydney, her mother wanted to be supportive – so she came to see the show multiple times. Each night, she booked a ticket in the middle of Row J; Stella could just about make her out from the stage.

Relatively Speaking was a farcical romp, and Pam, knowing all the lines, had to restrain herself from calling out some of Stella's punchlines, such was her excitement.

It made matters even worse that Stella didn't particularly enjoy performing in the show, favouring more dramatic roles over comedies of misunderstanding. When an opportunity to perform the lead role in Ibsen's *Hedda Gabler* came along, Stella believed she'd reached the pinnacle of her acting career. And in a sense, it was. *Hedda Gabler* was her last show before the assault, and before Madison died tragically around the same time.

The non-acting members of the Longhurst family were always pleased whenever Stella or Madison invited them to participate in script readings, but they each viewed this responsibility differently;

Fred, for instance, was always happy to play several roles if someone else was too busy to read lines.

Pam's input was always immediate, and sometimes, much to Stella's chagrin, she took over directing rehearsals. Fred imbued each character with detailed personalities, playing different physical and voice traits from the first reading. It always impressed Stella how little she needed to direct her father and how easily she could convince Alinta to play whatever character was needed.

Sometimes, when preparing for an audition and when she was satisfied that she'd perfected a character, Stella would call on the big guns – Madison – to assume the role, to provide her interpretation of the character. Madison was the first person Stella had called about the audition for *Hedda Gabler*, as she knew she would rely on her sister's acting ability to help secure the role.

She could admit, albeit grudgingly, that Madison could intuit subtleties for playing Hedda that Stella might have overlooked – and in doing so, make her performance better. As an actress, Madison had an inborn ability to be great, possessing an incisive, natural ability for performance, the kind of thing that couldn't be taught.

'I haven't read *Hedda Gabbler* since school,' Madison had commented when Stella told her about the audition. 'I remember her character, but not all the details about the play.'

Stella wanted Madison's natural analysis of the different colours of the character of Hedda – some of which she'd use to influence her performance.

'Stop being a purist, Stelz!' Madison had laughed with a roll of her eyes. 'I don't have time to read the play, only the monologue. Remind me what happens.'

'It's a suicide play,' Stella said. 'Hedda is newly bound in a meaningless and boring marriage. She can't stand her husband, and the fact that she's pregnant by him revolts her. It all ends badly.'

With this limited information, Madison had played Hedda's ambition, poshness, passion, and dirtiness with such precision that it made Stella cry – not from sadness but rather out of respect for her ability.

She knew Madison could have been great, but her sister had been snatched away far too soon, and now, as Stella began to consider a return to theatre, she could feel Madison's presence with her again.

***

Just as Stella was dragging herself out of bed to take a shower for work, another text arrived from her mother.

Ping!

Do it! Audition! You're THE perfect Blanche!

Stella resisted calling in sick, resolving that she'd spend the morning's event debrief reflecting on the weekend, texting Heath while earnestly pretending to take notes.

Steam condensed on the bathroom mirror as Stella pressed her face towards the glass, taking in her reflection. As she cleared a circle of fog the size of her face, her finger rubbing on the mirror made an amplified noise that sounded like squeaking strings.

The chocolate eyes staring back at her revealed light speckles of hazel in the iris. She tilted her head upwards and took in a deep breath as she turned her head from side to side, looking at her reflection. There was a considerable chasm between looking at oneself and seeing oneself. She hadn't truly *seen* herself since she gave up acting. Except for something she saw reflected in the way Heath looked at her, which made her feel happy, it was rare for Stella to ever acknowledge herself.

The car seat moulded itself to Stella's buttocks, or rather, she moulded herself into the seat. Over six months of commuting up to 15 hours a week to work, Stella's butt and back had merged into the car seat as though it were made of memory foam. She hated the commute to Brisbane, but there was scant work in public relations where she lived down the coast, leaving her little choice but to commute long distances to work in events.

Each Monday morning, when she sat back in the saddle of the driver's seat, she could swear the seat was already warm. Soon her butt would be sticky from sweat and she'd chastise herself for slouching, concerned that she looked like a truckie. On the plus side, driving so much had improved her short-sightedness, to the point that the optometrist had told her she no longer needed to wear glasses while driving.

She glanced at the dash and swore when she realised she was low on petrol. As she swerved into the service station, she silently scolded herself for running so late.

Great way to incite Oliver's ire at the start the week!

'Howdy, Stella!'

Like clockwork, Cassius, a 70-something semi-retired attendant, filled Stella's car and checked the oil. He reminded Stella of her father, who was always checking her car and called her kiddo; she specifically filled up at this service station to enjoy their brief exchanges at the petrol bowser. While her father had been an architect, he was also good with cars.

'How's tricks, Stella?'

'Tricks are terrible for the start to the week,' Stella confessed. 'I'm running late, and I fear that my creature of a boss will eat me alive for breakfast. How are you?'

'When was the last time you had your car serviced, kiddo?' You're completely out of oil. Go and grab two litres for me, please.'

'I'm guessing it was serviced about a year ago,' Stella called over her shoulder as she scooted off. 'It must be due for another one.'

'That boss of yours, you need to play him at his own game,' Cassius said, taking the oil from her. 'Hold the line and do not let him get under your skin.'

'Good advice. Thanks, Cassius.'

'Focus on the task at hand and take nothing personally,' he continued. 'You can't keep driving up the highway killing yourself each day. There's no point going through life being miserable. In the meantime, start looking for other work.'

With that bit of advice, Cassius closed the car bonnet, tapping on it twice to convey that she was good to go. 'Drive carefully, kiddo; I saw the speed you drove in here.' He shot her a wink. 'And get your car serviced!'

Stella blew Cassius a kiss and drove off, cautiously, knowing that he was like her dad, with eyes in the back of his head and a certain sixth sense about things.

Back on the road, arts, news, celebrity interviews, and binge-worthy crime podcasts helped to pass the monotonous highway drive. She also role-played different scenarios for how she'd resign once a better opportunity arose.

Her favourite scenario wasn't remotely feasible – unless she wanted to be sued for defamation; it just felt so tantalisingly good to fantasise about it.

Stella doesn't announce herself before striding into Oliver's office, possibly interrupting him mid-phone call.

'Oliver!' she declares. 'I'm resigning from my role at the Geoscientist Institute, effective immediately. You're losing my expertise, professionalism, and currency as a popular and valuable team member because you're a megawatt, micro-managing dick. I might not have another position to go to immediately, but it will be a great joy to no longer be obliged to endure your bile every day.'

She tosses her identification badge and office key on the desk before turning on her heel to walk off. Just as she reaches Oliver's office door, she pauses and slowly turns back towards her former boss to say, 'You're the most inept manager I've ever had the displeasure of working with – and you should know that my sentiments are shared by each and every employee and member of the Geoscientist Institute.'

With that, she breezes out the door, off to start her new life.

Stella allowed herself to savour this dream, which she had clung to and played through many times, massaging the edges of the reverie to suit her mood.

The second resignation, certainly more realistic, involved a little sucking up and an amicable departure. It was the least fun but the most likely to actually occur in real life.

Politely standing at the door to Oliver's office, Stella knocks to announce herself for a scheduled meeting she made sure to book earlier. Pretending not to see the pills in their assorted colours lined up on his desk, she takes a seat, compliments his jacket, and then proceeds with her resignation speech.

'Oliver,' she says politely, 'unfortunately, I've made the difficult decision to resign from my role at the Geoscientist Institute. I've been offered another role in my hometown of Sydney that better suits my experience. I'm happy to give you two weeks' notice and do a handover with whoever will assume my role.' She stands and offers her hand to

Oliver, who, Oliver being Oliver, declines to shake. 'Thank you for the opportunity to be part of the organisation.'

In the final scenario, Stella liked to skip speaking to Oliver altogether, daydreaming that she arrived at work to collect the contents of her desk, namely a framed black and white photo of her and Heath and some other personal items. She'd do a quick office circuit to bid farewell to her colleagues and exchange contact numbers, then walk out of the building a final time.

***

Stella's black Mazda Tribute screeched into the Geoscientist Institute's car park at 8.10 am. She scrambled to exchange the thongs she was wearing for heels, retrieved the lunch that had fallen to the floor at some point during the drive, and shoved it back into her bag, and scampered across the car park to the office lift.

Breathlessly greeting the receptionist on arrival, Stella took 15 seconds to plonk her bag at her desk and double-timed it to the boardroom, where a debrief about the Institute's recent industry conference was already underway. She tiptoed into the boardroom and mouthed, 'Sorry for being late.'

She'd warned Alison with a quick text on the way – *There's been an accident on the highway, I'm running late for the debrief!* – and, thank goodness, there was a seat reserved for her at the boardroom table, and a cup of freshly brewed coffee awaiting.

You're a goddess, Alison.

Oliver, dressed in head-to-toe black, cast an apathetic look at Stella. Several of the little black feathers on the collar of his designer shirt fluttered as he released a long, laboured sigh in her direction.

'Hello, Stella,' he said waspishly. 'Are you sure it's not an inconvenience to join us today?'

Opting not to respond, she pulled her computer out of her work bag and logged into the Institute's social media accounts, which allowed her to surreptitiously communicate with Heath during work hours.

Oliver's face visibly purpled at Stella's lack of response, demonstrating all too well his inability to conceal his seething anger.

She knew he'd attempt to humiliate her at some point during the debrief – maybe this time he'd compliment one of the other staff members' abilities over hers. He'd played this divide, conquer, and humiliate game several times before, and frankly, it was getting old. Not least because it didn't work. The junior staff members looked up to Stella for sharing her knowledge and the senior staff respected her boldness in standing up to Oliver – which all further contributed to why he detested her.

Ignoring Oliver, April continued providing feedback on the conference with a blow-by-blow account of sponsor and partner engagement.

Stella hid her boredom with busy taps on the keyboard. She uploaded countless photos of sponsor acknowledgements to the Geoscientist Institute's social media platforms throughout the remainder of the meeting, keeping a meticulous eye on each post to ensure that grammar and spelling were faultless, hashtags and tags were correct, and each post had exclusive content and was staggered to upload at different times throughout the day. It was a ludicrous amount of work for the 212 Instagram and 300 Facebook followers that the Institute had; Twitter's mere 15 followers were barely worth a mention.

Oliver selected Alison to take minutes at the debriefing session. In the six months that Stella had worked at the Institute, Oliver had never asked one of the male employees to take minutes, although he proudly wore bright purple on International Women's Day and professed himself to be a feminist.

Between taking minutes, Alison bombarded Stella with questions about her romantic weekend.

> Because you were late for work, I'm assuming it was
> a good weekend, gurl!

> No. It wasn't.

Alison shot her a wide-eyed look.

> What!? No! Don't tell me it was a flop?

It wasn't good.

YYY!?

It wasn't good, it was mind-blowingly brilliant.

Idiot. I'm risking my neck, messaging you in direct sight of Creature Human and you're pulling my leg.

I'll tell you more at lunch. Be a good girl and take the minutes, Ally.

As an exceedingly private person, Stella avoided telling Alison much at all at lunch about her weekend away, barely satiating her colleague's curiosity by providing only a few highlights. The spa scene was taboo, along with the night they'd shared naked on the balcony under a full moon, as was details about yesterday morning, when they'd woken up to an open fire and a complete rearrangement of their bedding.

'So, you recommend the Witches Falls Winery vineyard tour,' Alison commented, handing a bag of peanuts to Stella. 'And the three-course meal at the restaurant you say was divine.'

Stella chomped on a handful of nuts, nodding in the affirmative as she checked her watch.

'Whoops, we better get going,' she said, getting to her feet. 'Don't want to be late!'

***

Stella paused between uploading sponsor acknowledgements to social media platforms to shoot Heath a message.

Are you in the studio?

Yes.

Jesus, his economy of words is attractive.

By yourself?

Yes.

How can a single word sound so compelling?
She selected a photo from their growing catalogue of images to send, one she'd taken of them at lunch one day, smiling eyes and smiling mouths transfixed. If there were a competition to label the photograph, Stella had thought of several possibilities:
Ardour.
I want someone to look at me like this.
Eyes never lie.
Once-in-a-lifetime.

That is such a great shot.

It's my new favourite photo.

I just had a flashback to the weekend.

Listening.

***

Are you writing a second edition of the Bible?

In a debrief. Hamg on. I need to anrueswer Olivaaa

You do...but I don't.

I've been having flashbacks all morning also, Stelz.

Stop it. I'm in a meeting!

...no, don't stop. I could use the distraction.

I'm not as good with words as you, baby. It was a very romantic weekend.

Hmmm, flashbacks...

Trying not to trip over watching you on the bush track. Seeing the full moon reflect off your skin on the deck in the rainforest. Having three whole days with you and no disturbances.

Us lying in bed talking about us.

Dinner at the restaurant and how you were interested in my stories.

The spa. The spa. The spa.

'Everlong' playing in the background. Candles.

Baby, you're somethin' else.

It was the most Heath had ever texted Stella, and for a moment she forgot she was still in a meeting. A slight gasp escaped her lips, and she immediately looked up and pretended to listen to Oliver until he looked away again.

Wow, gorgeous. I bet your fingers are about to fall off!

You know I hate texting!

You forgot the part about how you nearly drowned us in the spa by using all four packets of bubble bath. Ha! What a great weekend.

It was exceptional, baby. I've never experienced anything better in my life.

The best is yet to come.

***

Within earshot of the other staff, Oliver ordered Stella to stay back while the rest of the team took a short break.

Stella exchanged a knowing glance with Alison, who moved at a glacial pace, fussing unnecessarily to arrange sponsor folders into alphabetical order. Then she went over her computer, cleaning its already pristine screen and checking the Institute's social media feed for engagement from the earlier posts.

'Would you like me to stay back also, Oliver?' Alison said at last. 'As Stella's conference assistant, I might be able to assist with any questions you have.'

A gentle smile spread across Stella's face as she sat back in her chair and stared into the distance, making a mental note to help Alison find another job, one where loyalty was respected and skills nurtured.

'If I thought you could add value to this meeting,' Oliver snapped, 'I'd have invited you to it, Alison.' He dismissed her from the room with a brusque flick of his hand, the movement drawing attention to the gaudy green nail polish he was wearing. 'Close the door behind you.'

As Oliver returned his attention to her, Stella could hear her father's voice in her head. *Don't tell the right hand what the left hand is doing, Stella. Hold strong, then look for a new job, pronto, and you can put this fiasco behind you.*

'What do you say about a certain junior staff member leaving the conference early to screw one of the sponsors, Stella?' Oliver's voice snapped through the quiet room.

'What do you want me to say, Oliver?' Stella asked, keeping her voice steady. *For God's sake, don't let him get under your skin!*

'Were you managing Vanessa at the conference?'

'Yes.'

'Was Vanessa in your charge?'

'Yes.'

'Did Vanessa leave the conference early?'

'I'm uncertain.'

'Was Vanessa at the conference at the end of the night?'

'I can't recall.'

'Were you managing Vanessa at the conference?'

'Yes.'

'It's on you, Stella.'

Stella leaned forward, looking squarely at Oliver. 'And how is that, Oliver?'

'We've established that Vanessa was on your watch,' Oliver said, ticking points off on his fingers. 'You should have always known where she was. When Vanessa should've been at the Convention Centre, she was on her knees at the Mantra.'

'I couldn't say what her sexual proclivities are, Oliver.'

Stella took a perverse pleasure in the fact that Oliver couldn't stop his face from turning scarlet whenever he heard something he didn't like. In this instance, she thought his nose might well combust from the blood rushing to fill its entire ruddy shape.

Taking a deep breath, Stella pressed her hands into the table and pushed herself back into her seat, hard, creating as much distance from Oliver as physically possible. The movement pulled her chin into her chest and arched her back upwards; her eyes wide, she couldn't look away from his nose as it seemed to swell to a near bruise from pressure. She turned her ear towards Oliver, sure that she could hear a thumping, pulsating sound – the sound of blood smashing into and out of his heart. She somehow restrained herself from giving in to the bizarre impulse to reach over and squeeze the bejesus out of his snout.

'Consider this an official warning, Stella.'

'I wasn't the one on my knees, Oliver.' *Hold the line. Right hand, left hand. Hold the fucking line, Stella!* 'I am not responsible for another staff member's choice not to fulfil their obligations or duties. I'll be taking this up with the Board.'

Stella sat back in her seat, finally breaking eye contact with Oliver as her colleagues re-entered the room.

CHAPTER 14

It was probably a good thing that Ray Stevens didn't bother to forewarn Stella to expect a call from internationally acclaimed theatre director Mark Henshaw, OAM – most recently recognised for his production of Sydney's *A Streetcar Named Desire*, imminently opening on London's West End.

If Ray had mentioned anything beforehand, nerves likely would have prevented Stella from answering the director's call.

She was midway through texting Alinta about her impending birthday lunch when Mark's phone call came through.

'Hello, Stella Longhurst speaking,' she said.

'Stella, Mark Henshaw calling.'

Stella barely managed to swallow her squawk of surprise. 'Mr Henshaw, hello! What a surprise. What can I do for you?'

Mark got right to the point. 'Melanie Tate had to drop out of the ATC's production of *Streetcar* in London.'

'Yes,' Stella replied firmly. 'I heard... It's such a shame.'

'We're in need of a new Blanche.'

Butterflies flittered about Stella's stomach, and she pressed a fist to her stomach. *Is it...could it...does he want me to audition?* The fact that Mark was calling her at all was unbelievable, given he'd been recognised for his contribution to the performing arts with a Medal of the Order of Australia; the idea he might actually want her to audition was almost impossible to accept as reality.

'Ray Stevens mentioned your name.'

It felt like fireworks were exploding in her brain, but somehow Stella managed to keep her voice steady and said, 'I would be honoured to read for the part. Of all the roles I've ever performed, Blanche remains my favourite.'

'Normally I wouldn't consider an unknown actor in a theatre production with such high stakes,' Mark said, voice gruff, 'but Ray speaks very highly of you. And, frankly, given the short period of time I have to cast a replacement Blanche and get her up to speed before opening night, I am at present more open to avenues that I wouldn't normally pursue.'

'I can't imagine how difficult it is for you and the rest of the cast, especially after so much time together,' Stella said, infusing her voice with the perfect degree of compassion and understanding. 'I did a play with Melanie when we were both at The Performers' Centre and we've remained friends. I was deeply saddened when I heard Melanie was unwell. It's such a tragedy for all of us.'

Was she shamelessly trying to draw a connection between herself and Mark's cast and crew? Yes. Was she sorry about it? Absolutely not. Was she aware Mark was granting an audition purely because of her friendship with Ray and nothing to do with talent? Yep.

'Six degrees of separation,' Mark remarked. Before she could respond, he continued, 'The most pressing matter is that the show opens in exactly one month. I'm running back-to-back auditions for Blanche with Australian actresses tomorrow in Sydney. Stuart Johnson, our assistant director, is on a plane from London back to Sydney as I speak. He'll be there in person for the auditions; I'll be joining him via Zoom from London. Whoever we end up casting must be in London by early next week.'

'I can be in London within 72 hours,' Stella said immediately.

'Let's see how you audition first,' Mark snapped.

There was a long pause on the other end of the phone before Stella stepped into the void. The confidence and surety in her voice would have surprised her if she hadn't been so focused. 'Blanche DuBois has been living rent-free in my head for years. You won't regret giving me an audition.'

'Well then. We'll see you tomorrow.'

Stella bit down on her lips to keep from screaming. 'That's great, Mark. I'll look forward to it.' She marvelled at how steady her voice was, given her body felt like it was about to bubble over with emotion.

'My assistant will forward you the audition details.'

'Thank you for the opportun ...'

Clunk!

She was so excited that she didn't even mind how abruptly Mark had terminated the call.

I'm auditioning for Streetcar! Tomorrow!

Mark-Fucking-Henshaw just rang my number!

Seventy-two hours to relocate to London.

That was enough to induce a tiny flurry of panic, and Stella promptly scolded herself. *Don't get ahead of yourself!*

She switched her phone off before dropping to her knees and letting out a decade's worth of pent-up creativity and anguish in an animalistic scream. She needed to immediately start thinking through the logistics of booking a flight and preparing for her audition – tomorrow! – but she allowed herself this moment of emotional release.

Before long, she was searching through a large wooden box for the copy of *Streetcar* she'd used when she played Blanche in The Performer's Centre's production. Countless scripts from failed television, theatre, and film auditions flew out of the box and onto the floor – each script a reminder of her dream to act. *The Seagull, Cowboy Mouth, Who's Afraid of Virginia Woolf...* The scripts went on and on, a sea of failure and the odd triumph. She picked up the nearest script and flipped it open. She'd walked into this particular audition with trepidation, since she hadn't done a lot of Shakespeare, but she'd felt confident in the preparation – until they asked her to read for Desdemona instead of Emilia, and she mangled the lines because she hadn't prepared for that role beforehand. Or the lead policewoman role she auditioned for in a prime-time television series, where she'd pulled off what'd she'd thought was a spectacular audition, only to hear back weeks later that they'd gone with someone else – and had refused to offer her feedback when asked... There was the television commercial for an airline – playing a flight attendant serving the late Scottish actor and comedian Ronnie Corbett – she tossed the reminder of failing to secure a simple TV commercial onto the floor. Or – oh, yes, Stella thought as she picked up the heavy vocal score to *Pirates of Penzance* – the utter humiliation of the threefold musical audition, where her acting was fine but the dance and singing auditions had gone so horrifically that she never wanted to see another music note or step-ball change in her life. Coordination was not her strong point.

She finally found *Streetcar* buried at the bottom of the pile of scripts. To save herself from despairing over the fruits of her failures, she immediately jumped to her feet and paced the length of her lounge room, flicking through the script. It was in worse condition than she'd remembered, dog-eared and littered with blotchy director's notes.

She would never understand bookmark users when a perfectly accurate and reliable system existed in dog-earing the pages of books or scripts; everyone knew bookmarks were useless, especially when they fell out.

A pink highlighter always underscored Stella's roles; no other colour would do. It was a habit she'd clung to over her years of acting, and it was a comfort to come back to it after so long away.

*****

Finally, Stella stopped pacing and dialled Ray's number. Unable to conceal her nervous excitement, as soon as he picked up, she shrieked, 'Ray! Mark Henshaw called! I got an audition! I'm auditioning for Blanche!'

She heard him chuckle. 'Excellent news, Stella. That's marvellous.'

'He said you mentioned my name?'

'Of course,' Ray replied. 'How could I not?'

'Ray – I – *thank you*!'

He laughed. 'Don't mention it, Stella. You deserve the chance.'

She sucked in a deep breath and then let her words out in a rush. 'The audition is tomorrow afternoon in Sydney – I only have 24 hours – it's ludicrous! I'll fly down this afternoon.'

'Would you like some assistance reading?'

'Yes!' she blurted out. 'Thank you – I would *love* your help with reading my lines. I'm planning to stay at a hotel around the corner from you, I'll buy you dinner and a bottle of champagne if we can run lines this afternoon, tonight, and tomorrow.' She hesitated, a sudden wave of insecurity rushing over her. 'If that's okay?'

'See you soon, Stella,' Ray said warmly. If he could hear her uncertainty, he didn't mention it. 'I'm looking forward to it.'

Stella hung up the phone and reflected on the proverb that a teacher would appear only once the student was ready. She was thrilled that Ray had agreed to come out of retirement to work with her. His belief in her had been steadfast since the first time he laid eyes on her during a student audition at The Performer's Centre.

***

It took Stella four minutes to book a flight to Sydney. A mere 52 minutes later and her bag sat beside her in an Uber bound for the airport.

In the Uber, she pulled out her phone to message Heath. She tried to think of a credible excuse for cancelling their date that night.

This is terrible. You're a cow... Lying and cancelling with Heath at the last minute!

> Hey, hon,
>
> I'm really sorry, I need to cancel tonight. I'm not feeling well at all. I'll message you later. X

Ping!

> Oh, no! That doesn't sound good. Headache? Stomach-ache? Where do you feel sick? I'll come over and take you to the doctor.

Shit... He's so bloody lovely... Of course he would offer to come over.

Stella scraped her shoes on the Uber floor in frustration and glared at the car's roof, thinking of what to text Heath. She needed her response to be brief and shut down further discussion of him coming over.

> Hopefully, it's only a 24-hour flu.
>
> I'm heading to bed. X

Stella bit her bottom lip and shook her head in disgust at herself. Heath continued angling to care for her:

Rest up, hon. I'm sorry to hear you don't feel well. I can bring some chicken soup over and pat you on the bottom until you fall to sleep?

Oh, thank you. X I should be fine.

I'm already half asleep. Going to switch my phone off and get some rest.

Ping!

Night. Hope you feel better. Talk in the morning. X

His response reassured her that her curt reply hadn't totally offended him.

As the Uber pulled into the airport, Stella blinked tears from the corner of her eyes, overwhelmed at the opportunity to audition for *Streetcar*. It was a little too ridiculous even to be real. If she was honest with herself, she was also crying about her inability to speak to Heath about the audition – and what it might mean for their relationship in the unlikely event that she secured the role.

***

Coming into Sydney, Stella snapped an aerial photo of Sydney Harbour before the plane touched down, just like she always did, capturing the radiance of the water with the Harbour Bridge and Sydney Opera House in the background. The steel arch of Sydney Harbour Bridge was a 'Welcome Home, Stella!' banner enthusiastically welcoming her back to the 'hood.

She'd spent hundreds of hours crossing the Harbour Bridge's glorious span during her adolescence and into her twenties and thirties on her way to work, or to theatre houses to perform, or for nights out with her girlfriends. While in the car she'd often talked out loud, sometimes prepping for a work meeting or presentation, at other times rehearsing a monologue from a play.

The Harbour Bridge knew some of Stella's deepest doubts. Like how she would berate herself for being nervous about presenting in front of work colleagues. How, on presentation days, she would take her eyes off the road to check in the rear-view mirror if a red rash had formed on her face and chest. She hadn't realised it at the time, but all the anxiety, all that fear – it had come directly out of what Jay and Steve had done to her. She hated that she lived with the torment they'd caused her, and the way that she hadn't fully understood their effect on her life until recently. Instead of laying the blame squarely at the feet of the man she'd trusted to be her acting teacher, Stella had blamed herself for having anxiety; the shame she'd felt then, and still felt now, was palpable.

***

The Jetstar flight landed on the tarmac five minutes early, nothing short of a miracle. Stella pulled down an overnight bag from the overhead locker and stood waiting in the aisle before the captain announced that seat belts could come off. After ordering an Uber while disembarking from the plane, she pinged a text to Ray.

> **I'm coming in hot, Ray. I'll be at your house in 30 minutes.**

> **Wonderful darling, we'll get straight to work when you get here.**

In the Uber, she scanned the cityscape, awash in nostalgic memories of growing up in Sydney. As far as she was concerned, the city was another family member – while she might complain and whine about its haughtiness, traffic congestion, and overpriced real estate, nobody else was permitted to say anything negative about the place she would always call home. While she enjoyed the more laid-back lifestyle of living in northern New South Wales, she still missed Sydney.

The Uber pulled up to Ray's driveway at Surry Hills 26 minutes later. The door to Ray's two-story terrace house stood open, the warm lighting highlighting the walkway to the entrance. Ray had developed an appreciation of good lighting from years of living and working with his partner Albert, a lighting technician, and Stella had been at their house often enough to enjoy their company. Over the years, the gentlemen had become like uncles to her.

The house was more elegant than she'd remembered – a fresh coat of white paint dramatically accentuated their glossy black front door – and the wrought iron fence was draped in delicate pink roses. Heritage, Hybrid Teas, and David Austin roses lined the pathway to the front door; and just as she did every time the roses were in bloom, Stella bent to inhale their scent.

At the end of the hallway, which was lined by an overpriced blue Persian rug, stood Ray, holding a well-worn script in his hand. Stella nearly tripped over herself, racing down the hallway to embrace him. She'd secretly been hoping for this moment ever since leaving the theatre, since Ray had first rung her up to hint that she should resurrect her dream to be an actress.

Ray motioned for Stella to enter the study and sit on the velvet green occasional chair in the corner of the room. He turned on an antique lamp with a frosted orange lampshade and pulled up a chair to sit opposite Stella. The study overflowed with shelves stacked with books, scripts, and autobiographies; the familiarity was comforting and transported her back in time to her younger, confident self. She sat upright against the stiff back of the chair, her chest expanding, her breath steady. She was hope personified.

'For someone living as a shadow artist and denying themselves of their creativity, you look exceptionally well, Stella.'

Stella grudgingly agreed, saying, 'I suppose I have been an interloper in my own life.'

'I'm curious, Stella – why the sudden urgency? Why have you all at once decided that you want to tread the boards again?'

'I haven't been able to think about anything else since I learned about the role,' Stella admitted. 'I need to make peace with my acting career. Anyway, it's only an audition. Let's not get ahead of ourselves.'

'Better still, let's get on with it. I see you've brought your old script.'

'I have.'

'I take it you speed read the play and the director's notations, on the plane.'

Stella nodded.

'You must erase every note you've read and any memory of directions I gave during our production of *Streetcar.*' Ray held out his hand. 'Please pass me your script, Stella.'

Stella resisted handing the play over.

'Ray! What? This script is like coming home for me.' She clutched the script to her chest. 'I recall every single nuance and direction. I could perform the entire role today, without hesitation.'

'Exactly.'

'Exactly? Exactly what?'

'You need to approach this audition as though you've never auditioned for the role of Blanche previously,' Ray said gently. 'Why? Because you're ten years older and with that maturity, you must play the character anew – to discover things about Blanche that you never appreciated or might not have understood previously. *When* you secure the role, you will perform with an entirely new cast and an entirely new director.' As he spoke, his voice grew stronger, he enunciated the 'wh' in *when* with so much emphasis that the silent 'h' could be heard. '*When* you perform the role, you will be performing for an English audience, not an Australian audience. *When* you perform this version of Blanche, you will bring an additional decade of life experience to the performance.' He fixed his eyes on Stella's face. 'You should not be approaching the role in any way that resembles the Blanche you were in the past.'

'I'm not planning to wholly *replicate* a beat-by-beat performance that I did years ago,' Stella said, and then protested, 'But the director's notes help me.'

Ray shook his head at her. 'Ultimately, the old director's notes will not assist you; they will only hinder your performance. You'll become bogged down performing the role as you did previously, and it will quickly become stale.' His voice softened. 'Trust me, Stella. Discard the old script and see the role with fresh eyes. Relying on what you did ten years ago is lazy.'

'Okay,' Stella said after a long moment. 'Okay. Take the script, Ray.' She couldn't help but be grateful for his bluntness – and for speaking to her as though she were destined to get the part. She'd come to Ray for a reason, and regardless of the fickle nature of the industry, it was nice to know he believed in her.

Ray took the script and tucked it underneath several scripts on the bookshelf for safekeeping. 'I'll give the script back to you when you return from London after a successful run.'

A little laugh escaped her mouth. 'I love your confidence.'

'While we're on the subject,' Ray added, turning back to her, 'do *not* watch the film version of the play, either.'

Stella held up her hands in mock surrender. 'Okay, okay! I promise!'

Ray's miniature poodle, Elizabeth, limped into the living room and laid down at Stella's feet.

'Aw, Elizabeth,' Stella said, bending down to pet her.

'She's a bit older and slower since the last time you saw her,' Ray lamented.

She picked up the old dog and cuddled her close. 'Hello, darling, Elizabeth. You're still very beautiful!'

The little white ball of fur had always sat at Stella's feet when she was preparing for an audition – and had proven to be better luck than any trinket or charm ever could.

For the *Streetcar* audition, Stella was to perform the dramatic monologue where Blanche makes a heartbreaking confession about her departed young husband. She was also required to perform the scene when the audience meets Blanche, when she arrives at her sister Stella Kowalski's home in Elysian Fields, in the French Quarter of New Orleans. Ray read the other characters in this scene.

Ray stood with his arms crossed tightly across his belly as he watched Stella perform the latter scene. If she hadn't known him so well, she might have intuited from his body language that he was annoyed, rather than simply being hyper-focused on getting the best from every nuance of her performance.

After a while, he held up his hand to stop her. 'Take a break, Stella,' he said gently. 'I appreciate that you can recite every word from these scenes, although you must think about where Blanche was before she arrived at Elysian Fields. You must intrinsically understand Blanche's emotional state before she left Mississippi.'

'We know her state,' Stella responded, a little frustrated. 'She's shot to bits and so is her reputation. She's a lonely, broke, and manipulative schoolteacher who feigns aristocracy and is run out of town.'

'What precisely was she was doing in the days before she was forced from Mississippi?'

Ray took a sip of water and crossed his arms in the opposite direction, then continued.

'How many men did she have sex with? Who was the last man she slept with? What alcohol was she drinking? Did she pass out in her bed? Wet the bed from being drunk? I want you to know Blanche's back story better than you know the script.'

Stella sat down on the velvet chair and absently scratched at her ankle before responding.

'The first time the audience sees Blanche, she's perfectly coiffed in head-to-toe white and presents as a put-together woman with an air of upper class. We don't immediately see her insecurity and fragility.'

Ray questions, '*Don't* we? Do not underestimate the audience and do not assume they are stupid. Blanche doesn't become untroubled simply because she puts a white dress on. She carries layers of complexity.'

'Of course. I'm saying we don't see every layer at once.'

'It's the layers of her character that we *don't* see that makes the performance interesting. Stop reciting and start being. From this point on, I want you to forget that you are Stella Longhurst. From now, wherever practicable, your every conscious waking thought, movement, and action will be as Blanche DuBois.'

When she first played the role, she'd fastidiously studied other actresses' portrayal of Blanche – right or wrong – observing performances by Jessica Lang, Faye Dunaway, Ann-Margret, Cate Blanchett, Glenn Close, Kim Stanley, Vivien Leigh, and Gillian Anderson.

But for this audition, she would rely on her own interpretation of Blanche. Her Blanche would be the only Blanche to ever exist.

CHAPTER 15

Stella woke up on the morning of the audition feeling unusually calm, yet also haunted by guilt that she had just given up her acting career when Madison had been entirely robbed of hers. Since she'd decided to resurrect her acting career, Madison had constantly been on her mind. There was a pervasive void now that Madison wasn't around to run lines with her, and her absence, especially for the most important audition of Stella's life, was almost too cruel to bear.

You must land this role, Stella – if not for yourself, do it for Madison.

After hours of rehearsing the previous evening, Ray had directed Stella to spend the morning of the audition alone, holed up at her hotel, to absorb their dissection of Blanche's character the previous night. She was indebted to him for his kindness; his belief in her ability fuelled her.

To help inhabit the character, Ray had instructed her to walk, talk, and dress like Blanche until the audition. She'd gone to bed the previous evening wearing the blonde wig she planned to audition in.

That morning, when she arrived at the hotel's restaurant for breakfast, the concierge had looked at her strangely, as well he might – she'd been wearing a white dress with matching gloves and a hat to order breakfast in a southern Mississippi drawl. Stella lathered herself in perfume and checked her hair and make-up in the mirror, akin to the perpetual panic Blanche experienced as a fading Southern belle. Blanche was a delicious character to play. In society's eyes, she was a fallen woman. She lost her young husband to suicide, along with her family fortune and estate. Along with a drinking problem, Blanche was a social pariah due to sexual indiscretion. Behind a veneer of social snobbery, she was an insecure individual and ageing woman, panicked about her fading beauty.

Today, the public relations version of Stella didn't exist; she was every inch Blanche DuBois. Hidden behind Blanche's mask, Stella was able to set her nerves aside.

***

Lined up in a mini-cattle call outside the audition room were another three hopeful Australian actresses. Stella thought she recognised an actress from her earlier acting days but resisted saying hello. The actresses only acknowledged one another with steely glances up and down each other's bodies, surveying suitability, or lack thereof, to play Blanche. A decade earlier, Stella might have been intimidated by this catty behaviour – actresses attempting to unnerve each other into a terrible audition. It was the psychological equivalent of cricket and football players verbally sledging one another on the field.

Today, Stella couldn't care less. She had nothing to prove. If she could nail the audition, it would go a long way to ridding herself of the shame felt for her failures to succeed as an actress, the shame for the reasons she failed; she hoped that facing her fears would help to extinguish the anxiety she'd kept a secret for years. It was a gamble she felt was worth taking.

Just as she was about to sit at the far end of the room, away from the other actresses, remaining in character, the director's assistant appeared.

'Stella Longhurst, reading for Blanche DuBois!'

Stella strode past the others, the only actress in full costume; a suitcase dangled from her hand, as though she were about to board a train to Elysian Fields…

The other actresses didn't laugh at Stella, or stare down their nose at her.

Blanche DuBois had just walked into the building, and everyone knew it.

Including Stella.

CHAPTER 16

Casting Changes in Store for Australian Theatre Company's
A Streetcar Named Desire

By HAMISH McLEOD

LONDON—The Australian Theatre Company, a month from opening night of its award-winning production of *A Streetcar Named Desire* at the Palais Theatre in the West End, has just found itself without a lead.

Melanie Tate's agent issued a statement to the media announcing Ms Tate will be unable to continue in the role of Blanche DuBois due to an undisclosed illness.

British theatregoers will be bitterly disappointed by the news of Ms Tate's departure from the production. Following her appearance in *A Doll's House* in 2018, Ms Tate turned her attention from the stage to her family. Her role as Blanche DuBois was to provide her much-anticipated return to the theatre.

Ms Tate's unexpected departure has forced director Mark Henshaw, OAM, to rapidly find a replacement capable of stepping into the veteran actress' shoes.

Mr Henshaw declined to comment on the nature of Ms Tate's departure, noting only that the Australian cast and crew has formed a close emotional bond during their time living and working together in London; whoever steps into Ms Tate's shoes will face the unenviable task of fitting herself into a tightly knit community.

Mr Henshaw, while unwilling to speak openly about the recasting process, has hinted that he not only intends to recast the role with an Australian actress, and indeed may have already done so.

Asked whether he has considered postponing opening night, or the production's run altogether, Mr Henshaw was adamant that the show would go on as planned.

London's theatre lovers will be waiting with bated breath for the announcement of the now highly anticipated replacement.

CHAPTER 17

Heath made Stella wait until after breakfast to give her his birthday present.

'I noticed that you don't have something like this,' he said shyly, handing over a large present wrapped in shiny silver paper. He'd put his heart into giving Stella a profoundly personal present – he knew it was a considerable risk, baring his soul, but he had wanted to do it. Now that she actually held his gift in her hands, moments away from revealing it, he was starting to have second thoughts about whether she'd like it.

He sat next to her and watched as she pulled the first layer of paper off the present, revealing a painting under a layer of bubble wrap. 'I might need to close my eyes before I finish opening this,' she said, looking up at him. 'I sense it's going to be very special.'

'I hope so,' he murmured.

Holding the present on the floor, Stella took a deep breath and tugged at the bubble wrap.

Heath watched as she unstuck one corner of bubble wrap after another. 'Careful. Unwrap it carefully, baby.'

'Okay,' she replied.

'Okay,' Heath repeated, the intensity of the moment making him feel at one with her.

Finally, Stella unstuck the last corner of bubble wrap and slowly turned the canvas over. She covered her mouth with both hands as she stared down at her lap, '*Oh, my!*' escaping from her lips in a low, happy, muffled cry.

A celestial painting of her father Fred strolling down a beach rock wall at sunrise, his back facing the camera, shone out from the canvas. The morning's first rays of sunlight broke through a cloud above Fred's head to light a pathway, stretching into the horizon. Or, perhaps, into heaven.

Heath had procured the image from Stella's Instagram account and had painted a replica of the photo. He'd hoped she would love it but had still been afraid it was too big a gesture.

'It's so beautiful,' Stella said. '*Thank* you.' She picked up the painting of her father, put it back down, and picked it up again, tears spilling down her cheeks as she lost all composure. Her tears brought tears to Heath's eyes, emotion he tried to choke back with deep swallows.

The funny unicorn birthday card he gave her for her 39th birthday provided enough comic relief for him to confidently write in the card, 'Love you to pieces.'

***

A group of Stella's friends, plus her mother, and Alinta, sat shoulder to shoulder at a small Italian restaurant for Stella's 39th birthday lunch. Pam and Alinta had travelled from Sydney to celebrate Stella's birthday with her. The guests swapped large bowls of pizza, pasta, and salad back and forth, washed down with bottles of Italian Chardonnay and classic Lambrusco. Heath sat next to her during lunch, sipping on a glass of Chianti, proudly enjoying the celebration of Stella.

A light on Stella's phone flashed, alerting her to a new text message. Though aware of how rude it was to check her phone during lunch, she couldn't resist sliding the phone onto her lap and tapping the glass, hoping to see a message from Mark Henshaw – only to be disappointed by a birthday cheerio from a colleague. Hiding her impatience, she put the phone back on the table and re-joined the festivities.

Gina, one of Stella's school friends, needed no particular occasion to drink, instead taking advantage of the opportunity to flirt shamelessly with their waiter.

'Signorina? You're so sweet,' she said, fluttering her eyelashes. 'I am *flattered* that you see a Signorina before you.' She knocked back the last of her wine. 'You know, I did a sightseeing tour of the Amalfi

Coast several years ago. It's quite a gorgeous view –' her lips tipped up at the corners – 'a bit like you.'

The waiter, flustered, cast his eyes around the table before fixing on Gina's empty glass. 'Can I fill up your vino, Signorina?'

Gina thrust an empty wine glass towards him. 'You can fill me up any time.'

Stella closed her eyes and dropped her face into her hand. 'Gina, you're old enough to be Marco's mother,' she hissed as the waiter made his escape. 'He should be addressing you as Signora!' The guests burst into laughter.

'Oh, Stella, don't tell me you're too old to have fun now that you're 39!' Gina teased. 'Maybe your new boyfriend has some friends he could introduce me to.' She waved at Heath from across the table, 'Heath! Do you have any nice friends who might like to meet me?'

'Gina!' Heath grinned as he replied, 'I have a few friends that might suit you. Is 20 too old?'

Gina threw her head back, laughing hysterically, and then gulped down another glass of wine. 'You're pretty sharp, I'll give you that. You make sure you send some of your 20-year-old friends my way.'

'Consider it my next task.'

Stella rolled her eyes and watched as Heath was drawn into conversation at the far end of the table. About to join the conversation herself, she realised that opposite her, Gina had lowered her voice to whisper to Alinta; Stella pricked up her ears, just barely able to hear what they were saying.

'Heath has looks, class, and a quick wit,' Gina said to Alinta. 'Your sister seems to have scored a perfect gentleman in her new boyfriend.'

Alinta murmured a noise of assent. 'He's smart, attentive, and adores Stella.' She dropped her voice even further, so it was barely audible. 'She says she's smitten! I haven't seen her this happy since before Madison and Dad died. It's wonderful to finally see her happy.'

'So, Heath has no skeletons in his closet,' Gina said. 'He's actually perfect? There's nothing that you've been able to find out about him?'

Alinta frowned. 'I haven't been *trying* to get dirt on him. Why would I do that?'

'Because, Alinta,' Gina said patiently, 'every man has a flaw, and nobody wants to see Stella hurt. She's been through way too much to have to face any more heartbreak.' She sighed and then continued, 'Look… He seems nice enough, but…'

A laugh down the table momentarily brought both Gina and Alinta's heads up, and Stella immediately pretended to be engrossed in that conversation instead of shamelessly eavesdropping.

'Seems nice enough, but… But what?' Alinta commented.

Gina bent her head back towards Alinta. 'Look, Heath and I have a mutual friend, Fleur, and according to her, he still keeps in contact with the American woman he was seeing a while ago.'

'Jesus, Gina,' Alinta snapped. Eyes flickered in their direction, and she waited until everyone had turned away again before saying, 'He's allowed to be friends with an ex-girlfriend. It doesn't mean anything, so stop fabricating issues where they don't exist.' She let out an annoyed huff of air. 'Nobody knows more than me what Stella's been through. Heath is an amazing guy. He obviously adores her.'

'Well, yes, that much is obvious,' Gina said. 'I just hope she's the *only* woman that he adores. He's exceedingly private, and it makes me suspicious.'

Alinta considered Gina's statement for a moment before responding, 'Being private isn't a crime.'

This is a totally inappropriate setting for these two to be discussing my love life, Stella thought.

As Gina glanced around to make sure everyone else was still occupied, Stella busily occupied herself with checking her phone again. Nothing.

'Unless you have something to hide,' Gina whispered, 'there's usually no reason not to talk about your past.'

Stella couldn't see her face, but Alinta's annoyance came through in her voice. 'Stop being suspicious, Gina! And stop questioning the guy, for heaven's sake. Just be happy that Stella is finally happy.'

Gina topped up her wine again before slumping back in her chair and grudgingly muttering, 'I suppose so. It's just… Oh, look.' Her voice returned to its normal level. 'Cake!'

'I took the liberty of organising a surprise birthday cake,' Heath said, pressing a kiss to Stella's cheek. 'Salted caramel popcorn.'

It wasn't a cake Stella would have chosen for herself, but she was overcome by the thoughtfulness of the gesture. She could feel her cheeks press upwards as she smiled when the cake was placed in front of her. Gooey French caramel dripped down the side of a vanilla sponge cake adorned with an assortment of chocolates. Love on a plate.

The lunch guests broke into a rousing and tone-deaf rendition of 'Happy Birthday,' and as they sang, Stella realised that Alinta had captured her expression as she received the surprise birthday cake. Alinta slid her phone across the table to Stella, a grin on her face.

As Stella looked down at the photo, love washed over her. Alinta had captured a timeless moment: Heath and Stella declaring without words their unspoken love. The image was as quintessential to Stella as Alfred Eisenstaedt's iconic photo 'V-J Day' – a big, bold, and overly inflated statement though it might be, but that was what the birthday cake photo represented to Stella.

At that moment, the clichéd saying 'a picture is worth a thousand words' seemed all too true – who needed words when love could flame so brightly in a photograph?

She looked upwards on the screen, softening under Heath's loving gaze, the cake sitting between them. Although the photo didn't show it, her hand rested on his leg, his trousers smooth under her fingers. His arm gently wrapped around her waist and rested on the small of her lower back. They'd accidentally worn matching clothes – the white embroidery of her dress accentuated the brilliance of Heath's long-sleeved white shirt. For a shot taken spontaneously, it was a remarkably technically honed photograph, though no amount of technical aptitude could match the emotion emanating from the image.

As the last clashing notes of *Happy Birthday* trailed off, Pam got up to stand behind Stella and raised a glass without clinking it, waiting for the guests to come to a natural hush.

Pam cleared her voice. 'I thought it suitable to make a toast in honour of our beautiful birthday girl, Stella, who turns 39 today. It's hard to believe that she's a year off turning 40. It feels like only yesterday that I gave birth to my darling girl.'

Blushing, Stella said, '*Really*, Mum? Thanks, but please don't …'

Gina burst out, 'Lap it up, Stella, it doesn't last forever, luv!'

Ignoring the interruption, Pam continued, 'Your beloved father would be so proud of you, Stella. You were the apple of his eye. Madison would be proud too. We *all* love you very much, Stella, darling. I'm extremely happy, as they would be, that you've recently made the important decision to pursue your childhood dream.' She fanned an arm out to the side, stepped back as though to bow, and then paused dramatically, as Stella realised a moment too late what her mother was about to say. 'Our Stella has decided to resume her acting career. If – I should say *when* – Stella lands the lead role in a new play that she recently auditioned for, she'll be relocating to London, as, very excitingly, the play is being performed on the West End.' Pam beamed, clearly oblivious to the silence that had descended over the table at her news. 'Now, I can't announce much more right now, but suffice to say that the relocation will be a small sacrifice to enable our Stella to showcase her immeasurable talents to the world. To Stella!'

You could have heard a pin drop before several people belatedly raised their glasses, looking as stunned as Stella felt. Emotions, too many to count, washed over her; she wasn't sure if she was about to faint, have an anxiety attack, or both.

Everything around them slowed to a glacial pace, the restaurant feeling dim and hazy and small. She looked down at the table, the choice easier than raising her eyes to see the questions in Heath's gaze.

Why would Mum do this? Inside, Stella wailed at the position her mother had put her in. *I don't even have the role secured yet. Why? Why would she announce this news? Here. Today. In front of Heath… In front of everyone.* And then she realised. *To be sure I can't back out. That's why she did this. Christ.*

Stella finally looked up and met first Alinta's eyes, then Gina's. They were the only other people who knew of her plan to resume her acting career.

At least she knew that her adoring younger sister wouldn't be photographing this excruciating moment.

After lunch, they walked the short distance from the Italian restaurant to Heath's apartment, Stella nearly tumbling once or twice, having had a sufficient supply of Chardonnay to merry her step.

Heath was withdrawn and quieter than usual on the walk, only speaking to check if she was okay each time she tripped.

The familiar smell of incense and fresh linen greeted them as they entered the apartment. Heath put the remaining cake in the fridge and turned the stereo on to Eddie Vedder's album *Into the Wild*. The words to *Setting Forth*, a song Stella interpreted as about leaping into the unknown, seemed poignant and was somewhat uncomfortable.

She flopped on the lounge in a boozy haze, her mother's ill-timed announcement ringing in her fuzzy head. She hoped Heath would support her, whatever she chose, if she got the role.

Really, Stella thought hazily, *it's confounding that a person can love another so much, to such a degree, that they'll support an excruciating decision while sacrificing themselves.*

The final scene in *Sophie's Choice*, which won Meryl Streep an Oscar for Best Actress in 1983, wriggled its way into Stella's mind. Standing in line for the German concentration camps, Streep's Sophie was informed by a Nazi officer that she had to choose which of her two children would survive – the other would die. There was no way to save them both.

Gosh, comparing your impending career versus a relationship decision to Streep's performance in Sophie's Choice *is dramatic, even for you, Stella.*

'Stella,' Heath said softly.

She opened her eyes to see Heath extending a hand, inviting her to dance to Vedder's *End of the Road*. She let him pull her close and the two fell into an anti-clockwise trance, rocking heel, toe, heel, toe – rising, falling, and rising again in a melancholy version of a Viennese waltz.

She wished she could say something about the audition and apologise for being deceitful, but no words came to mind. Instead, she rested her head on Heath's chest, grateful to him for reaching out, and that they were cocooned in his apartment.

***

Heath wasn't sure how they ended up on his lounge, devouring large chunks of Stella's birthday cake. Yet there they were, plying themselves with caramel sponge to the verge of being sick.

The food fight started with Stella smearing a piece of cake down the side of Heath's thigh.

'Oops-a-daisy. Sorry!' Stella stared dovelike at Heath – butter wouldn't melt in her mouth – as though the cake sticking Heath's leg hairs together had found its way there by accident.

She was too cute to be annoyed with her, but…

He loaded a hunk of cake onto a finger and filled Stella's ear with soft sponge. Before she could move, he dolloped another portion of cake into her mouth and pressed her chin shut.

Stella chased him into the kitchen to re-arm herself with leftover cake from the fridge. Too late. Creamy splats of cake rained down on her. If she could stop laughing, Heath thought, watching her, she might have had a chance of defending herself against his cake assault. It was a wonder she managed to scrape a chunk of cake from her thigh to slide it beneath his jeans and into his underpants.

'Yuck!' he exclaimed loudly, picking his legs up in exaggerated movements, as though he'd been in the saddle all day, trying to stop the cake from gluing his bum cheeks together.

'Truce?' Stella asked, then quickly turned the question into a statement. 'Truce. Truce!' She laughed as Heath peeled his jeans down his legs and hopped to the shower like the odd person out in a three-legged race.

From around the shower curtain, Heath called out, 'Truce! That's it. If you've called it a truce, there's no more funny business from you, Stelz!'

'Promise,' she said, following him to the shower. He turned to adjust the water and, while distracted, found her hand smearing the last glob of caramel cake onto his face.

'You little shit!' he said before grabbing and kissing her.

The day ended as it started, with them both in their birthday suits in Heath's bed.

CHAPTER 18

The following morning, indiscriminate oily handprints had climbed their way across the span of the pale green wall behind Heath's bed, offering clues to their activities into the early hours of Stella's second day orbiting her 39th year around the sun.

With an impending property inspection looming, Heath needed to wipe their handiwork off the wall – but not, Stella was delighted to learn, until they completed a post-mortem of which handprint correlated to what position.

'Mmm… I wouldn't be dead for quids,' Heath drawled.

He wrestled her to the base of the bed, where they set up a pile of cushions and continued examining their wall-to-wall artwork. Stella claimed ownership of the little pillow; she'd had possession of it since the first time she stayed at his house – nestling against it when sleeping, infusing the pillow with her scent. Heath had confessed that when she didn't stay overnight, he took custody of the little pillow, curling against it to remind him of her.

Heath perked up, turned his head upside down, and pointed to two handprints glistening on the wall. 'Those hands are upside down.

He went to the wall to touch the prints. 'Ahhh, these are still warm.'

She laughed again.

'We might need to take an intermission. I'll make us a cup of tea.'

He stepped back to take in the wall. 'Jesus, Stelz. This oil painting is gallery-worthy. You couldn't buy what we have.'

His comment rang through the air like a goodbye and they fell silent, far too conscious of the enormous dilemma posed by the resurrection of her acting career.

Stella snuggled into Heath and whispered, 'I'm sorry you found out about the audition the way you did. I was going to tell you but…' Her voice trailed off as she struggled to find the right words. 'I was just – I'll know very soon if I got the role. Maybe we can talk about it more then?'

When Heath slipped into character as Mr Hyde Park, Stella knew he was hiding behind the character's bravado.

'Well, my darling, Stella, we all know that you are destined for lofty heights. Of course, you will land the role, and you will take it, as you must!' Somehow Heath managed to say this with genuine enthusiasm.

Mr Hyde Park continued, 'I anticipate you'll receive notable awards and metamorphose into Dame Stella Longhurst, one of the West End's most beloved actresses. Dame Longhurst shall win a slew of Olivier awards, receive triumphant reviews, and enjoy a legion of adoring fans!'

'Heath,' Stella whispered, 'please stop. This isn't a time to joke. I feel horrid… My heart is breaking into more pieces than I knew was possible.'

Hearing the unfamiliar pleading note in her voice, Heath dropped the mask. 'I'm sorry. I know it's important that we discuss this situation, but can we do it another time soon, please? Let's just be in this moment. Every moment we have ever lived has brought us to this very minute. I want us to enjoy it.'

As they lay in their quiet familiarity, Stella doing her best to honour Heath's request to be present, she contemplated the innumerable forever-seconds they'd shared. When, first thing in the morning, they were tightly wrapped around one another and it was hard to tell whose belly was grumbling; debating for hours about the evils of politicians, pop culture competitions, playing wrestle-the-thumb under the bed covers; tracing bodies through sheets; the humming sound they echoed at one another to indicate they were awake; the way Heath always awaited Stella's arrival and buzzed her in before she had a chance to use her key.

Not breaking the silence, Heath jumped up and sloped off to the kitchen to make tea.

Stella eased herself to a seated position and surveyed the oily wall one last time, and said quietly, not realising that he could hear her, 'The oil stains are my love letter to you, Heath.'

CHAPTER 19

Sometimes, real life was better than fiction. Of all the scenarios Stella had dreamed about regarding resigning from the Geoscientist Institute, never had she conceived of this one.

She sashayed unannounced into Oliver's office and waited for Dragon Man to raise his eyes from the computer screen to meet hers.

'Yes, Stella, what is it?' Oliver asked, with the enthusiasm of a manager who wanted to sack an employee but was bound by too many pesky rules.

'I'm resigning, Oliver.'

Oliver's eyes lit up with excitement. In all the time she'd worked for the Geoscientist Institute, Stella had never seen him look at her with any level of interest. The way he was looking at her now, though, almost bordered on affection.

The irony of being in his favour, for once, for the act of resigning.

'Do you have a timeline for the resignation, Stella?' Oliver asked, keeping a poor check on his enthusiasm.

'Effective immediately.'

Embarrassingly, Oliver's expression had morphed into such adoration that Stella looked away, feeling uncomfortable.

Oliver probed further, no doubt desperate to know if her resignation was politically geared and might affect his influence with the Board. 'Do you have a new role to go to, Stella?'

'Indeed.' Stella didn't bother to keep the smug note from her voice. 'I'll be playing the role of Blanche DuBois in the Australian Theatre Company's production of *A Streetcar Named Desire...* in London's West End.' She paused for dramatic effect and then added, 'I shall be replacing the much-revered actress Melanie Tate in the part. Very sadly, Melanie is terminally ill. I leave for London imminently.'

Stella's gaze never left Oliver's as she watched his expression transform from astonishment to disdain to something resembling capitulation.

And with that, Ms Longhurst left the building.

CHAPTER 20

For a man who stood six foot two inches without shoes, Heath felt tiny – his shoulders slumped as he folded into himself in his truck, the wind taken out of his sails.

He wouldn't normally catch up with Stella on a Monday night, but he'd intuited from her text that she'd been successful in landing the role of Blanche in *Streetcar*.

> Can we catch up this evening, beautiful man? We
> need to talk ASAP.

He stared down at the message on his phone, feeling numb. *My baby doll is moving to London.*

He'd intentionally been avoiding the topic. Their impending talk would be sobering, and part of him wished he could postpone it forever.

Sitting in the car looking out at the ocean, even four-foot waves couldn't entice him to get up the energy to surf before work. Instead, he sat, lifeless, unable and unwilling to move. For once, he didn't immediately respond to Stella's text. What could he possibly say? What was one supposed to say?

He started crafting a text message from Mr Hyde Park, thinking this it might lighten the situation, or at least articulate something without being too glum.

> My dearest and one and only Stella,
>
> It's appropriate that I'm reminded of the Pearl Jam
> song called Black where Mr Vedder refers to his love
> having a beautiful life and being a star. My wish is

that you don't become a star in someone else's life.
That, my dear, would kill me. I know you're going to
be a huge success.

You will be loved.

You will be adored.

Heath stopped short of sending the text message to censure himself.

You're clutching at straws, Heath. Firstly, Stella will see straight through your stupid Mr Hyde Park text and know it's an awkward attempt to avoid your feelings. Secondly, she'll tell you that Mr Hyde Park wouldn't have heard of Eddie Vedder – Miles Davis, maybe – but not Eddie Vedder.

Realism even in pretend, he supposed.

Eventually, he responded to Stella's text with a single squid emoji.

One time, Heath remembered, he and Stella had been feverishly texting one another using emojis as intimate references.

Stella, thinking herself to be a on roll, sent Heath an emoji of an octopus. He hadn't been able to make sense of the octopus emoji. And then Stella explained that the octopus represented them in bed, their eight limbs – four arms and four legs – entwined around one another in a loving embrace. From that point on, she'd identified as an octopus and assigned Heath the squid emoji. Some mornings, an octopus would land in Heath's messenger, its presence saying, 'Good morning,' from Stella. Sometimes he'd ping Stella a squid emoji at random times throughout the day, just to let her know he was thinking about her.

The squid that Heath messaged Stella in response to her request to talk that evening said everything and nothing. It was a love note, a death knell, a speechless man, a deflated soulmate – and a desperate clinging to anything familiar before everything became unfamiliar.

***

Stella arrived at Heath's apartment at 7 pm. With the security fob to Heath's apartment, she could easily have let herself in; there was no need to announce her arrival. Instead, she pressed the intercom, as she always did, and waited for him to play the game of buzzing her in. The urgent sound of the intercom being pressed sounded for longer than normal, suggesting that he was impatient to see her right away.

Heath answered the door, his right foot turned slightly in, long arms dangling by his side. Stella's usual bounce was replaced by a soft tiptoe as she entered his apartment.

They embraced, saying nothing as their hands moved up and down the familiar curves of their backs. She rested the side of her face against his chest, listening to his heart. The familiar smell of onion, dough, and cheese announced that he was cooking pizza for dinner – the same meal he had cooked when she first visited his apartment.

As the party responsible for potentially blowing up their relationship, Stella knew she had to be the one to break the silence and address the issue of her impending move to London. Yet, any semblance of eloquence was proving a challenge this evening. A pastiche of emotions – excitement, despair, terror, and something verging on self-assurance due to her satisfaction at securing the role, soared through her body, wreaking havoc on her rationale.

Part of her wanted to ask Heath to run away with her to London; the other part was quietly relieved, knowing it would be impracticable for him to leave, especially with his upcoming exhibition. She knew to succeed in the role that she'd need to be hyper-focused; if Heath were in London with her, he'd be a distraction.

Finally, Stella spluttered an inarticulate jumble of words. 'It's – It's imposs – impossible. I don't… Honestly, I don't know how to start this conversation…' She took a deep breath. 'Everything feels like a dream. It all happened so quickly.'

'I'm not going to pretend that I know how to deal with this, Stella. I don't.'

Caught in a crossfire of colliding emotions and at her most vulnerable, Stella shocked herself by almost confessing the secret of her assault. 'Heath, I need to tell you… I need to do this – there's more to it, deeply personal reasons. It's complicated –'

Heath cut her off. 'It's not complicated! You got the part. So, you're going.' He closed his eyes briefly, and his jaw momentarily locked. 'Look, I know what it's like to have a creative calling… I just – this came out of nowhere, Stella, and it's all been so sudden that it's knocked me for six.'

'You're not hearing me,' Stella said, desperate to get her words out. 'It's not just that – I need time to work through some things –.'

'I'm not an idiot, Stella,' Heath said shortly. 'I worked it out as soon as I received your text. Although –' his voice softened '– you were destined to get the part before you even auditioned. I know how capable you are.'

'But –'

'I suppose saying congratulations is a good place to start,' he said, cutting her off again. 'I know it can't have been easy to secure the role, particularly given it's been a long time since you acted. You're amazing.'

'That means the world to me,' Stella said, trying to rein in her enthusiasm at having landed the part. 'I'm happy. Terrified. Excited and scared. And I was scared about us. I adore you. I don't want this opportunity to jeopardise our relationship.'

'Sorry,' Heath said shortly, 'but you know my feelings about long-distance relationships. They're hard work, and I have a business to run. I can't move to London, Stella, let alone visit.'

Stella flinched. 'Heath, we're talking about us! We have to find a way to make it work. You could visit after your exhibition opens!'

'I can't commit to anything right now,' he said. 'I need to process everything – I need to focus on my work.'

'At least commit to visiting me?'

Her question went unanswered as Heath went to the kitchen to check on the pizza. 'To be honest, I'm a little bent out of shape, Stelz,' he said after a moment, busying himself with wiping down kitchen benches as he spoke. 'I feel like I've been punched in the gut. Everything has moved at lightning speed. Don't get me wrong,' he continued, keeping his eyes on the table, 'I know this is your dream, and I'm genuinely happy for you. Really. I am. It's just – I don't see how to make a relationship work with you over there and me here.'

Stella joined Heath in the kitchen and gently tugged at his arm, turning him to face her. 'Heath, we need to discuss this. It's important. I – I leave –'

The oven timer interrupted her, signalling that the pizza was ready.

'Oh, fuck!' Heath snapped, burning himself taking the pizza out of the oven and dropping the pan on the bench with a clatter. 'For fuck's sake, that hurt. The prick of a pizza!'

'Are you okay?' Stella asked.

He stepped around her to the sink to run water over the burn. 'Let's talk … logistics. Yeah. We need to discuss logistics first. You need to get yourself organised – to resign from work.'

'Um… Yes… There are things to organise…'

'You need to book your flight.'

'The Australian Theatre Company has booked the flight… It's all already in…' She reached for his arm. 'Heath –'

Heath continued, 'You need to resign. No, I said that already. When do you think you'll resign, Stella?'

Stella hesitated before answering, then blurting out the words so quickly that she was barely understandable. 'I resigned this morning.' She stared at his face, hoping for some indication of his thoughts, but his face remained blank. 'Oliver took the news well, to no one's surprise. You should have seen his face when I announced that I was leaving to perform in London!'

Deafening quiet.

Shit.

'Riiight. So, Dragon Man, Oliver, received the news that you got the part before I did?' He plonked the pizza down on the table and slid an upside-down knife and fork to Stella. 'Did everyone know before me, Stella?' He tore too many hand towels off a roll to use as serviettes, the force of his action knocking the roll over, and disappeared back into the kitchen, fossicking for salt and pepper.

'I had little other choice than to tell him,' Stella said. 'I got a call from Mark Henshaw – the director – this morning at work to tell me I'd got the part, and I wanted to tell you first, but time being of the essence… I had to resign quickly, and I just – I thought it would be better to have this discussion in person.' She prodded at the pizza in front of her. 'I'm sorry. I wanted to tell you everything – about the audition and resigning, and –'

'It's a lot to take in, Stelz,' Heath said, returning to the table with salt and pepper. 'Frankly, I'm in shock.'

'Heath, I'm so sorry,' she said earnestly, reaching over to put her hand over his. 'I was scared of failing the audition. I was also worried I'd be confused if I spoke to you about it. Not in a million light-years did I think that I'd get the part.' She shook her head. 'It felt like there was no reason to mention the audition until I knew for sure – I didn't want to tell you for no reason, you know? And anyway, it's ludicrous. I feel like I have imposter syndrome – as though I'm going to get found out for being a terrible actress at any moment. There's enormous pressure riding on this, and I'm feeling it. I have no idea how the press will receive the news that I'm stepping in for Melanie Tate. It won't be easy.' She sucked in a quavering breath and admitted, 'This is possibly the most stupid thing I'll ever do, the biggest mistake I'll ever make.'

'I wish you would've told me you were auditioning,' he said softly. 'There should be no secrets between us.'

There should be no secrets between us. Stella wanted to cry.

After a pause, he continued, 'To be honest, this has left a bad taste in my mouth, Stella. I get that you were nervous and have your reasons, but none of it really seems to be enough. I just can't get past the fact you kept this from me. I just don't understand.' He absently turned his pizza around in circles on the table and then looked up at last to meet her eyes. 'I'm going to need to have some space, Stella, to recover from this. I feel like I'm playing second fiddle to your career. I've been there before, and frankly, it's not a place I want to be.'

In that moment, Stella realised she'd done the same thing as Candice. She'd loved Heath – and was now leaving him, except unlike Candice, it seemed there was no chance of even trying to keep the relationship going despite the distance.

'You leave for London tomorrow, don't you?' he said abruptly as she fell silent.

'I leave in the morning.'

'For fuck's sake,' Heath snapped, pushing back from the table with such force that his glass of water spilled. 'Really?' He scoffed. 'Look, I'm happy for you, but I don't know what this means for us. I need time for this to sink in.'

The remainder of the evening was one of the worst in Stella's memory, everything that had come before being reduced to excruciating and paralysing politeness. She was heartbroken at how quickly the de-escalation of their relationship had begun, and while she wanted to bring up the idea of Heath visiting her in London again, it was clear he wasn't interested.

Hoping to win him over at least a little, Stella told him about auditioning for Blanche; he listened courteously, nodding in all the appropriate places, but remained aloof. There was no sex, and they agreed without saying it that she wouldn't stay the night; she opted instead to head home early to prepare for the flight to London.

She told herself it was easier that way.

CHAPTER 21

London, September 2022

It was a mild autumnal day in London, and Stella was enjoying a quick stroll through Camden Square Park for the meeting with Melanie Tate. Her small, quirky hotel in Camden was a short walk from the Palais Theatre in the West End.

Due to Melanie's illness, and with the announcement that Stella was replacing her in the role of Blanche yet to be released, Mark had suggested the actresses meet for breakfast at a chic London café near the theatre.

Stella's love–hate relationship with coffee had turned lukewarm two days after her arrival, and now she ordered a pot of black tea while she waited for Melanie to arrive. She peeked at her phone to see if Heath had sent her a message, even though, knowing the time difference, it was pointless to expect anything, as he hadn't contacted her since the last time they spoke when she was at his house. She blinked away the tears pricking at her eyes as she imagined Heath tucked into bed. She had loved quietly observing him as he slept. She would trace the profile of his peaceful face, light speckles of grey beard catching what little light eased through the window, the mole on his left cheek near invisible but there nonetheless, one of the many adorable features on his face.

Her thoughts about Heath vanished when she saw Melanie Tate float into the café, ethereal and mysterious and looking almost exactly as she had ten years earlier. Stella envied her for her thick blonde hair; unlike Stella, Melanie wouldn't have needed to wear a wig to play Blanche. The dark rings under Melanie's eyes and the listless way she greeted the waitress as she sat down were the only clues that she was unwell.

Stella closed her hands around Melanie's outstretched one, the simple touch renewing a friendship they had forged years earlier while studying at The Performers' Centre.

'How are you?' Stella asked. 'You look beautiful, as always.' The compliment came easily, not least because it was true, but also because there wasn't a fibre of competitiveness between the women, despite the circumstances surrounding their meeting.

'Oh, Stella. It's like a dream, seeing you here in London. I'm so thrilled that you're acting again and taking the role. The whole cast is. It's crazy and surreal and wonderful all at once.' Melanie covered a yawn with her hand as she took her gloves off, shaking her head from side to side in apology.

'Thank you, Mel. I'm thrilled and terrified, more terrified, I think... Anyhow, this isn't about me. I want you to tell me how you are. Honestly, how are you?'

'I'm petrified, Stelz. It's a particularly virulent type of liver cancer. And it's metastasised.'

Melanie turned to look at the ground; a thick vein bulged at the side of her forehead.

Stella pressed her palms together and rested the edge of her hands against her chin, not saying a word.

After a few moments in silence, Melanie lifted her eyes to meet her friend's, her palms turned upwards indicating uncertainty. 'I'm going to keep putting on a brave face for Victor and Desdemona. She's only four. Far too young to be a child soon to be without a mother.'

Stella leaned in closer, 'Is there anything – *anything* – I can do to help?'

'Thank you, but no. There's nothing you can do. Victor's taken time off work and is caring for me around the clock. It'll be lovely for you to meet Victor and Desdemona.'

Stella stroked Melanie's hand.

'Anyway,' Melanie said, moving on, 'I couldn't possibly perform Blanche in this state. Tennessee Williams would kill me before the cancer does! The role is too arduous and emotionally taxing. Blanche's breakdown and the rape scene... I had little choice than to pull out.'

The actresses shared a contrived laugh and sat quietly. Stella busied herself with pouring tea to stop from bursting into tears. The thought of losing another person she cared about made her throat close over; she knew that her voice would be strained when she went to speak.

'I am, however, utterly joyed that you will be playing the role,' Melanie said, using both hands to steady her cup, straining under its weight. 'I wish you'd told me you were acting again.'

Unbuttoning her heavy trench coat and draping it over a decorative floral armchair, Stella commented, 'I'd barely decided to give acting another try when the audition came up. I mean, what were the chances of me landing the part? It doesn't seem plausible, even now… If I'm honest, it's a little ridiculous, but I'd be lying if I said I wasn't thrilled.' She added a spoonful of honey to her tea and topped up Melanie's cup. 'It's a massive risk.'

The sides of Melanie's mouth crept upwards into a gentle smile, 'You've always taken risks.' For someone so sick, she suddenly became animated as she recounted a memory from their younger acting days.

'Remember when you pitched to Sydney agents to represent you?' Melanie's fingers tapped the table gently, excited at the memory. 'Remember?'

Stella looked off to the side, slowly nodding as the memory came to her.

'Oh, it was brilliant, Stelz,' Melanie continued. 'Creating a fake interview with *Variety* magazine to stand out was genius. Pretending you were already an established actress and quoting how fantastic your agent was. Then you cut and pasted the *Variety* masthead, tailored the article to different agents, and posted the interview off with your black and white head shot.' She took a few deep breaths and leaned back against her seat, the flurry of words and excitement tiring her.

'I'd nearly forgotten that.'

'I wish I'd thought of that to score my first agent.'

Edging her chair closer, Stella took Melanie's hand again. 'It's so bloody good to see you. I am incredibly proud to play this role on your behalf, Melanie. I am doing this as much for you as I am for me. I will do everything, absolutely everything, to make you proud of my performance.'

'You will be brilliant.' Melanie drew in a deep breath. 'Okay, let's not waste another minute discussing my health. I need to give you the lowdown on the cast and playing to a British audience.'

'The press conference is at midday,' Stella said. 'Will you come? I completely understand if you don't want to.'

'No, I won't attend. There's no point in me being there. Besides, it's your time to shine, my friend.'

MEDIA RELEASE: 1 SEPTEMBER 2022
LONDON, ENGLAND

Stella Longhurst Replaces Melanie Tate in A Streetcar Named Desire; Lead Actress Exits Production Due to Illness

LONDON—Australian actress Stella Longhurst is replacing Melanie Tate in the role of anti-heroine Blanche DuBois in the Palais Theatre's upcoming production of

A Streetcar Named Desire. Longhurst takes over following Tate's unexpected withdrawal due to health concerns.

Director Mark Henshaw said: 'It's regrettable that Melanie cannot continue in the role of Blanche, but she has the full support of the cast and crew in making this difficult decision. Understandably, at this time, Melanie's health must take priority and we wish her a speedy recovery.

'The ensemble is delighted to have the talented Stella Longhurst join our cast.'

Tennessee Williams' *A Streetcar Named Desire*, written in 1945, became more widely known due to the 1951 film adaptation, starring Vivien Leigh and Marlon Brando. Leigh won an Academy Award for her portrayal of Blanche DuBois, an unhinged and ageing alcoholic Southern belle.

The play is set in a rundown house in New Orleans and obtains its name from the streetcar that delivers Blanche DuBois, an anxiety-stricken former schoolteacher, to the home of her sister, Stella Kowalski (Delia Turner), in Elysian Fields. The production follows Blanche as she leaves her small-town world and moves in with Stella and her husband, Stanley Kowalski (Johnny Marsden). Stella and Stanley's already volatile relationship is exacerbated by Blanche's flirtatious presence, leading to greater conflict in the Kowalski household.

Bookings are open for *A Streetcar Named Desire*. The play opens on 1 October 2022.

Media contact:
Vikki Milligan
Senior Publicist
[003 871 7628]
Palais Theatre Publicity Department

CHAPTER 22

For the press call at the Palais Theatre, Mark strategically seated Stella in the centre, between himself and Johnny Marsden, who was playing Stanley Kowalski. Delia Turner – Stella Kowalski – was seated on Mark's other side.

Feeling like a deer in headlights, without a character mask to hide behind, Stella reminded herself to take long, measured breaths to calm her nerves.

Despite it only being a press call, Stella absorbed the powerful energy of being back on stage and pressed her feet hard against the wooden floorboards she'd soon become intimate with.

The press call had been orchestrated by Vikki Milligan, the Palais Theatre's senior publicist, with precision timing, commencing at 12.00 midday sharp and concluding at 12.30 pm, allowing the journalists ample time to file stories for the evening news bulletin.

'Alfie Knox, senior arts writer for the *Guardian*,' the first journo said, addressing Stella. 'Ms Longhurst, congratulations on being cast in the role of Blanche amid the difficult circumstances of Ms Tate's departure. What's your process is for inhabiting Blanche, one of theatre's most challenging female acting roles, with less than a month until opening night?'

The stage manager handed Stella a microphone. Before responding, she sat upright, took a deep breath, and pressed her feet firmly into the ground. As instructed, she was conscious of keeping her answers brief and to deflect questions about the decade-long gap in her performing biography.

'Thanks for your question, Alfie,' Stella said, resisting fidgeting with her fingers. 'To assist with wholly imbuing the character, I'm taking a method approach to performing Blanche.'

Alfie spoke over the top of the journalist from the *Sunday Times* to direct a follow-up question to Mark.

'Mark, why have you taken such a big risk in casting Ms Longhurst, who is undoubtedly talented but is nevertheless an unknown Australian actress?'

'Stella's audition was exceptional,' Mark said, 'and frankly her ability to channel Blanche DuBois with such ease was more than enough to convince me that she is capable of stepping into Melanie's shoes.' A subtly different expression crossed his face as he continued, 'Obviously we miss Melanie, and wish her personal circumstances were different, but we are privileged to welcome Stella to our production of *A Streetcar Named Desire*. Stella also has worked with several cast members previously, which will help to ease the transition.'

'Mark, sorry, just a follow-up,' Alfie said, again talking over his fellow journalists. 'Might you sleep easier if you'd cast a well-known actress in the role?'

Mark chuckled. 'You're assuming I'm not sleeping easy now, Alfie. I have full faith in Stella's abilities, and while a known name can have its advantages, the fact is that we aren't making an American blockbuster film that relies heavily on star power. We're creating theatre, and I'd prefer any day to cast talent over stardom.' He leaned forward, pinning Alfie down with an intense gaze. 'After so many years on this beat, Alfie, you should know I don't play safe. I don't hedge my bets. Hiring so-called stars as a ploy to ensure a production's success is cheap, tardy, and not worthy of the Palais or the West End.'

Vikki allowed Mark's response to linger in the air before nodding to the next journalist to ask a question.

'Ms Longhurst, Davey from the *Sunday Times*. I appreciate there will be difficulties being dropped into the production at the eleventh hour. What are the main challenges for you in performing the role?'

'Thanks for your question, Davey,' Stella said, crossing one leg over the other and letting herself relax as she answered. 'It's easy to sound rubbish – or exaggerated – with a Southern American accent, so I've been brushing up on my accent skills with the help of a dialect coach.'

Davey stepped forward as he questioned Stella, 'Did you use an accent coach...' He referred to his notes and continued, 'ten years ago when you first performed the role?'

In her peripheral vision, Stella saw Vikki shift to observe her response. 'Yes, the first time I played Blanche I worked closely with a dialect coach. This time it's more a case of brushing up on the accent.'

'You make it sound so easy,' he said with a smile that reminded Stella of a shark. 'Er, refresh my memory, Ms Longhurst, what other roles have you performed over the past decade?'

Any journalist worth their salt would have dug into her past; he knew the answer but was clearly hoping to catch her out.

Stella paused momentarily and took a deep breath. She clasped her hands discretely and pressed the webbing between her thumb and index finger. She'd workshopped a response to this question with Vikki – the two publicists forming a formidable team. Stella wasn't about to tell Vikki the real reason she'd stopped acting; she wasn't proud of choosing to rely on the tragic deaths of her father and sister to excuse her absence from acting instead of being honest about the assault and reliving the trauma on the eve of returning to the stage.

'I had a break from acting...' she said, keeping her voice level but friendly. 'I'm sure you've seen that my family experienced several traumatic events in a relatively short period of time, and with all due respect, I don't wish to discuss the past. And while it's lovely to be back, Davey, I have no delusions that playing this role will be easy. That said, once you play someone like Blanche, the character never leaves you, which is an advantage.'

'In any case, I'm only one actor, and I shouldn't be monopolising the questions. We're here to discuss the production and its entire fantastic cast, with whom I'm so privileged to work.' She settled a smile on her face, ready to captivate her audience, and continued, 'Does anyone have a question for another cast member?'

You could hear a pin drop at the Palais Theatre.

CHAPTER 23

Heath scoured the internet for news of the London media's reaction to Stella replacing Melanie Tate as Blanche DuBois.

'Aspiring Australian wannabe has high hopes of being the next Naomi Watts,' read the *Sunday Times'* headline, with a by-line by Davey Booker.

Alfie Knox's cover story for the review section of the *Guardian* led with, 'Australian director resurrects fallen production of *Streetcar* with a credible casting choice.'

Davey Booker sounds like a tosser, calling Stella a wannabe. Prick. Alfie is on the money – 'Credible'. That's more like it.

While he was still reluctantly coming to terms with Stella's relocation to London, and with keeping her audition a secret, the fact was, he still had her back, and he always would.

He squinted at the photo in the *Sunday Times* of Stella sitting front and centre with the *Streetcar* cast, on stage at the Palais Theatre press conference. As he scrutinised the photo, his attention was grabbed by how closely Stella and co-star Johnny Marsden were seated together – closer than the rest of the cast. The back of her hand seemed to be half-resting against Johnny's thigh. They looked awfully familiar for two people who hadn't seen one another for a decade.

Are their legs touching? He leaned into the computer, expanding the image to full size, and inspected the image so closely that he could see tiny blue grid lines on the computer screen. *Their thighs are definitely touching.* While he wasn't usually the jealous type, he had read enough about Johnny to know the actor dated and discarded actresses quicker than new socks.

Heath noted that Stella had elevated her style, looking chic yet foreign among the actors. Seeing such a difference in her appearance made her feel so far removed from where he sat at his computer, wearing only boardshorts; grains of sand still stuck to his feet from his time on the beach.

Usually on the weekend, he and Stella would wake up early and grab a coffee at the Bean Pod en route to the beach – a routine that had been shattered with little warning by her sudden departure for London.

Heath could see her sitting next to him, enjoying freshly made poached eggs, wearing cut-off denim shorts and a white singlet top stained with wet triangles from her damp bikini, her long hair tangled in salty knots.

They'd once gone to a beach wearing only oversized, broad-brimmed hats. Lying on cotton Moroccan beach towels, hands and knees pressing against one another as gentle raindrops peppered their bodies, neither could be bothered to lift their hat to check if the sun shower would turn into a rainstorm. Instead, they'd lain still, acquiescent and stoned by the sun's heat, the pitter-patter of raindrops stimulating nipples and skin. He'd declared they were free as birds, revelling in a bare-skinned rebellion. They hadn't cared if they got caught in a heavy downpour, much less about anything. They only cared about being together.

Seeing Stella's blue steel theatre gaze staring back at him from the screen put roughly 10,000 miles and different life choices into perspective.

It was already 28 degrees at 8 am, and Heath was trying to decide if he could be bothered to go for a run. Stella had forgotten to pack her runners, which sat lonely in the corner of his living room. She'd liked to challenge him to a race and bolt off down the beach pathway ahead of him; more than once she'd mentioned it was her way of relieving stress and maintaining good mental health. The runners were a reminder that she'd left him for London, although he didn't have the heart to move them, not an inch.

Giving up on going for a run, he queued relaxing music and turned on a recorded yoga class on the TV. He kicked open a well-worn yoga mat and lay motionless, staring at the ceiling, arms tightly folded against his chest.

He willed himself to do some stretches before it became too humid, too unbearable for physical movement. He'd started practicing yoga years earlier to become flexible in his surfing, but over time it had become more of a habit than anything else, a way of centring himself. With any luck, yoga would help lift the funk he'd been in since Stella left.

With his eyes closed, Heath listened to the instructor's voice on the TV. She had a matter-of-fact yet knowledgeable teaching style and avoided some of the weird alignment cues he'd encountered with other teachers, things like, 'Articulate your vertebra,' 'Liberate your shoulders,' or 'Let your collarbones smile.' The country boy in Heath couldn't help but quash alignment cues as absolute hogwash.

'Let's start in Balasana or child's pose.'

The instructor's voice settled around him as he rolled from his back to sit on his heels, separating his knees wide towards the edge of the yoga mat. Sinking his hips back towards his feet, he stretched his arms forward to rest his chest on the floor. The sponginess of the mat supported his forehead as he moved his head from side to side.

He could still smell Stella's perfume from the last time she'd been over, only a few days earlier.

With each breath, he surrendered deeper to the mat, his nervous system thankful for respite after a stressful and distressing 48 hours. Remaining in child's pose much longer than he usually would, he allowed the smell of Stella's perfume to fill every cell of his body. Each one of his senses was in overdrive – overrun with memories – the essence of Stella cruelly fresh in the air.

'Stretch your arms further forward to get the full length of your spine,' the instructor said.

He didn't stretch his arms further.

'Press into your hands into the mat,' she said, 'lift up onto your toes, and press back into downward facing dog.'

Still, Heath didn't move, not even to wipe away the sweat gathering pace down the side of his neck or the single tear leaking from his eye.

The instructor continued, 'Let your head and neck hang free; press your heels back as far as they'll stretch to the ground. Don't worry if they don't quite reach the floor… Roll your shoulder blades away from one another.'

He couldn't tell if it was his heart or his head thumping. Both, probably. Except for the tears, coming increasingly faster to keep pace with the sweat pouring down his neck, no part of him moved, submitting to the ground in a quasi-genuflexion, crushed by emotion and the reality that Stella was gone. Unmoving, he let the instructor's voice flow over him, registering the words but not bothering to follow the directions.

'Stretch your hands forward and breathe deep into your belly. Press your hips backwards and upwards. Take broad and deep breaths to the four corners of your lungs. Expand your ribcage.'

'Breathe in for four and breathe out for four… Slowly in, slowly out. Expand your breath, broaden your ribcage. Breathe in… Breathe out… In… Out… There's no place to be and nothing to do. Allow yourself to settle into the pose effortlessly. Breathe. Deeply.'

A kookaburra's low, hiccupping chuckle lifted into raucous laughter on Heath's patio, breaking the trance of the instructor's voice.

The bloody kookaburra's laughing at you, mate. Get up and sort yourself out. Stella walked out on you. It tells you everything you need to know about how she truly feels about you. The relationship is a hoax!

Notwithstanding chastising himself, Heath didn't immediately get up. Letting out a guttural groan, he curled himself into the foetal position and lay still for a while, ruminating over his and Stella's relationship going askew.

A howling, gut-wrenching primal scream tore from his throat, competing for airplay above the music as unbearable grief coursed through his body. Moving for the first time, he reached to turn the music to total volume – the sound of tribal drums and Indian chants blaring through the speakers – drowning out the sound of crying. A loud bass drum shook the room as rhythmical and repetitious prayer sounds consumed him; his whole body convulsed in waves of mourning as shocks of music jabbed at him, hypnotising him into an exorcism of emotions – the beginning of the expulsion of Stella.

This relationship isn't going to work. Fuck this. I can't do this.

CHAPTER 24

Stella wasn't as nervous as she'd thought she'd be; it probably helped that she'd at least already met the rest of the cast for the press conference, though she knew that backstage was often a far cry from the smiles in front of the camera.

She'd got the tour of the theatre the same day as the press conference, so she was able to walk through the theatre doors and head backstage with confidence, striding down the corridor until she found her dressing room. She paused and brushed her fingers against the name card, tracing the 'S' of her name, before pushing the door open and going inside.

Ten minutes later she joined Johnny on stage; he flashed her a grin and then both turned their attention to Mark, who was sitting a few rows back in the house, a scowl on his face as he flipped through papers. Hearing Stella's heels click against the stage, he looked up and said, 'Good, you're both here. We'll start with your first meeting in scene 1 to establish Stanley's animalism and brutal forthrightness compared to Blanche's deception and sensitivity. I want their conflict honed before we jump to Blanche and Stanley in scene 2. I'd like to get through both several times before Delia arrives.' He flicked open his script and then snapped it shut again. 'If we have time, we'll move on to block the rape scene, but I'd prefer to get these two down and leave the rape scene to focus on its own.' He leaned back in his seat and propped one ankle on the opposite knee. 'As you are both aware, we have a very short timetable and a lot of work to get done. I have no time to coddle you, Stella, and I have very short patience for wasting time.' Clapping his hands together, he sat forward and said, 'That said, let's begin.'

***

It made sense to rehearse the play chronologically to help establish dynamics between the characters that would evolve throughout the play.

Mark started blocking the scene from his seat in the auditorium, 'I want to see immediate curiosity – chemistry and a hint of menace – when Stanley and Blanche's eyes first meet. Say the initial lines in close proximity.' He gulped down the last of his coffee and continued, 'Run lines up until when Stanley brings up Blanche's first husband. Then I want Blanche to sit down immediately.' He pointed his forefinger at an occasional chair near a dressing table. 'Okay, go!'

The theatre fell deathly silent as Stella stood on stage as Blanche and waited for Johnny to enter as Stanley, clad in a sweaty singlet and trousers, his hair greasy and lathered in Brylcreem.

Knowing the power of silence, Stella resisted the urge to rush Blanche's first line when Stanley arrived in the apartment he shared with her sister. Instead, she took a moment to survey his chest, moving up and down under the muscle shirt, flecks of oil catching under the stage lights.

One...two...three seconds passed after Stanley walked onto the stage. She sized him up with flickering eyes and a subtle shoulder lift before introducing herself as Blanche. She resisted diving immediately into being overly flirtatious – instead, she projected coquettishly coy-edged with prim reserve. Overt flirtation would come soon enough.

Within moments, Stanley assumed the upper hand in the relationship, questioning Blanche about her former marriage and triggering a deep sadness at the memory of her husband's death. She sank into the occasional chair, her shoulders hunched; Stanley stood over her, his dominant presence almost overbearing.

Blanche reached for a tissue and dabbed at the corners of her eyes. She folded her face in her hands before looking back up at Stanley to confirm that the boy – her former husband – had died, her chirpy spirits quickly dashed.

Mark's voice rang through the space, pulling Stella and Johnny out of the scene. 'Stand up, Stella. I don't want you to stay seated for too long. You're using the chair as a crutch. Just pause for a brief respite, and then get straight back up.' He settled back into his seat. 'Go again.'

After a long day of rehearsing that had reminded Stella just how much hard work acting was, she was just about ready to go home and tip herself into bed. But the cast at the theatre invited her to come out with them to the pub – to welcome her properly and celebrate making it through her first day of rehearsal. As tired as she was, Stella decided to go; she badly wanted her castmates to like and respect her.

It didn't take long to realise her mistake.

As they settled around a large table in the back corner of the Crown, Danny Rice, who played Mitch, leaned forward and said,

'So how did you find the first day of rehearsals, Stella? I mean, this must have been such a whirlwind for you! Coming in at the eleventh hour and thrown straight into the lion's mouth!'

The idioms reminded Stella of Heath, and a sharp pang of sadness shot through her. Shaking off the feeling, she smiled at Danny and said, drawling her vowels, 'It's been a mighty whirlwind, that's for sure.'

There was a long silence when she stopped talking as the rest of the table stared at her.

'Hey, you've really got Blanche's voice down,' Kurt Brown who played Steve said. 'I mean, most of us leave it at the theatre, but props for the commitment.'

'Yeah, anyway,' Danny said, 'are you the only actor in your family, or are you a legacy like Delia here?'

Delia quipped, 'Legacy. Cheers, I'll take that, even though it makes me sound like I'm dead.'

'My beloved sister, Madison, who *is* dead, was also an actress.'

Another silence descended over the table, this one fraught with so much awkward that Stella wished she'd just gone home instead.

'I mean, you don't…you don't really need to keep it up,' Danny said.

'I don't, but I will,' Stella said with a gentle smile. 'I intend to stay in character throughout the entire rehearsal period. It's the best way for me to access Blanche.' She took a sip of her drink and pretended not to notice her castmates exchanging glances and rolling their eyes. She tried to let it wash over here, and stayed around for a bit longer, but finally cited jet lag and first day fatigue for an early departure.

It was the first time she wondered if she'd made a mistake to commit so thoroughly to method acting. She hadn't really anticipated the possibility of so clearly alienating her castmates.

But she was committed now – and committed she would stay.

CHAPTER 25

The first few days of rehearsal had gone relatively well, with formative scenes between Blanche and Stanley and key scenes between Blanche and Stella Kowalski shaping their relationships.

Stella had to admit rehearsal was going better than expected. Mark had run them through the first scenes repeatedly, snappish but seeming satisfied with how scenes were shaping up.

Then Stella went into a spin.

From Row D, where Mark liked to watch rehearsals in the house, he barked, 'That's a wrap for today. Except for Stella and Johnny, the rest of the cast is called for midday tomorrow. Stella and Johnny, I need you at the theatre by 7 am for the rape scene.'

Stella had been dreading this moment. She knew rehearsing the rape scene was imminent, but the knowledge really hadn't prepared her for the shock of its imminent arrival.

'I see you nodding,' Mark barked out, 'but I don't hear a response… Stella. The rape scene. You'll be prepared for it first thing tomorrow?'

Glancing nervously at Johnny, Stella replied, noting the quaver in her voice: 'Yes. I'll – I'll be prepared.'

She had the whole night to come to confront the anxiety that Mark's announcement had triggered. Whether that was a good or a bad thing, she had yet to decide.

***

The following day, Johnny caught Stella as she was entering her dressing room, his expression serious.

'Hey, today might get pretty intense,' he said. 'Let's take it slowly up there. If you need a break at any time, just say the word. Mark will need to go at *our* pace, not his, today. Okay?'

Stella's hand slipped on the dressing room door as she edged it open; she hoped Johnny hadn't noticed that her fingertips were shaking. She flicked on the make-up lights and turned to face him, her eyes blinking rapidly. His instinct to check on her was touching; the fact that he cared about her comfort was… unexpectedly soothing.

Steve Crosley might not have raped her all those years ago, it didn't mean the rape scene in *Streetcar* wasn't a palpable reminder of that day and the humiliation and trauma that had followed.

'Thanks, Johnny,' she said, meaning it. Taking a moment to breathe deeply, she continued, her Southern accent twanging, 'I'll be calling on my nerves to perform the scene.'

Johnny still looked worried.

'I'm not going into this with my eyes closed,' Stella said, flicking on the electric kettle in the corner of her dressing room. 'I've read what other actresses have said, and I know it'll be taxing. You know better than I do how far Mark intends to take the physical side of it, and I'm not ashamed to admit I am a bit nervous about this.' She sifted through her costume rack until she found the correct outfit for the scene – a rhinestone tiara and satin dress – what Stanley Kowalski would later disparagingly liken to an old Mardi Gras outfit. 'Even if Mark chooses to black the scene out and leave it largely to the audiences' imagination, it still requires a lot emotionally, and I'm acutely aware of that.'

Johnny reached out and took Stella's hand. 'If we need to stop, we will. Okay? I promise.' He waited for her to smile and nod, then winked at her and walked out of the dressing room calling over his shoulder, 'See you on stage, superstar.'

Stella was grateful for the trust she shared with Johnny. She was even more thankful that the acting world had come so far since her early acting days – so long before the rise of #metoo.

***

Taking a deep breath, Stella stepped out onto the stage, sinking into drunk Blanche, channelling her own anxieties into Blanche's trembling psyche.

She successfully managed the nerves right up to the point where Blanche called Western Union, in order to send a message that indicated her desperation after being caught alone by Stanley, her feeling of being trapped.

When Johnny's Stanley started to slowly advance on her as Blanche, Stella desperately wanted to run from the stage, but she couldn't. It wasn't the actual rape scene that triggered her; it was more that she felt trapped, unable to move, unable to escape – just as she had in the room at Central Casting.

By the time they got to the part in the scene where Blanche broke a bottle and threatened Stanley, Stella had dropped out of character, shaking so badly she could barely get the dialogue out.

'Hey, let's take a quick break,' Johnny suggested to Mark, drawing the director's attention away from Stella. 'I need to catch my breath for a second and I desperately need a coffee.' Before Mark could say anything, he continued, 'Look, I want to block the scene line by line and not ad-lib it. I want to know exactly where we're going in this scene.'

When Mark nodded in agreement and turned his attention to his notes, Johnny shifted position to stand in front of Stella and block her from Mark's view.

'Hey,' he said gently, brushing a knuckle against her cheek. 'Deep breath, okay? All you need to do is breathe in and out. That's all you need to do right now.'

As Mark directed them to take a coffee break, Stella slowly started to come back from her panic attack, more grateful than she could say for Johnny's intervention.

***

Down the road at the Café Emporium, Johnny settled Stella into a chair with a coffee and said, 'Do you want to talk about what just happened?'

Stella flinched. 'No. I… I really don't.'

He frowned, his gaze intent on her face. 'Are you going to be okay? I hate to be an arsehole, but are you going to be able to get through the play?' When she didn't answer immediately, he continued, 'Look, I don't want to make you talk about anything you don't want to talk about, but if this is going to impact your performance, we need to talk about it sooner rather than later.'

'I've been working with this stuff for many years,' Stella said, after another minute of using carefully measured breathing to regain her equilibrium. 'I'll get through it.' She sighed and finally looked up at him. 'I'm sorry. I wasn't sure –' She stopped, sighed again. 'It's not going to be a problem. Just know that I truly appreciate your support.' She met his eyes with hers and offered, with heartfelt sentiment, 'Thank you.'

That Stella had momentarily dropped out of Blanche's character, coupled with the sincerity in her voice, reassured Johnny.

***

Later that night, Stella picked up the landline in her hotel room and called her long-term counsellor back in Australia. She knew Katrina wouldn't participate in a counselling session if Stella pretended to be Blanche, so she broke her promise to remain in method acting mode, with little regret, to spend the next hour being expertly guided by Katrina with techniques to help her through the rape scene. They'd briefly talked about it before Stella left for London, but it was good to build on the coping strategies they'd already discussed.

'I've had anxiety long enough to know I wasn't actually dying, Katrina,' Stella said, 'but honestly, being back on stage and in a compromised situation, I truly believed I was dying. It was like that first time having a panic attack. There was a complete loss of control – my throat closed over and I felt like I was burning. All the techniques you've taught me over the years flew out the window. I just froze.'

Katrina took several long, slow breaths before responding. 'I hear that what you experienced is terrifying. I hear you're in a new country with an enormous challenge and away from your family and loved ones. These circumstances would be enormous pressure alone.

Add to this that the scene is triggering the experience that happened years ago.'

Tears streamed down Stella's face. 'I can't do this.'

'It's not a case that you can't do this,' Katrina said. 'You can – I know how strong you are. It's a case of if you want to do this or not.' She paused, then continued, 'This could be the ultimate exposure therapy. Yes, there is an element of danger in exposing yourself in this way, and it isn't particularly safe, but it might help you to reduce your fear and decrease avoidance behaviour. This could help you to stare down the anxiety you've run from for most of your adult life. We've talked about you being confronted by the scene when you were in Australia. It's very risky, but if you can get through this, it could have enormous benefits.'

'Keep going,' Stella ventured.

'Make no mistake,' Katrina said, 'if you go ahead with this, it will take enormous courage, and you may not get through the experience. You also might not feel up to the challenge some days. Some days will be worse than others. I want you to feel comforted in the knowledge that I'm here if you ever need to speak to me. Keeping you as healthy as possible throughout this experience is critical, and not something you should brush aside.'

There was a long pause as Stella stared out her window, thinking about her therapist's words.

Katrina broke the silence first. 'Are you sitting in a comfortable position?'

Stella pulled herself upright and pressed her back into the lounge, just as she'd done countless times since their counselling sessions began.

'Feel your feet as they press into the floor,' Katrina said quietly. 'Find your hands in a comfortable position on your lap – facing upwards for openness or downwards for grounding.'

Stella's chin dropped ever so slightly, and as she sank into breathing deeper and deeper, into an almost trancelike state, she decided there was no turning back.

CHAPTER 26

The central heating in Stella's London hotel room turned to high was an extravagance she couldn't live without. It was kept company by a blow heater and electric radiator she'd already learned to leave on during the day to keep the apartment warm – damn the expense.

She was hoping a cup of turmeric chai latte and three hours of poring over Mark's notes from rehearsals would lull her into a deep sleep, something that stress and jet lag had prevented since she'd first touched down in London – made worse by late-night phone calls from her mother, who had yet to successfully negotiate the time difference between Australia and London.

Lying in bed, Stella repeatedly replayed the scene she'd rehearsed earlier that day: Blanche's first appearance. Mark had given explicit directions for Blanche to almost glide onto the stage when she first arrived, but in that particular rehearsal, everything refused to come naturally. She knew her performance hadn't been convincing, and that she'd dragged her body around the stage like a dead tree trunk – she was all too aware that a wooden performance could signal a certain death knell to an actor.

At 10 pm and just as Stella was drifting towards hopeful sleep, her phone pinged.

> **How is rehearsal going, darling!?**
> **What's Mark like to work with?**

She'd hoped she might be able to update her mother on all happenings London-wise the following day, instead of dragging herself away from temptation of sleep.

Pam Longhurst had other ideas.

I haven't heard from you today.

Several minutes later…*ping*!

It's a bit rude, Stella, that you haven't responded to my texts. I'm excited for you. And worried. Are you warm enough? Do you need some jumpers sent over? You packed in such a hurry, I'm worried you didn't take enough warm clothes.

Stella peeled the teal and gold *Breakfast at Tiffany's*–inspired sleeping mask from her eyes and knocked a glass of water off the side table as she fossicked for her phone to switch it to silent.

'For heaven's sake!' Stella exclaimed; her words drawled in Blanche's Mississippi accent.

Sleep deprivation hadn't wearied Stella's unshakeable commitment to fully inhabit Blanche's character. Her goal was to remain in character at all times during rehearsals; once the play opened, however, she could relax and resume being herself whenever she wasn't on stage.

She'd had long been a fan of method acting – an emotion-oriented acting technique. Established in the early 1900s, method acting was based on some of Russian actor and theatre director Konstantin Stanislavski's Method of Acting. It was designed to encourage actors to use subconscious behaviour to activate emotional experiences from memory. Stanislavski had described the technique as the 'art of experiencing.' In the 1930s, the technique had been introduced to American acting studios by Lee Strasberg and Elia Kazan, who subsequently collaborated with Tennessee Williams on the screenplay and directed the 1951 film adaptation of *A Streetcar Named Desire*. The rest was history.

The instant Stella's hand landed on her phone to turn it to silent, it started ringing. Without thinking, she answered the call, sounding chirpier than she felt, her voice breezy – despite her words, Blanche's socially elite Southern twang was irrefutable.

'Howdy, Mama!'

'Stella, darling. How *are* you!? Did you get my text messages?'

'Aw, come on now, Mama. I answered the phone in two rings and you literally just sent me text messages.'

'So, you did receive my texts. Why haven't you replied?'

'Mama, do y'all know what time tis? I was jus' fixing for bed and the phone went and rang.'

Pam paused, recognising her daughter was in method mode, 'Don't go hiding behind the character, Stella. I know what you're up to. I was concerned.'

'Now don't you go gettin' sassy with me, Mama. From here on in, it's Blanche. Lemme inform you, it won't do calling me Stella. Understand, Mama, that I just won't answer to that name. I am Blanche.'

Hearing her accent out loud, Stella recognised that she needed to refine Blanche's accent. While she'd been fairly successful, she knew she needed to slow down her words and draw out her vowels to realistically portray Blanche's thin veneer of social snobbery.

'Blanche, then,' Pam said. 'Mighty nice to speak to y'all,' she said, her voice pitching so high it was almost a squeal. 'As it happens, darling, I have a script of *A Streetcar Named Desire* in my hot little hands. I bought a copy of the play online and it arrived in the mail today. I would *love* to run lines with you. Just like we used to do before, when you rehearsed with your father and Madison.' Her voice earnest, she added, 'I can play any character you need to rehearse your lines with.'

Initially, Stella hesitated to accept her mother's offer. It had been a long time since she last ran lines with a family member, and even though she needed all the help she could get, she was acutely aware that running lines with her mother would only emphasise her father and sister's absence.

If they'd been alive, she would have called on them rehearse with her from the start.

'What do y'all say?'

Despite her exhaustion and the late hour in London, Stella accepted her mother's offer. She hung up the phone and called Pam back via Zoom to run lines together. Rehearsing with her mother gave Stella another perspective for playing Blanche; Pam had always been intuitive, especially given her long-held interest in being, and failure to become, an actress. Pam's lack of formal training hadn't diminished her natural acting ability or intuitiveness.

For as long as Stella could remember, her mother had provided hours of entertainment through mimicking people – Stella's friends, the local shopkeeper, relatives, and strangers – nobody was safe from her incisive character assassinations. Pam was always perfectly coiffed, never leaving the house without first fixing her hair and make-up, and would joke, 'You never know if the television cameras will be out today. I need to look good in case I'm caught on camera.'

Mother and daughter would sit attentively, watching a live telecast of the Academy Awards annually, sizeable celebratory glass of champagne in hand. Regardless of work commitments the following day, all four of the Longhurst women watched the ceremony late into the night until the main awards, including Best Picture, were announced, and they often correctly guessed the winners in the major categories.

After Madison died, the tradition began to fade. As much as Stella, Alinta, and Pam enjoyed sharing cheese and champagne, watching their favourites win, the experience now came with a degree of sadness – particularly for Pam, who each year became less animated and finally stopped watching it altogether.

'I don't support the Academy Awards anymore,' Pam had told Stella one year. 'The problem with the Oscars is they've lost integrity. For what should be the most coveted honour in all of cinema – the Oscars aren't relevant anymore.'

Pam had started saying this around the time the Best Actress award was announced; she would disappear to the bathroom straight after the acceptance speech was over. At this stage of the evening, Pam's hair, which she often fashioned similarly to Joan Crawford's, would hang loose around her face, the curls drooping, the slick of red lipstick faded. Stella had thought that the Best Actress award came as a slap in the face to Pam because it rubbed salt in the wound that she was a failed actress.

Even though she considered herself a true cinephile and had previously loved the Academy Awards, Pam increasingly clung to the idea that the Oscars had become bogus. Her reasons for citing this weren't implausible – ranging from timing the release of films to increasing the chances of generating an Oscar buzz, to how momentum for a particular actor to win in their category could quickly shift to another actor for seemingly meaningless reasons.

Pam would scoff, 'The narrative around the Oscars is ludicrous. There's no credibility anymore. The distribution company spending the most money on marketing campaigns wins.'

The truth was, Pam had stopped watching the telecast because it hurt too much.

It was sad, and painful, for Stella to see her mother's dream shrivel inside her. While nothing had made Pam happier than the fact her daughters had pursued careers as performers, she sometimes failed to mask the pain of her curtailed amateur acting career.

On the late-night Zoom, the immense trust Pam and Stella exchanged – picking over *Streetcar*'s various acting monologues despite being on different continents, making character enquiries, experimenting and pushing boundaries – came easily.

Stella satisfied Pam's predictable request to first rehearse the scene between Stanley and Stella Kowalski, which had been parodied for decades. It was the scene that many people were familiar with, even if they hadn't seen the play or watched the film. An argument ensued between the sisters and Stanley, which prompted Stella Kowalski to take off from her husband. In the famous subsequent scene, Stanley yelled, 'Stella!' in the pouring rain on a New Orleans street. In the 1951 film adaptation, Marlon Brando's performance of the famous 'Stella!' line was so powerful and memorable that it cemented his stardom. Brando's heart-wrenching calls were enough to win his wife back after she left him. In a single moment, Brando created enough conflict for the audience to sympathise with Stanley – in spite of his godawful flaws – and for the audience to see in Stanley everything that his wife saw in him.

It would have been almost impossible for Stella not to satiate her mother's desire to perform this iconic scene – not least because it was Pam's favourite but also because it was the inspiration for Pam naming her middle daughter Stella. Since the minute she was born, Stella had had a lot to live up to. Her mother's first words to her were, 'A Stella is born,' a clear play on the well-trodden phrase, 'A star is born.'

Pam would play both Stella and Stanley Kowalski in the scenes.

Ray had once told Stella it was good practice to rehearse the monologues or scenes of the other main roles to help understand the characters' psychology. Even though Stella was performing Blanche and not Stella Kowalski, she afforded her mother the indulgence of acting in the scene.

Pam bumped the computer as her arms stretched forwards and shot upwards. She dramatically clamped her hands on either side of her forehead, not holding back as she hollered 'Steeellla!' into the computer. She broke out of character briefly to comment, 'Stella Kowalski should take her good ol' time before she reunites with Stanley at the end of this scene.'

With the computer repositioned, Pam leaned into the screen, providing a close-up as Stanley Kowalski – a man fearful of losing his wife. She picked the computer up and stood up, her face prominent on the monitor. As Stanley, she paused for several heartbeats before asking Stella Kowalski never to leave him.

Pam injected so much passion and generosity into her performance that it nearly made Stella cry.

The two Longhurst women analysed *Streetcar's* characters until the early morning hours in London, spurring each another to delve into the characters' nuances, layers, and depth.

Pam spoke so excitedly and loudly that at one point Stella thought her mother's excitement might wake her neighbours.

Guzzling mouthfuls of water and dabbing at her cheeks and chest with a cloth, presumably because she was hot or excited or both, Pam babbled so quickly her words came as an onslaught.

Shaking her hands ferociously at either side of her ears, Pam exclaimed, 'Blanche! I need to play Stanley as a force of energy. We know Stanley has no patience for Blanche's delirium and distortions of truth. Oh, I would love it if you would pass on to Johnny Marsden that he should play Stanley with horrifying force. Particularly in the rape scene. You must inform him to play the part with lurid immodesty – to exhibit Stanley's violence as verging on exhibitionism. The stage directions call for a quick fade-out, but the audience knows Stanley will rape Blanche. The build-up to the fade-out must be certain and apparent, specifically when Stanley says to Blanche, "We've had this date with each other from the beginning!"'

Stella, continuing to experiment with her Southern accent, replied, 'Yes, Mama. Well, I sorta agree but not entirely. First and foremost, I surely will not advise Mr Marsden how to play the character. I shall never do that…'

Artistic differences evident, Pam let out a long, defeated sigh and nodded.

Carrying on, Stella said, 'Mama, it's appropriate to illustrate Stanley's menacing nature in the rape scene. However,' she continued, drawing out her vowels, 'as you read the part, you need to be sure'n show all Stanley's terrible traits but be jus' as sure to leave a liddle mystery in reserve. The character can't be all bad or the audience will jus' never warm to Stanley! It might help if you give Stanley a secret to play against.'

Pam's dramatic eye roll did little to dissuade Stella.

'Perhaps think of something he might be wrestling with to show a softer side,' Stella added, trying a slightly longer drawl, 'something that might help the audience empathise with him. Nobody is all good or all bad. Y'all know the first lesson in acting is to layer the character, Mama. For gawd's sake, you know this. If Stanley is only bad, the audience will hate him, and the play will be over after the first scene.'

One of the best pieces of acting advice Ray had ever imparted to Stella was that every character must have a secret – big or small – that nobody else knew about.

'My darling, *talented* Stella,' Ray had said, 'a character must always be an enigma.' He continued, 'Every character should have a riddle they're trying to solve – a personal quest they are wrestling with – something unknown that they need to resolve. It might be a dream or ambition they are harbouring. It could be a secret. People have secrets of all sizes – a small secret could be equally as powerful as a big one. And not all secrets are inherently bad. Please think about this. You need to think about the hidden motivators for why a person keeps a secret – for instance, are they acting odd around their partner because they want to propose to them? People are always motivated by things in their life that others might not know – even if they seem to behave out of character; internal motivations contextualise the actions. The character must hold something back but always be on a knife's edge of revealing something. This confidential information will colour and influence the character's actions – knowingly and unknowingly – so that the character is motivated, almost galvanised at an unconscious level. An undisclosed truth is what separates good and great performances.'

The steely gaze in Ray's eyes that day indicated how important he felt this was.

He went on, 'And remember my dear, *talented* Stella. Play your cards close to your chest. Don't ever tell anyone what your character's motivation is – *not* the director, *not* the producer. *Nobody* must know. The best performances come from an actor grappling with an internal issue and coming to a resolution about the problem themselves.'

Stella didn't need much effort to give Blanche's character depth; she used her own trauma. The only good thing to come of the assault was that she could use the emotional turmoil it had caused her to intensify her portrayal of Blanche's character.

Blanche DuBois experienced personal losses, scandals, and humiliations that left her homeless and with no money in her thirties. While Stella wasn't penniless or itinerant, her assault added a level of shame to her portrayal of Blanche. She would draw on how she felt when Jay said to her, 'When you're hot, you're hot, and when you're not, you're not.' On that day, she had been reduced to nothing in front of her peers. Now, she wondered if Blanche felt a similar indignity when she was run out of her hometown by the townsfolk.

Over the years, she had also wondered why Jay's words had seemed to impact her more than Steve's actual physical assault.

Stella had never revealed to another person why she'd stopped acting, that the humiliation that day had made her run. The reality of grappling with spontaneous panic attacks, privately certain she was going insane, was an entirely different story, and one she was afraid to tell. To add insult to everything, she was ashamed for not legally pursuing Styler and Crosley for ruining her career and inflicting her with at-times debilitating mental health.

After being demoralised in front of her acting peers, fear of being viewed negatively or judged by others became as natural to Stella as her former innate confidence.

She knew it wasn't unusual for actors to be introverts and quite shy in person – more comfortable performing or presenting to 100 people than communicating in smaller, intimate groups. She also knew what she had been like before the assault, when it had never been difficult to express herself in any setting, small or large. Now, if she felt restricted in a situation – being in a confined space – she sometimes re-experienced the trauma from that day.

She'd summoned the courage to act again because she could hide behind the mask of being an actor. Over an extended period, with the help of Katrina, she'd developed a toolkit to manage her anxiety. Running, meditation and counselling had proved to be a blessing.

CHAPTER 27

The final week of rehearsals at the Palais arrived all too soon: the dreaded tech week. With just ten days until opening night, when the cast would hand their arses and reputations to arguably the world's most elite theatre critics and audiences, nerves were starting to fray.

The actors started to doubt their abilities and reverted to performing parts as though it were the first time they'd ever seen the script. Lines were forgotten, clearly noted stage marks were ignored, props were misplaced, and jokes fell flat. It was a rough week.

It was that awkward time between not rehearsing enough and over-rehearsing, when it could be almost impossible to find another way to deliver a line, or a physical performance became stiff, the actor walking with all the grace of having wooden legs.

During tech week, Stella forced herself not to overthink the first scene she appeared on stage – she'd been grappling with it throughout the entire rehearsal period. Despite being required to perform the scene repeatedly to get the lighting right, she knew something was still off. But she couldn't indulge in any negative thinking for fear of jinxing her performance from the first moment she set foot on stage, instead steeling herself to believe that she would perform the scene brilliantly to a live audience and that it would be entirely different when she wasn't under the scrutiny of the lighting director, who'd weirdly taken to telling her to perform the scene, even though it wasn't actually required as part of the tech run. She should be conserving her energy for the real performance; Neil was simply being a bully.

At this critical time in a production, some directors chose to rest their actors, to give them a chance to return to rehearsals feeling fresh, composed, and invigorated, a few days out from opening night. More than rest, the cast mainly needed performance pay-off – to have an audience take their performance to a new perspective and new heights. Nothing commanded an adrenaline-induced performance like the energy of a live audience.

The cast dreamed of the exhilaration and critical acclaim of a successful opening night. They were all praying for the first performance to end with robust applause to acknowledge a job well done. Equally, the cast feared opening night with anxiety-fuelled terror that the audience might receive the show negatively.

Psychologists would have a field day in trying to understand why actors are compelled to work in an industry that causes this much anxiety and distress. To knowingly force themselves to experience a full-blown panic attack night after night, standing in the wings, anticipating their time on the stage. Stella thought that American psychologist and philosopher Dr Frank Barron had been onto something when he described the psychology of creativity – how the creative person has measures of sanity and insanity, along with destructiveness and constructiveness.

Not all actors lived up to being big-mouth show ponies; they were just more adept at covering up their timidity.

Nicole Kidman spoke about experiencing crippling stage fright and shyness, finding red carpet occasions particularly awkward. Alan Rickman had similarly acknowledged the commonness of the fear factor in theatre, which he likened to a gremlin that sat on your shoulder and never went away. Multi-award-winning Sir Johnathan Pryce had talked about the fatiguing and dizzying effects of stage fright that he experienced early in his career, acknowledging that he was more nervous when he was required to present as himself, unable to hide behind the façade of an actor or a character in a play.

Throughout her career, Stella had drawn on acting skills to cover her nervousness when presenting in front of colleagues or sometimes when in the spotlight at gatherings.

She had once loved the spotlight. Since the assault, she had come to loathe it.

***

Mark was strict with the cast and crew in the final stages of rehearsals. Except for occasional guidance, his job was largely done once opening night was over. While he would attend opening night to gauge the audience's reaction, and might offer small performance notes, once the show had opened, it was up to the cast to take ownership and solve problems independently.

In the final week of rehearsals, he removed the stage prompter and forbade the cast from apologising if they forgot a line, making an horrific example of Stella early in the week when her mind went blank mid-monologue.

'Can I get a prompt?' Stella called out. 'Sorry, I can't for the life of me remember my line…'

Mark sat upright in his seat in the house to admonish Stella, the rest of the cast either on stage or in the wings, treated to an up close and personal view of her castigation.

'*Sorry?* Sorry is the least useful word for an actor to use. Never. EVER say sorry. You should never apologise when on stage. Ever! If you apologise during rehearsals, you will apologise during a live performance… If you forget a line, you must train yourself to wait. Wait! Do *not* speak. Do not break the excruciating silence – wait – regather your thoughts and then carry on.'

Suddenly feeling silly for her commitment to stay in character for the duration of rehearsals, Stella found herself transported back to that tiny room at Central Casting. Part of her enthusiasm for staying in character had been to avoid being re-traumatised by *Streetcar's* rape scene. Now though, the Palais felt as though it were closing in around her, and she regretted accepting the role of Blanche DuBois.

Her Southern accent sounding feeble and ridiculous to her ears, Stella said, 'I won't forget my lines during a performance, Mark.'

'What you won't do, Stella, is ever say *sorry* on stage again!'

Mark turned his attention to the rest of the cast, his words exploding from his mouth, rapid-fire, his face strained with fury. The droplets of spit careening from his mouth glistened and danced in a streak of light from a beam on the stage. 'Lesson Number ONE,' he spat in Stella's general direction. '*Never say sorry!*'

Since Mark's public flogging, Stella's credibility as an actress had come under intense scrutiny by the cast and crew. Her choice to remain in character as Blanche throughout rehearsals had in particular become the focus of unconcealed facepalming, eye rolls, and sniggers. Except for Johnny Marsden and stage manager Lilly Dickson, she had largely lost the confidence of her peers which, with opening night looming, couldn't be worse.

Soon after Mark's bollocking, Stella inadvertently overhead an animated discussion between co-star Delia Turner and Lilly in the wardrobe department that articulated the general mood towards her.

'Fucking diva,' Delia commented as she came into the room.

Instantly knowing that Delia was speaking about her, Stella slipped behind some long coats to hide. She held her stomach in, making herself small.

'She thinks she's the next Marlon Brando,' Delia continued, 'with her method acting and staying in character for weeks of rehearsals.'

Lilly responded, 'Cut Stella some slack, Delia. She's come into the production one month from opening and is doing a very credible job in the role. I support why she's staying in character. She's clearly trying to perfect the role to the best of her ability and live the character with the little time she's had to rehearse. It's brave.'

'Bullshit!' Delia snapped, hanging one of Stella Kowalski's sensible past-the-knees dresses on the clothes horse. 'She's an upstart wannabe. Who casts anyone that hasn't performed in a decade!? She's embarrassing herself, the entire cast, and also will probably manage to embarrass the Palais, too.' She rolled her eyes and added, 'Neil and I were sitting in the green room the other day having a cup of coffee, and she talked to him all sassy and flirty in that stupid Southern accent. She asked him to pour her a tea, like she was royalty. It was cringeworthy.'

Covering her face with her hands, Stella hunched into herself, tears streaming down her cheeks.

Delia continued, 'Honestly, Mark made an enormous mistake casting Stella as Blanche. It's evident that she has little chance of performing the part with any credibility. I hope Melanie Tate doesn't come to opening night. She'll be mortified.'

'That is ridiculously scathing,' Lilly protested. 'We're supposed to be an ensemble theatre company working together, not against one another, to create excellent theatre. You've been around actors long enough to know they each have a different way of approaching their work. The poor woman is probably buckling under all the negativity.'

'She's over the top,' Delia insisted. 'All show and no substance. I'm not going to pander to her method acting, not when it makes it impossible to form a relationship with her. Her aloof bullshit doesn't convince me. Stella needs to come down to the proletariat and deign to get to know the cast, for fuck's sake.'

'Have you watched the documentary about *Man on the Moon?*' When Delia didn't respond, Lilly continued, 'It's a mind-blowingly brilliant display of method acting at its finest. Jim Carrey remained in character for the duration of filming *Man on the Moon.*'

'What's your point?'

'My point,' Lilly said, 'is that he had the courage to stay in character to develop the role, and it's the bravest approach to any performance I've seen.'

Delia, checking her props were in the right order, practically shouted, 'For Christ's sake, Lilly, it's a bit much to compare Stella simpleton Longhurst to the genius that is Jim Carrey!'

'Watch the documentary, Delia,' Lilly said, 'and you might better appreciate what Stella's trying to achieve.' She added, 'Danny DeVito, Paul Giamatti, and Courtney Love are also in the film. If those kinds of stars can suffer Jim Carrey staying in character, then we can suffer Stella doing the same.'

'Apples and oranges, my friend. Apples and oranges.' Delia let out a scornful huff of air. 'Mark my words, Stella Longhurst is going to ruin this production and the company's reputation along with it. The production is doomed with her in it.'

And with those final words, Delia stormed out of the wardrobe department.

***

That night Stella sat alone in her apartment with the lights off, a large glass of wine empty on the table next to her, her anxiety rendering her immobile as she reflected on Delia and Lilly's conversation. She was moments from calling Mark to tell him she was withdrawing from the show when Ray's voice whispered in her head.

Acting is a game of psychology. You have to stay upbeat. If you don't water a thought, it dies.

In that moment, exhausted from years of running, Stella decided it was time to take a stand. Her relationship with Heath was in tatters and she'd managed to ruin her reputation with the cast and crew, but...

No. She wasn't going to drop out of the play.

Otherwise, she'd have blown up her entire life for no reason.

CHAPTER 28

Stella sat on a bus en route to Johnny Marsden's house in Notting Hill with a Louis Vuitton suitcase stuffed with vintage clothes, including hats, jewellery, coats, dresses, and a variety of silk tops. Despite being dressed in head-to-toe white and wearing a bodice, silk shirt, gloves, hat, and a fake pearl necklace and earrings, she almost broke out of Blanche's character.

With her head bowed, browsing a 1940s *Vogue* she'd purchased in a second-hand store in Camden – her favourite haunt since arriving in London for finding high-end, vintage clothing – it was the all-too-familiar smell of Lomani Essentials, Heath's preferred aftershave, that drew her attention to a man who had just boarded the bus.

For half a second, Stella thought it was Heath – that he had come after her – before logic kicked in and she realised that of course it wasn't him. Regardless, the strong scent the gentleman was wearing made him immediately attractive to Stella. And she hadn't even looked at him. Her body perked up as it recognised the cologne – essences of musk, bergamot, and subtle sandalwood – and captivated her heart; trying to be discreet, she inhaled deeply, drawing the fragrance into every cell of her body.

Her eyes widened as the scent surrounded her, glued to an image in the magazine in front of her of Vivien Leigh, seeing the actress' stylish black pencil skirt without really registering what she was looking at. Everything around Stella became cloudy, an emotional onslaught provoked by the scent.

For a moment, she closed her eyes and saw herself lying in bed next to Heath. In her memories, it was late in the afternoon on a summer's day, and the two of them had just come off the beach, after they'd spent hours in foreplay, idolising one another's bodies, expressing what they'd do to each other if they weren't on a beach surrounded by people. Heath's hand gently stroked her breast as she nuzzled into his chest, inhaling the aftershave he'd just applied after showering. She loved the smell on his damp skin – it was altogether sensual, a sign that sex was to come, and had a slight air of formality about it. She loved it in the same way she appreciated his confidence in lighting a candle when they went to bed, his unspoken way of inviting her to make love. During their time together, there hadn't been many nights when a candle went unlit.

Though focused intently on the man's smell and her memories of Heath, Stella was aware that she was drawing attention; out of the corner of her eye she saw a couple sitting nearby exchange a concerned glance as she continued to breathe so deeply that she could be mistaken for hyperventilating. There wasn't anything sexual in the way she breathed at the memory of Heath; it was more that she was on the verge of a panic attack. The intensity of smelling the man's aftershave, being on a bus – a relatively small, enclosed space – and reminded that she had left the love of her life whacked Stella with the consequences of her choices.

The female passenger from the couple hesitated, in the polite way of the average British person reluctant to interfere, before tapping Stella on the shoulder. 'Excuse me, dear… Are you quite well? You seem…somewhat distressed.'

As luck would have it, the stop for Johnny's house was next, saving Stella from too much embarrassment. 'I'm fine,' she said, quickly gathering up her belongings, and then caught herself and dropped into her Southern accent to repeat. 'I'm fine. I was just remembering a friend.' She offered the woman a smile and added, 'Thank you for asking, ma'am.'

Stella flung a gossamer and white feather scarf around her neck, filled her lungs to the brim with the smell of the aftershave, and alighted from the bus without ever looking at the stranger wearing Heath's cologne.

***

When Stella arrived at Johnny's apartment, Adele's *Easy on Me* was blaring loudly from the stereo.

The sound was jarring; to remain faithful to the period in which *Streetcar* had been written, she'd decided to listen to music only from the 1940s or earlier. She'd initially used her computer and iPhone after landing in London to research the play or to speak to her mother and Heath, but after a short period of time she'd stopped using any form of technology that wasn't of the period. Given that Alexander Graham Bell's revolutionary invention of the telephone received a patent in 1876, she'd approved use of a landline phone as a satisfactory means of communication, when deemed absolutely necessary. Her iPhone sat in a drawer in her apartment, switched off, making a long-distance relationship near impossible. She'd even disconnected the landline in her hotel room. The only way for Heath or anyone else to contact Stella was to leave a message at the hotel reception where she was staying. It had annoyed Pam immensely that Stella had made herself nearly inaccessible. When Stella had called Heath to say she planned to go offline, he didn't take the news well, either, snapping at her that he couldn't decide if her behaviour was more selfish or bizarre, but whatever else it was, it was certainly ridiculous.

Their conversation flashed through her mind as she went to knock on Johnny's front door.

'It's like you're rubbing my face in it,' Heath had said during one of the few phone calls she'd made to him while in London. 'I despise long-distance relationships, and you *know* that, yet here you are telling me it's okay that you're not accessible via your mobile phone because – because there's a method to your madness with this method acting thing. What the hell?'

'I'm sorry, Heath,' Stella said pleadingly. '*Streetcar* is set in post-World War II Louisiana, and there weren't any mobile phones then. I need to remain true to the character. You could always leave a message for me in the hotel lobby... My focus is ...'

'Lobby? Christ, Stella, this whole Blanche thing is ridiculous. We say *reception* in Australia. Not *lobby*. I can hardly even recognise you at this point.'

'It's part of my acting process,' Stella replied, her voice wobbling. 'Please, please have patience and try not to take this personally. It isn't something I'm switching on and off. I'm staying in character... I...'

'Staying in character and eroding our relationship,' Heath smarted. 'I'm astounded.' After a brief silence, he said, 'I've got to go,' and abruptly hung up.

***

Johnny casually opened the door, a picture of health, holding what Stella guessed was a gin and tonic in hand, even though it was only 4 pm.

If Johnny were an Instagram hashtag, Stella reflected, it would be #weekendgoals. He'd got the *how-to-wear casual wear if you're a guy* memo in spades – opting for adjustable slim grey track pants, a navy sweater with a white t-shirt underneath, and floppy, oversized grey woollen socks.

Classic black Ray-Bans perched on his head, a place they left only to cover his eyes for photographs. He'd cultivated his signature look years earlier, masking his deep blue eyes with sunglasses and wearing a white t-shirt, and was rarely ever photographed in anything else.

He was perpetually cool without trying.

Standing at Johnny's front door and smiling up at him, Stella thought, *He's always been beautiful.*

She wasn't the only one to think so. The *Streetcar* cast and crew affectionately referred to him as Jimmy – his matinee idol good looks all too similar to late, great actor and cultural icon James Dean.

'Hey Stella!' Johnny beamed. 'It's great to see you. I'm so glad you came.'

'Johnny,' Stella said, the drawled word dripping of Blanche. She intentionally avoided referring to him as Jimmy, lest his ego get any bigger. She really wanted to refer to him as Stanley, as Blanche would, but thought better of it. 'Darling, you know better than that.' She tapped his hand and sent him a disapproving look. 'It's Blanche, not Stella.' She softened her words with a small smile and added, in a gentler tone, 'You needn't worry; I won't refer to you as Stanley.'

'Nope,' Johnny said firmly. 'Sorry, *Stella*, but I'm not going to call you Blanche, and I'm not going to play along with you being in character.' He crossed his arms and leaned against the wall inside his apartment, blocking Stella from entering the apartment. 'From one actor to another, Stella, I appreciate the logic behind the deep-dive method acting approach. But you have to admit it's a lot.' He shook his head. 'Here's the thing: I'll only indulge your method during rehearsals at the theatre, as we run lines, or during a live performance. Outside of that…nope. Not happening.'

Plonking her suitcase at the front door, Stella pleaded, 'What? Why, Johnny? Why not?'

'Because it's exhausting, Stella,' he said shortly. 'We need to connect as friends in order to build and ultimately enhance our trust of each other on stage.' He paused and then added, 'We have excruciatingly intimate scenes to perform, and frankly I'm not entirely comfortable with them unless I know my co-star and know we have confidence in one another.'

'Johnny, that's just silly,' Stella protested. 'I came here to run lines. Our characters are enemies in the play – we'd be better served not to be friendly until the show is over.'

'Since you landed in London, we've spent no personal time together,' Johnny pointed out. 'Something is lacking in our performance, and you know it as well as I do. So, while you're visiting me in my home, unless we're running lines, we are Stella and Johnny, not Blanche and Stanley. Just a couple of knock-about mates from Australia getting to know one another.'

Even though she trusted Ray implicitly, Stella had begun to doubt his advice to remain in character to access Blanche quickly, especially given its disastrous implications for her relationships with the cast. She questioned if method practitioner Konstantin Stanislavski had advocated for living the role outside of the rehearsal and performance setting.

'I'm not sure I can, Johnny,' she said after a moment.

'Stella, stop it!'

'But, Johnny… I made a commitment…'

'The two days Mark's given us off are a gift to reset and refresh. Let's shoot the breeze, have some fun. Get to know one another.' He readjusted his sunglasses on his head. 'It's all for the good of the show. Trust me.'

'Shoot the breeze?'

'Look,' Johnny said, frustration creeping into his voice. 'I want to get all my cards on the deck about how I feel about this, straight up.'

Stella wasn't sure what Johnny meant, but he'd always had a way with words. She'd liked how he spoke from the moment they first met, a decade earlier. He was like a verbal meme, summing up a situation – good or bad – in a word or two. That was the thing about Johnny Marsden – he somehow could get away with saying inappropriate things while convincing people to bend to his whim…like telling Stella he'd only support her choice to method act on his terms.

Grudgingly, Stella picked up her suitcase and moved towards the lounge room, accidentally brushing against Johnny's chest as she walked past him.

She plopped down on the couch and tossed her hat to the side, announcing as she stripped off her gloves, 'Truth be told, Johnny, I'm happy to ditch Blanche for a while. I've been living, eating, breathing, and shitting that tortured, insane Southern belle for weeks.'

That she was willing to drop the facade for her fellow actor but not for the man she loved made her question her integrity – but just at that moment, she couldn't bear to think about it.

'Glad I could make you see it my way.' Johnny grinned at her from the doorway.

'I don't wholly submit to your thinking,' she admitted, 'so the one thing I do request is that you dim all the lights, to honour Blanche's vanity.' When he didn't say anything, she added, 'Come on, Johnny, that's a fair compromise.'

Asking Johnny to turn the lights down served Blanche's vain and crippling insecurity about her fading beauty. It also happened to flatter Stella, something that she couldn't object to when under Johnny's intense and somewhat intimidating gaze.

Johnny dimmed the lights and walked towards the kitchen. 'Can I offer you a drink, Stella?'

Stella dropped her head against the back of the couch, saying, 'I thought you'd never ask.'

***

By 8 pm, Stella and Johnny were two drinks from being fall-down drunk.

Johnny had shared his iPhone password, and they had been passing his phone back and forth, playing song requests in a game of *Guess That Song*. The game's rules were basic – whoever had the phone selected a song, and their opponent had to guess the artist, plus the name of the song, before it ended. Guessing incorrectly resulted in missing a turn, with the winner granted two successive song choices.

Stella opted to play pop and grunge hits from the 1980s and 1990s, while Johnny's eclectic musical taste ranged from old crooners to classic songs from the 1960s, 1970s soul, and an assortment of blues, big band, and jazz songs. He was obsessed with singers from the 1920s and 1930s.

Since they had started playing *Guess That Song* two hours earlier, Stella hadn't stopped dancing, as though she couldn't stop her feet from moving even if she wanted to. Too much alcohol mixed with weeks of rehearsal tension, plus her relationship with Heath hanging precariously by a thread, collided in a cataclysm so momentous that she had to let her hair down. Given that most of the cast had lost faith in her acting ability, she felt like this was an incredibly valid reason to get exuberantly and obscenely drunk, in the hopes of blocking it out and forgetting how much their opinions hurt.

Phone in hand as the current Master of Music ceremonies, Stella popped on a 1990s grunge song for Johnny to guess. It was a breathtakingly easy selection – even with his minimal interest in this music genre, he should have been able to identify Nirvana's *Smells Like Teen Spirit* and break her six-track winning streak.

'Awwww, come on, Johnny,' she laughed. 'I *know* that you know *this* song!'

Waiting for him to guess, Stella started shouting the lyrics, bouncing up and down, teasing Johnny by adding a question mark to the word hello, a central word in the song's chorus. By adding the single punctuation mark, she turned the chorus from a succession of statements into one of the most annoying phrases to come out of America of all time: Like, *hello*!?

"Hello? Hullo? Hello?' Stella continued, slurring and singing the words to the chorus out of order. 'Low. How low. *Hello?*'

Given his encyclopaedic knowledge of music, Stella was pretty sure Johnny was intentionally letting her win, and she wasn't fooled as to his motivations – the man clearly enjoyed watching her bounce excitedly around his apartment, wearing only a cream satin slip. In her defence, it was all she could find to wear given her suitcase had been filled entirely with Blanche's clothes, since she'd anticipated they'd be rehearsing. Plus, his apartment had turned out to have excellent central heating, which was now turned to low after starting out at a temperature that felt near boiling.

'The heating in your apartment works a treat,' Stella said, running her hand over a concrete wall.

'Doesn't it? It makes the place very cosy, just how I like it.' Johnny grinned at her and added, 'I also like the crimson pink your cheeks turn when you dance, Stella Rock Star.' He shot her a flirty wink.

Drunk though she might be, she had no interest in playing into Johnny's amorous advances. Tripping over the portable speaker and its disco lights, she replied, 'Crimson!? More like bright beetroot!' She added, 'I can tell you from experience that I don't look in the least attractive at the moment. I'm certainly no Blanche in real life — she wouldn't let herself get into such a state.' She burst out laughing at the irony.

Johnny intercepted the phone as *Smells Like Teen Spirit* came to an end, before Stella could select another song, momentarily breaking up the game.

'Wait! Stop! I want to do something.'

'Huh? What?'

Oh, no. Please don't tell me he wants to kiss me.

'Wait,' he said, scrolling through his music. 'I want to play you something…'

Thank God. He doesn't want to kiss me.

'You *need* to hear *Crazy Blues* — Mamie Smith, from the 1920s. I love Mamie almost as much as Ella Fitzgerald, but not nearly as much as Louis Armstrong. You know what I'm sayin'?' Finding the correct track, he hit play as he said, 'Listen to this, Stella Rock Star… You're a star, Stella. Hope you like your nickname.'

Before she could respond, Johnny turned the volume to full, topped up the white wine he'd swapped to drinking, and used his wine glass as a microphone to sing the words to *Crazy Blues*.

He glided up and down the hallway on socks – half dancing, half falling over – singing and yelling out musical trivia as he goes.

'Mamie catapulted the popularity of blues music in American culture.'

'Johnny, you're a veritable musical almanack.' Hiccups prevented Stella from speaking for a few moments. 'I'm afraid I'm a musical mutant in your company, Johnny.'

Excited by the acknowledgement of his musical prowess, Johnny continued articulating his love for music, among other things, with the enthusiasm of a toddler making sandcastles at the beach.

'Stella Rock Star, did you know that Mamie was the first female African American singer to record and release a blues song, single-handedly revolutionising the blues genre?'

Stella responded, 'Said musical mutant did not know this pertinent piece of trivia.' Hiccups.

Laughter rang out from opposite ends of Johnny's apartment.

A musing, brief silence, and then, 'Okay, Stella. What about this? Did you know that Elvis Presley's hometown is located in the same state as your tormentedly insane Blanche DuBois is from? Mississippi!'

'Oh, Christ, Johnny!' Stella wailed. 'Why did you have to remind me about the play? I'd forgotten it for a moment. Shit!'

Johnny bolted in from the hallway to wrap Stella up in a tight hug.

'Hey, hey, I'm sorry,' he said. 'I shouldn't have mentioned the play. Don't mention the war! Don't mention the play.'

'I need to go, Johnny,' she said, pulling away. 'I'm drunk. It's getting late. I can't be hungover tomorrow. We need to rehearse. I'll come back tomorrow.'

'Don't be a party pooper, Stella. I'm having a great time. How about this – how do you spell Mississippi? It's a tongue twister and a brain bender. Spell Mississippi in two seconds – go!'

'Stop it, Johnny,' Stella said, turning to look for her belongings. 'I can barely say Miss-usss-a-siii-peeee right now, let alone spell it.' She tripped over the rug and fell onto the lounge. 'I need to go home,' she said, her voice muffled against a pillow.

'Aww, don't go,' he pleaded. 'I am so happy to be hanging out with you – you funny, smart-as-hell, rock star actress.'

'That's not what the rest of the cast is saying,' she said, hating how pathetic her voice sounded. She turned her head so she wasn't talking into the pillow. 'They don't think I'm a star; they think I'm a train wreck.'

Johnny topped up their drinks and said, 'Screw them, Stella – I know how talented you are. *Mark* knows how talented you are, or he bloody well wouldn't have cast you.' He snorted. 'Honestly, they should be applauding your conviction. Just wait until the reviews come out, raving about your performance. I can see the headlines now – *Stella Rock Star Longhurst achieves theatre immortality for her stellar performance as emotionally delicate Southern belle Blanche DuBois!*

'Thanks, Johnny,' Stella said on a sigh. 'The way the cast has turned is so depressing – I'm tempted to throw myself in front of the tube.' She groaned. 'Seriously, can we stop talking about it. I don't want to think about the play right now, and I guess I don't really want to go home, either.' She flicked her eyes up at his face. 'Clearly, this means it's your turn to play a song. Play something from when you were in a band.'

In his younger years, Johnny had had a fledgling career as a guitarist and songwriter, forming the band Johnny Marsden and the Stiffs with two best friends and touring Sydney's inner-city pub circuit for several years.

As a lyricist – or poet, as he preferred to be called – Johnny had displayed exceptional talent.

On the eve of signing a major recording deal, his best friend – and the lead singer of Johnny Marsden and the Stiffs – died, making him a literal stiff, throwing Johnny into a creative drought spiral that lasted for several years. He'd only pulled out of the stagnation when a friend suggested he try acting lessons, which proved to be the chance he needed to kickstart his creative life again.

Johnny Marsden was one of those people innately gifted with the ingenious ability to turn his hand to anything creative. He played guitar, drums, and piano, wrote hauntingly poetic songs, and sang with a light lyrical tenor. A highly regarded acting career had won him several acting awards during the four years he'd performed in theatrical productions on London's West End.

He was also a painter. Except for several prints by Salvador Dalí, the walls of Johnny's apartment were adorned with his own artworks

– paintings inspired mainly by the styles of neo-expressionist Jean-Michel Basquiat and abstract expressionist Jackson Pollock.

Johnny was an artist's artist, and if Stella were honest with herself, this made him very attractive.

Johnny lit a few candles and settled onto the futon next to Stella, rejecting her request to play something from his band days.

'Those days are well and truly over, Stella,' he told her. 'Instead, here's a treat: I'll play you one of my finest playlists. It features some of my favourite artists – Rita Coolidge, Rod Stewart, Helen Reddy, Captain and Tenille, Simon and Garfunkel, Donna Summer, Bill Withers, The Carpenters, Gloria Gaynor, Kris Kristofferson.... Too many to list, really.'

Stella opened her mouth to respond but was immediately cut off as he exclaimed,

'Actually, no! Changed my mind.'

She laughed and knocked her glass, spilling half of her wine down her slip.

'I want to play you a song by one of my favourite musicians of the '70s,' Johnny said. It's called *Still the Same*. It's from rock singer Bob Seger's album *Stranger in Town*.'

Stella tucked a cushion under her head and enquired, 'Why *Still the Same*? Why that song?'

'The song reminds me of you,' he explained. 'Sorry if I'm being presumptuous, but... in a relationship, someone always leaves first, often breaking their partner's heart to smithereens.' He hesitated and then continued, 'I suspect this is the case with you. Nobody would ever leave you. You would leave them first. Anyway, this is what I think the song is about. It's about you.'

'What a strange thing to say.'

She squeezed the pillow under her head, regretting her decision to leave Heath in Australia for what increasingly felt like the most stupid decision of her life.

'I've nailed it, though, haven't I? Nobody would walk away from you... Anyway,' Johnny said with a shake of his head, 'they'd regret it if they did.'

'That sounds portentous.'

He laughed so hard that he spat, 'That's why I like you, Stella Rock Star. You've got the combination. Hot, intellectually amazing, and the kicker: you're emotionally deep. We cut through some stuff tonight.' He grinned. 'I'm looking forward to seeing our chemistry once we're back on stage.'

'Don't mention the play!' Stella wailed.

'Sorry. I'm just saying that some people can churn the numbers but can't articulate what those numbers mean, whereas you cut through stuff. A lot of people can't do that! You know what I'm saying?'

'You're being terribly cryptic.' She closed her eyes. 'Just play the song, Johnny.'

He settled next to her on the lounge and played *Still the Same*, setting it on repeat. Hearing it a second time, she wasn't convinced that Johnny being reminded of her was particularly flattering. The central character was a gambler resistant to change, whose charisma was both a gift and a curse, who walked away from a card game – insert relationships as a metaphor – to maintain the upper hand. Stella recognised that she, too, walked away from relationships, leaving before the other person had the chance, as Johnny had said. She wasn't in the least proud of it. And, too, she was achingly aware how she'd badly bungled the situation in moving away from Heath to London; the way she'd handled it was appalling – indefensible and bordering on cruel.

Perhaps she was taking the lyrics too literally. Perhaps Johnny was trying to say it reminded him of her as someone who always shoots for the stars, that bad things couldn't happen to her as she was already on her way to the next big thing.

Moments later, as Stella slipped into sleep, she barely registered Johnny as he said, 'That was a perfect first chapter to our renewed friendship, Stella Rock Star.'

***

The Commodore's song *Easy* woke Stella. Notwithstanding a headache she could photograph from too much wine, it was the deepest sleep she'd had since arriving in London. The smell of bacon from Johnny's kitchen wafted into the lounge room, and she forced herself to sit up. She found herself shaking off a soft blanket she couldn't remember draping over herself, her body clammy with dried sweat from hours of dancing, and her hair annoyingly tangled around her neck.

The night was mostly a blur. Presumably Johnny had put the blanket over her after she'd fallen asleep.

Johnny's enthusiastic singing, interspersed with whistling, trilled throughout the apartment.

Why is he so happy?

The small faux sheepskin rug in the middle of the lounge room was twisted over itself, and Stella remembered twirling around on the rug like a mad banshee the night before.

God. I was so drunk.

A smattering of actor's biographies and memoirs, pulled from a bookshelf, lay strewn across the coffee table. A music sheet stand held a dog-eared copy of *Shakespeare Monologues for Men*. The audition manual was held open by two unlit candles at the famous St. Crispin's Day monologue from Shakespeare's *Henry V*.

Staring at the lounge room mess, Stella recalled Johnny standing on top of the coffee table, performing Henry's impassioned speech to his troops before the battle of Agincourt, speaking with rousing enthusiasm to capture his imaginary troops' comradeship and patriotism in light of the upcoming battle, in which they were outnumbered by the French.

Oh, no... We were so drunk. What the hell did we do last night?

The whistling from the kitchen became louder.

She flung herself back onto the lounge, buried her face in a pillow, and pulled the blanket over her head. Electric shocks of guilt pinched at her nervous system, even though she had no idea if the guilt had a foundation or if nothing had actually happened.

Oh, please, dear God. Please, beautiful Buddha. Please don't let anything have happened between Johnny and me.

More dull and unclear images began to fill her head. Flashes of Johnny cavorting about his apartment impersonating Elvis Presley's controversial dance moves, with gyrating rubber legs and pulsating hips. Stella, play-acting a love-struck groupie, fawning over Johnny's impersonation of the King.

Surely nothing happened. I would never do anything to hurt Heath.

Johnny's phone, sitting on the coffee table, caught her eye. An image from the previous night slammed into her with such certainty that it was a blow to her heart. In the midst of her drunken reverie, she had signed into her messenger account on Johnny's phone and rung Heath.

The blow to her heart fractured, cracking open her ribs as tiny shards of bone pierced her lungs. Wheezing for air, she curled into herself on the lounge, barely able to breathe.

What have you done, Stella!?

The memories flooded back in. Last night, at 10 pm London time, she'd thought it would be fun to surprise Heath with a phone call. Given her pointed non-use of modern technology during *Streetcar's* rehearsals, Heath had been understandably bewildered to receive the call, and yet had answered so quickly that the phone barely had a chance to ring.

'Stella! … What's that? I can barely hear you. Are you okay? Where are you? I can't hear… Are you at a nightclub!?'

Stella, oblivious that he'd already answered the phone, slurred, 'Hey, Johnny! I've had enough of those old-time ditties. Play a Powderfinger song! It's one of Heath's favourite bands. Let's rock 'n' roll!'

'Stella?' Heath said again. 'What the hell's going on?'

Johnny had grabbed the phone and held it up, bringing both he and Stella into view. He tapped the camera icon and an instant selfie of Johnny and Stella was sent to Heath's messenger.

'Who is Stella? There is no Stella here, only someone who happens to go by the name Stella Rock Star!' Johnny burst out laughing before continuing, 'Hey, you must be Heath… It's Johnny here! Stella and I are old friends; we're having a long and overdue catch up. It's all innocent fun. Promise.'

Though not in full command of her faculties, Stella had suddenly realised how impossibly terrible the scenario might look. Her senses slowly kicked into gear as she snatched the phone from Johnny attempting to salvage the situation.

'Hey, Heath! Honey.' She squinted at the screen and the blinding Australian sun emanating from it. 'You must be on your way to work. Soz. Sorry, hon. I wanted to surprise you with a phone call.'

The apocalyptic look on Heath's face and a mirage of sand and sun behind him had made him look like an actor on a spaghetti western film set.

At the memory of the phone call, a thin layer of sweat coated Stella's skin as she continued to lay in Johnny's lounge room, the gentle tenor of Lionel Ritchie's voice singing the final words to *Easy* assaulting her senses. She was terrified she'd irretrievably broken Heath's trust and ruined their relationship.

'My head is pounding, Johnny!' she called out. 'I can't bear the music any longer. I'll give you ten pounds to turn the stereo bloody down!'

Johnny's whistle preceded him as he strutted out of the kitchen, a cup of coffee in one hand, two Panadol and a glass of water in the other.

'Goody morning!' he said, trying not to laugh. 'Seems Stella Rock Star is a tad hungover! Get these Panadol into you and you'll feel better in 20 minutes.'

Without saying anything, Stella sheepishly took the Panadol and examined his face, hoping for an explanation of why his spirit happened to be so buoyed this morning. She scrutinised him for clues of familiarity that hadn't existed before their drunken night of debauchery. A patchy memory of the evening's frivolities had her doubting herself, even though she'd never been one for casual sex-charged drunken abandonment.

Johnny stopped mid-whistle, taking in Stella's demeanour. 'Ahhh... You think we had sex last night,' he said, a bit too gleefully. 'Oh, Stella. I could have fun with this.' When she just stared at him, he continued, 'Goddamn, stop looking at me like I'm Jack the Ripper. Hmm... I can attest that Heath is a fortunate man to have a woman as wonderful as you.'

Practically chewing the last of the water instead of drinking it, Stella knew her abhorrence must be evident across her face. Afraid of vomiting and finding it too difficult to speak from alcohol-saturated adrenaline coursing through her body, she remained mute, continuing to search for signs of informality in Johnny's body language.

'To borrow a well-known phrase from the Bard – "To sex or not to sex, *that* is the question!"'

Seeing the distress on Stella's face, Johnny put an end to his teasing. 'Stella, stop this misery! Alas, it wasn't to be! As much as I would have liked something to happen – I would have loved to have my wicked way with you – I can assure you, albeit sadly on my part, that nothing happened. The lady doth or did protest too much. Not even my best Elvis dance moves could convince you to rumba, cha cha, or tango with me.'

The announcement did little to lift her spirits or to right any sense of decency, let alone erase the all-too-clear memory of Heath's tortured expression looking at her from Johnny's phone. Remorse immobilised her as she imagined what Heath might say to her if they were together in person – *Once bitten, twice shy, baby girl; there's no coming back from this* – as she accepted that moving to London to resurrect her acting career indeed was the stupidest decision of her life.

With no hint of a hangover whatsoever, Johnny attempted to pick up where they'd left off last night, his indomitable energy trying to coax Stella out of her deflated mood.

'Can I tempt you in a bloody mary, Stella Rock Star?' he called over his shoulder as he wandered back to the kitchen to fix himself a drink. 'You know, the hair of the dog lessens the effects of a hangover.'

'Christ, no!' Stella responded. 'I need to rehearse today. Not that I want to. I wish I'd never agreed to perform in this bloody stupid play. And I wish we'd never gotten drunk last night and I'd gone home instead of sleeping on your lounge.'

'What's that, Stella!? I can't hear you!' Johnny yelled over the sound of a blender. 'What about an Irish coffee? Can I tempt you into one of those? It occurred to me that you've done very little sightseeing since you've been in London Town. We can have a drink and duck out to see the sights.'

He returned from the kitchen with a tall bloody mary garnished with a long sprig of wilted celery, two green olives balancing on a toothpick and a slice of lime. 'Here's a morsel of trivia for you, Stella. Did you know that *Easy* is considered by most people to be a love song? People don't realise it's a break-up song. Fact!'

Johnny clearly had no plans to spend the day rehearsing and wasn't in the least concerned about the opening night of *Streetcar* looming, and finally, Stella couldn't take it anymore.

'Shut up, Johnny. *Please.* Just. Shut. Up. My life is a goddamn nightmare and you won't shut up!'

CHAPTER 29

Stella's choice to stay true to method acting – an obstinate quest to access Blanche quickly and authentically – and ploy to shield her anxiety at returning to the stage, had become increasingly unsettling for her friends, family, her co-workers, and, if she were honest, for Stella, as well.

But her mood was lifted as she sat tucked away in a quiet corner of the hotel reception where she was staying, on a landline phone call to Pam, discussing her mother's impending arrival.

'I'm not going to lie, Stella,' Pam said, her voice not as chirpy as usual as it came down the telephone line. 'It's been challenging not being able to speak to you or text you on your mobile phone. I'm also disappointed that Gina and I won't be able to see you before opening night. However, I respect your choice to stay in character and not see us until after the opening performance. I understand your wish to stay true to your acting process. I've booked a hotel for Gina and me to stay at before opening night. We'll stay with you afterward.'

'Thank you for understanding, Mama,' Stella drawled. 'You and Ray are about the only people to understand my logic… I am so glad you'll be here soon.'

The familiar sound of Barry Manilow's *Can't Smile Without You* played in the background from the Longhurst family home. It made Stella homesick, wanting to be back in the lounge room with her mother right then and there – to be anywhere but the situation she was in. The chorus sang out before Pam responded.

'I wouldn't miss opening night for the world, darling.' She cleared her throat, her voice adopting a more serious tone before she continued, 'I'm sorry to hear things aren't working out with Heath. The few times you've contacted me while away, it's been all you've wanted to talk about. Hopefully things will get back on track when the show is finished. For now, you need to focus on the show.'

Stella moved the phone away from her face and took a couple of deep breaths, the crease in the middle of her eyebrows deepening.

'No,' she said at last, bringing the landline receiver closer again. 'I'm pretty certain I've done my dash with Heath.' She looked down at the envelope she'd collected from the hotel reception earlier that day, flipping it over and over in her hands, pausing occasionally to admire the penmanship. Heath had a beautiful hand – his handwriting was sweeping swirls of confident elegance – an artist through and through.

Pam's only response was a noncommittal 'hmph' – Stella knew her mum was resisting indulging her in a pity party – emotional ruin would be a disaster this close to *Streetcar*'s opening.

'It was stupid, going offline and being drunk at Johnny's,' Stella said, and then quickly added, 'It was innocent fun, honest. The only fun I've had since I arrived in London but the result... Oh. My. Gawd. There's absolutely nothing there, but to Heath... Gawd, he must have taken it in the worst possible way.'

'While I'm sorry to hear this,' Pam said, cutting her daughter off, 'you must *not* dwell on it. You need to focus on the job at hand! If your father were alive, he'd tell you not to lose sight of your dream – it's so close, Stella.' When Stella responded only with a self-pitying grunt, Pam practically yelled, 'Stop wallowing about a boy, dear girl, and step it up! Step it up for yourself, for Madison, and for your father, Stella. Hell, step it up for me. Just damn well step it up!'

With that, Pam hung up.

The helicopter mother had sounded every bit the stage mother as she delivered an uncharacteristic lesson in tough love.

***

As inviting as Heath's letter looked, Stella couldn't help but believe it was meant as a goodbye, rather than a good luck message.

She left the letter unopened.

CHAPTER 30

London, October 2022

It was opening night, the electricity throughout the Palais Theatre almost palpable. Surreal yet radiant energy brought inanimate objects to life; the original red velvet upholstery on the theatre seats looked renewed and fresh, the chairs sitting upright, just waiting for applause.

With *Streetcar* opening in a few hours, the cast was feverishly aware that the critics' attention was homing in on them, as was Mark's.

The production wouldn't have had a chance of success without its wholly competent stage crew – the set and costume designer, wardrobe staff, music and lighting director, and stage manager all formed a crucial part in a jigsaw puzzle of a much bigger picture. Mark had allowed the faithful stage prompt to return, although each actor had silently pledged that the prompt's role would be redundant. One of the great mysteries of theatre was how actors who had previously stumbled over lines and missed their cues somehow never again needed the stage prompt past their first word on opening night. Still, it was comforting to know the prompt was hidden in the darkness of the wings, waiting to feed a line to a flailing actor with all the enthusiasm of a vulture eyeing its opportunity to pounce.

The fine line between nerves and excitement ensured the cast was the most alive they'd ever be. The only time they would feel this alive again was the opening night of their next play. Or the birth or death of a loved one – those rare moments when life wasn't taken for granted – when people said philosophical things about living in the moment and talked big about fulfilling their dreams. Today, the actors would ride nervous energy – conscious of shutting down negative thoughts as they arose – and yet, all the same, would indulge in irrational, superstitious routines in an attempt to control the outcome of their performance.

Some actors were so troubled by superstitions that it could lead to obsessive-compulsive behaviour. Stella knew from previous experience that she couldn't give in to obsessive thoughts about needing to do a pee before going on stage and allowed herself only a single wee stop before show time. She waited until she received the ten-minute stage call, then dashed to the toilet – after that, she'd made a pact with herself to refrain from further thinking about toilet business.

The cast bustled past one another from make-up to wardrobe and to their respective dressing rooms, the minor cast members sharing a dressing room between them.

In the rehearsal room, half-hidden behind a partition, Stella watched as Johnny and Delia, preparing to play Stanley and Stella Kowalski, practiced voice exercises, stretching their vocal cords like an athlete stretches their muscles before a game. Like the rest of the cast, they'd been sure not to consume milk or dairy products over the last day to avoid mucus forming in the nose, throat, or sinuses.

Pre-show rituals – group and individual physical warm-ups and facial and vocal exercises – were crucial to prepare the cast to deliver their best performance. The exercises helped equip their main instruments – the body and voice – to transition to performance mode. Gentle physical stretches released tension, taking their focus from the inner critic – nothing spoke death to performance louder than an actor inwardly judging themselves on stage.

Some actors performed lip trills and flutters – some of Stella's favourite vocal exercises – making 'trr' and 'rr' sounds, exhaling slowly and humming, yawns, and singing.

Other actors might do the cork exercise for several minutes: placing a cork between the upper and lower teeth forced open the actor's mouth and helped to improve enunciation and diction, develop vocal strength, and encourage voice projection, so that audience members in the last row of the theatre could hear easily, without straining.

Johnny held a hard, wide grin for several seconds, then pursed his lips, quickly stuck his tongue in and out several times, and then held it at the back of his teeth for five seconds. He repeated the exercise as Delia delivered tongue twisters with the precision of a strict schoolmarm.

'How much could a woodchuck chuck if a woodchuck could chuck wood?' She spat the words out quickly and efficiently, and then moved on. 'A skunk sat on a stump and thunk the stump stunk, but the stump thunk the skunk stunk.' Taking a deep breath, she continued. 'He threw three free throws.' Repeating this tongue twister several times, Delia's smug expression made clear how pleased she was that she hadn't tripped over a single word – a good sign for her upcoming performance.

Johnny paused to interrupt Delia's routine. 'Damn! Badass! You're smooth, Delia! A tongue twister pro – your vocal cords will be so limber they'll be able to perform a ballet!'

She looked at him, opened her mouth, and did three long consecutive fake yawn-sighs.

'You are a master,' he said appreciatively. 'I see that you can do warm-ups and simultaneously insult me. You're a genius.'

'Try and be good, Johnny. Just focus on your exercises and ensure your Gene Simmons-sized tongue gets a proper workout,' she said before sounding out descending nasal consonants.

'I'll Gene Simmons you, if you're not careful,' he replied, flirting shamelessly.

The playful repartee helped to settle nerves and establish a rhythm ahead of stepping out on the stage.

Delia interlaced her fingers behind her back and stretched her arms upwards, opening her chest. Lifting her arms above her head, she slowly pushed her hips from side to side, opening her ribcage and expanding her lungs.

Lying flat on his back, Johnny stopped humming scales. 'You're an agile little bird. However did you become so elastic?'

'When, if ever, aren't you a cheeky shit, mister?' she responded. 'Go and prod at someone else. Actually, where's Stella? Why don't you go hassle our drama queen-extraordinaire and leave me to my own devices? I want to warm up.'

Johnny jumped to his feet, his mood immediately turning serious. 'As if I would hassle Stella, unlike the rest of you miserable jerks.'

'Wow! That's an over-reaction. I was joking.' She rolled her eyes and said, 'Why don't you ask her to join us in some warm-up exercises?'

'You were not joking and it's too late to be inclusive,' he said shortly. 'You should have befriended the poor woman weeks ago.'

'What!? I did try.'

'You didn't try hard enough, Delia! None of you tried, and this dysfunction could threaten the show. Do you even care how awful this experience has been for Stella? Have you taken a second to consider how unprofessional you have been? If I'm truthful, I applaud her tenacity and guts for not giving up.' Johnny shook his head, frustrated. 'Anyhow... Let's not talk about this. It's a fucking preposterous discussion to have mere hours before curtain.' He chucked the wine cork he was holding into a bin.

'Johnny,' Delia said, sounding worried, 'for shit's sake, settle down. I did try, it's just —'

'It's pathetic form!' Johnny snapped.

'What planet are you from?' Delia demanded. 'The way she carried on was so...ugh, burdensome. Fanatical! *Come on*, admit it — you found the whole method acting thing bloody pitiful.'

'You've done yourself a massive disservice,' Johnny said shortly. 'I'll leave it there.'

'Disservice?' Delia's voice echoed with frustrated annoyance. 'What are you implying? You can't say *disservice* and leave it there. It's like cutting off a confession mid-sentence.'

'Look Delia, you're a superb actress,' he replied, gentling his tone. 'I acknowledge we were handed a shit sandwich with Melanie abruptly leaving the show, but that is *not* Stella's fault. Your performance would be *much* stronger if you'd connected with Stella from day one. I don't remember you ever trying to get to know her. It's obvious every time you're on stage — chemistry cannot be faked.'

'Oh, for Christ's sake,' Delia snapped, 'there *is* no chemistry to fake! It's not like our characters are in a relationship. We're playing sisters! As well, you *rape* my sister and commit her to an asylum in the play, so how does that account for *chemistry*, Jimmy?'

'Calling me Jimmy isn't going to soften me up, Delia.' Johnny turned away and blew out a harsh breath before swinging back around and demanding, 'Are you an idiot? Every actor is in a relationship with each other! Chemistry doesn't necessarily mean allure – it's trust, confidence, and connection. As sisters, your rapport can NOT be faked. The audience will look for authenticity – particularly in the sisters' relationship – you know this, of course! Hang about, here's something from the archives: do you *think* Vivien Leigh and Kim Hunter would've won Best Actress and Best Supporting Actress Academy Awards for *Streetcar* if they hadn't had an incredible bond?'

Johnny took a big breath. 'Delia, it's bad enough that you drove a wedge between you and Stella from the outset, but to make disparaging remarks about her today – of all days – is indefensible. Speaking ill of a co-actor on *opening night* is like a black cat walking under a ladder – forget the curse of saying 'Macbeth' – you've just rained rotten juju all over your performance!'

Sucking in enormous gulps of air, Delia pressed a hand against a wall to steady herself and said through gritted teeth, '*You!* You just said Macbeth!'

The lighting director, who had been crossing the room towards the door, stopped dead in his tracks at Delia's words. Eyes the size of dinner plates and hands pressing against his ears to drown out the actors' raised voices, Neil silenced them both with, 'This is *unholy*. You *both* just said the M word. Last night's disastrous dress rehearsal is the only thing saving tonight's performance.'

Everyone knew that a crummy dress rehearsal ensured a successful opening night – just as everyone knew that the word 'Macbeth' escaping an actor's lips cursed the play.

Ignoring Neil, and terrified that her performance was now ill-fated, Delia screamed, 'Stop! Stop speaking!' Strangely, she ran around in circles like a puppy chasing its tail and flailed her hands in the air in distress, hoping to shake off her sins. 'Johnny,' she said at last, dropping his nickname, 'if you keep up this behaviour, I'll believe you *are* Stanley Kowalski – an out and out BULLY!'

'You've been bullying Stella for weeks, Delia,' Johnny spat at her. 'You're an A-grade bully extraordinaire. And fuck you very much.'

'Stop talking! I don't want to see your face again until we're on stage. Piss off!' Delia yelled before running off to the solitude of her dressing room.

From the other side of the room, behind the partition, Stella drew in a shaky breath and waited until Johnny disappeared through the door to stand back up.

CHAPTER 31

Vanity lights framed the large rectangular mirror in Stella's dressing room – white bulbs glowed brilliantly, accentuating her high cheekbones, and providing lighthouse illumination for Stella to apply 1940s-inspired stage make-up for *Streetcar*.

Stella had insisted on applying her stage make-up for the production, declining to use the Palais Theatre's skilful make-up artist, which Mark had reluctantly approved. She knew it made her appear even more diva to the cast and crew, but she spent hours researching make-up tutorials in magazines of the period to perfect an authentic everyday 1940s aesthetic – including how to apply a strong brow, accentuate lashes, and create the classic overdrawn hunter's bow – a look that had become Joan Crawford's signature lip.

Although Stella had managed to annoy most of the cast and crew by staying in character during rehearsals, nobody could deny her commitment to the role. Her reasoning for micro-managing every detail of playing Blanche – down to doing her make-up – was calculated. If she ended up being lauded for her performance, she could genuinely own the accomplishment, and what a joy that would be. Similarly, if the British media ravaged her acting, she would truly own the failure. Her audaciousness – true to being her father's daughter, meant that even with the cast's negative feedback, she'd plough on to do things her way.

Fortune favours the bold, kiddo.

Her father had had an endearing habit of saying encouraging words to her whenever she faced a challenge; exciting or terrifying, he always knew the right thing to say, brief though it might be. Fred had almost always offered words of encouragement on his way out the door to work, to avoid the embarrassing crime of being sentimental, and never failed to select an appropriate card for a special occasion. He could write things; he just couldn't say them in words. The big stack of unique birthday cards that Stella kept tucked away – not a Hallmark greeting card among them – many with embossed cartoon characters of women slaying it in life, screamed that he cared.

There was no other explanation for her father's words coming to her just now, sitting alone in her dressing room, other than to cheer her on to a successful first performance. Thinking of her dad made her think of Madison, as well; she wondered if her sister might also visit her in spirit.

She dabbed her nose with a powder puff, enjoying how comforting the powdery smell was. Her late grandmother used to squirt a dash of powder into her shoes before putting them on, with puffs of rose-scented talc then smoking from her feet as she walked.

Stella sprayed Miss Dior behind her earlobes and gently dabbed the scent onto her wrists. Another squirt of perfume to the back of her head filled the dressing room with floral tones of gardenia, lily of the valley, and jasmine. Unlike Blanche, who would never leave the house without first applying a fragrance, Stella rarely wore perfume – at least not a sickly floral scent, timeless though it was said to be.

The scent still wet on her skin, she floated a hand to her face, gently gliding her nose up and down the soft underside of her wrist, with movements more delicate and refined than usual. It was sometimes said in character development that once you had the walk, you had the character, or sometimes the costume might galvanise a character. The second Stella sprayed herself with Miss Dior, Blanche lived within.

To compensate for the harsh effects of stage lighting and to highlight her facial features, Stella applied heavier and darker than usual foundation – she checked that the make-up was blended from the jawline to the neck and top of her forehead. Cheekbones were emphasised with just enough red blush to maintain the natural look of the 1940s; red lipstick became an exclamation mark on her face. She was careful to apply lipstick with precision as was done in the '40s, using two single slicks to outline the upper lip dramatically, then applying a single coat to the bottom lip, filling them in with up and down strokes before blotting excess lipstick with a tissue. If Miss Dior breathed life into Blanche, applying make-up and then crowning herself with a blonde wig might have been the equivalent of administering mouth-to-mouth. Add clothes as a device to express social class and Stella Longhurst's transformation into Blanche DuBois was complete.

Stella shifted a make-up compact, silver vanity brush set, Elizabeth Arden lipstick and its caddy, a string of pearls, and matching earrings to the side of the dressing table.

She gazed at herself in the mirror, this time not to examine her make-up but rather to square herself up. Reflected in the mirror, a row of good luck cards cramming for a position on a shelf behind her caught her attention. There was a card from Melanie; she'd used the entire left side of the card to write a heartfelt sentiment about knowing Stella would do a magnificent job performing the role. It must have been harsh for Melanie to face her mortality, Stella reflected, knowing she would never act on a stage again.

In the middle of the cards was the only bouquet she'd received, a loving although possibly undeserving gesture from Heath; he didn't know that giving flowers before opening night and not after the performance was lousy luck in theatre land. The arrival of the flowers earlier that day had dashed her hopes that maybe Heath might surprise her by jumping on a plane to see her perform.

When the blooms and card were delivered to her dressing room, Stella knew Heath wouldn't be joining her mother, Gina, and Ray in the audience for opening night.

Heath's card read:

Dear Stella,

There are a lot of 'I'm-a-gonna' type of people in the world – you are not one of these people.

You deserve all the success coming to you.

Go the whole nine yards …

I think I'm meant to say break a leg, so do that.

With love,

Heath

Lovely gesture though the flowers were, the apathy in Heath's words was undeniable. Sure, he'd said the right things, but for two people that cherished one another, there wasn't much investment in what he'd written, to say nothing of the fact he hadn't bothered to make the effort to be at opening night in person. With Heath's letter still sealed, she couldn't know that their relationship had already ended, the flowers being a gesture of politeness.

With love, Heath… He didn't say baby girl. Stella traced a finger over the words. *The flowers are a token, a duty Heath felt obliged to send.*

I wish he hadn't sent anything.

Despite being tempted to switch her iPhone on to check if Heath had sent her a more personalised good luck message, she resisted. To be truthful, she was scared there might be a message breaking off their relationship – if their affiliation was even still considered one. In part, she was looking forward to getting the first performance out of the way, not to relieve herself of the pressure but so she could switch her phone on and communicate freely with Heath, if that was what he still wanted.

More than her decision to stick with method acting and thus receive immense scorn from her co-actors, Stella regretted her choice to refrain from using technology. Even a man as sturdy as Heath might have questioned her motivation for disallowing communication between them, considering it driven more by secrecy than her commitment to the part.

Before she could spiral into despair over Heath's detachment, she pulled her attention back to the mirror and sat erect in her black velvet chair, the decorative metallic buttons on the side of the cushion pressing into her back as a reminder to improve her posture.

She remembered Mrs Brown's words on her final day of school – 'Burn your talent until it's reduced to ash, dear girl' – and closed her eyes for several moments, a smile forming at the memory of the words.

Stella called on the mantra she had coined many years earlier. The power of the saying was that it was deeply personal – a prayer – her meditative rosary, which she repeated to surround herself in spiritual armour before going on stage. Acting could very much be a religious experience, and certainly her mantra was for her.

The ritual that she couldn't circumvent was to say, exactly 20 times, *confident, cool, composed Capulet.* Despite not playing Capulet in this show, it nevertheless was a custom she had to observe. She'd first say it 20 times, looking in the mirror – eyes blazing and brazen. Then she'd repeat the mantra in her head another 20 times, waiting in darkness in the wings, heart pounding in anticipation of going on.

In some way, there was a joyful mystery in the ritual. It paid loving respect and reverence to her belief in her ability as an actress. While she might have doubted herself in other ways – doing presentations at work or in some social settings – she had never doubted her ability as an actress. Confidence in one's ability could breed hatred. Perhaps that had been why the cast turned against her from the get-go.

On saying the mantra for the twentieth time, Stella paused to take in her reflection – and saw only Blanche.

***

The knock on the dressing room door was too early for a stage call. Stella stopped making short 'ha, ha, ha' sounds and relaxed her diaphragm before drifting to the door, cream silk gloves in hand, wearing a knee-length cream dress with a matching cropped jacket and round faux tortoiseshell sunglasses.

Ray took a step back as Stella opened the door. He pointed at the bright gold star standing out against the black dressing room door.

'Hello, Stella, darling.' Ray tapped twice in the middle of the star and said, 'I always knew your star would rise.'

Setting her emotions aside, Stella didn't miss a beat welcoming Ray into her new world, Blanche's drawl emerging perfectly. 'Oh, dear, Ray. I am thrilled you could come; it means the world to me.

Can I fix you an aperitif?' She checked her delicate 9ct solid gold Swiss windup wristwatch and announced, 'Of course, I can't join you in a drink, I'll be called to stage in 20 minutes.'

Ray sat on the plush low lounge, placed a card on the coffee table, and watched as Stella fixed him a large dram of rum.

'Chin-chin,' she said, handing Ray a drink. She sat on the occasional chair opposite Ray, meeting his gaze with long, coquettish blinks. She would never flirt with Ray, an uncle figure to her. However, moments from treading the boards, Stella was enmeshed with Blanche, the poor dear who turned to sexual promiscuity and alcohol to help her forget her young husband's death.

Ray politely accepted the drink, yet after the first sip he only turned the glass in his hands. 'I saw your mother in the foyer,' he commented. 'She looks well.'

'Fabulous. I haven't seen Mama yet. She arrived yesterday and is staying at the Savoy. I needed to ensure I had a clear head for today's performance.' Despite being deep in the character of Blanche, Stella was looking forward to spending time with her mother. 'Mama will stay with me for the remainder of her time in London post-opening,' she continued. 'I'm very much looking forward to exploring some of the tourist sites with her. I've mostly only been inside these theatre walls since I arrived in London. I'll start sightseeing after tonight. My first place to visit will be Shakespeare's Globe Theatre, of course.'

Employing a method technique sometimes altered an actor's behaviour, urging them to follow impulses foreign to their nature and making it challenging for them to return to their essence. In *Birdy*, Nicolas Cage pulled out two of his teeth without anaesthetic for the role to understand the Vietnam War soldier experience more intimately. In *Vampire's Kiss*, in which his character descended into a mental decline, Cage ate a cockroach.

While banishing her mother to a hotel before the opening wasn't quite like eating an insect, it occurred to Ray that Stella might have been taking method acting too far. He shouldn't have coached her from the sidelines, but she was his protegee, and he couldn't help himself from doing so.

For now, he was careful not to mention his concerns and omitted saying he knew the cast had given her a terrible time; there would be time to discuss these things post-opening.

'I'll get going, Stella,' Ray said after a moment, rising to his feet and setting aside his drink. 'I just wanted to wish you the very best for this evening's performance. I know you will be marvellous. I'll see you after the show.'

In her now finely honed Southern accent, Stella responded, 'Thank you, Ray. I so appreciate your long-time support and belief in me. I keep telling myself that the nerves are just excitement.'

Ray was already partway down the corridor when Stella popped out of her dressing room and called out after him.

'Oh, Ray! Sorry, I forgot to say – would you be a dear and ensure that when you see Mama, to remind her not speak to the media. She has a terrible habit of talking me up to journalists!'

'I certainly will do, Stella. Don't give this another thought. Chookas, dear girl!'

A few moments later, Lilly knocked on the dressing room door. 'Ten minutes, Ms Longhurst.'

Stella looked up. 'Thank you, Lilly.' She took a final look at herself in the mirror, pulled in a deep breath, and made a furious run for the toilet.

***

Standing in the wings, halfway through reciting the almighty mantra, a vivid memory came to Stella.

She was a young girl sitting in the audience at the Sydney Opera House; her father had surprised the Longhurst girls with a performance of *The Phantom of the Opera*, an interesting choice for her architect father.

Madison had pulled on Stella's dress sleeve, telling her to watch the lead actor psyching himself to go on stage. Stella had observed the actor with fascination – visibly off his mark, as the audience shouldn't have been able to see him – a voyeuristic moment, a cataclysmic experience.

From that minute, Stella had wanted to be an actress.

Now she knew with complete certainty that this memory coming to her, at this time, signified that her big sister Madison was waiting in the wings with her.

The instant Stella stepped on stage, transmogrified as Blanche, the intimate space so familiar and sacred and filling every cell in her body with electrified energy, she was home.

***

Magical energy crackled in the air in the foyer at the play's afterparty. There was an inexpressible knowing when performers successfully captivated an audience. A storm of applause and a standing ovation at the end of the play had confirmed a triumphant opening night.

The cast, changed out of stage costumes into civilian clothes, greeted audience members, including family, friends, respected theatre reviewers, and a smattering of celebrities. The audience, with beaming smiles and starry eyes, vied to meet the performers to praise their performance.

The cast's challenge would be to maintain the excitement after the thrill of opening night faded and the repetitive nature of performing set in.

CHAPTER 32

Pam could barely contain herself while reading theatre reviews to Stella the morning after *Streetcar* opened.

'"A Stella Is Born!" reads the *Guardian*,' she proclaimed. 'This is better than my wildest expectations, Stella. The audience completely ate up our performance.'

Stella ignored that her mother said *our* performance, not *your* performance.

Pam enthused, 'I am thrilled, although, I'm somewhat annoyed that Alfie Knox stole my line – "A Stella Is Born!" – I coined that phrase the instant you opened your eyes. How dare that smug little journalist plagiarise me?'

Stella sighed. 'Mum, you and Gina were inebriated last night, so I doubt you remember yelling out, "A Stella is born!" at the top of your lungs midway through Mark's afterparty speech. I was *so* embarrassed. Honestly!'

'Well, Stella, it worked in your favour. The little peewee journalist stole my line and ran it on the front cover of today's Arts section. You simply couldn't wish for a better headline, darling.'

Pam continued to scour the internet for reviews of the production.

'Oooh, excellent! The *Sunday Times* headline is superb, although not as good as my headline in the *Guardian*. The caption reads "Stella Longhurst Shines in *A Streetcar Named Desire*."'

Stella appreciated her mother was excited, but couldn't resist commenting, 'Mum, next you'll take credit for writing the article.'

'I had a good chat with Alfie about the play last night,' Pam said, ignoring her. 'Journalists need to be spoon-fed. They are *so* lazy these days. For an arts writer, Alfie should have more respect for Tennessee Williams as one of America's most seminal writers – honestly after our chat, I sensed he doesn't have much regard for Williams at all. He kept wanting to talk about Arthur Miller, of all people!' She sniffed with disdain. 'I set Alfie straight about *Streetcar*'s significance as one of the most important pieces of theatre in the twentieth century – and beyond. I also briefed him about how we prepared you to play Blanche. Once I check to see if I made the social pages, I'll read Alfie's review to see how much he learned.'

We! She just said, 'How we prepared you to play Blanche.'

Let it go, Stella. This is your mother's proudest moment. Let it go.

Incredibly, Pam went on, 'I educated Alfie about how the original 1947 Broadway production of *Streetcar* caused a fuss of nuclear proportions due to its complex themes of truth versus illusion, passion and sexuality, death and destruction, rape and addiction –'

A knock on the door at Stella's apartment interrupted Pam. At the same time, Stella's phone pinged. She checked her phone and laughed; Gina, impatient as ever, had felt it necessary to message while knocking on the door in stereo.

The near month-long stint sans mobile phone had made Stella less dependent on it.

How did we ever survive without using mobile phones?

Considering her relationship with Heath might not survive due to not using her phone, it was a pertinent question to consider as she went to answer the door. The thought of their haemorrhaging relationship brought her mood down, her faultless performance at the opening of *Streetcar* overshadowed by this truth. With the show underway and the ability, finally, to relax somewhat, she had dropped living and breathing every moment in character as Blanche. She was desperate to speak to Heath, who still hadn't returned her call or message after last night's performance. She'd been careful to ring him immediately upon coming off stage at 10 pm, hoping to reach him, as it was Saturday morning in Australia. When he didn't answer, she reasoned he must've gone for an early surf – instead of confronting the possibility that he was ignoring her on purpose. The only clue to his existence was his online status. It didn't require a sixth sense to know something was off. Heath's silence was deafening.

Stella opened the door to her apartment to find Gina, slumped against the wall next to the door with a large bunch of flowers at her feet, balancing a tray of coffees and assortment of pastries as she adjusted the sunglasses that sat askew on her nose. A dull paleness had replaced the dewy glow Gina had radiated the previous night; it was anybody's guess where she'd ended up after Stella left her and the cast in the early hours at the Royal Hotel.

Practically choking on a sip of coffee as she stumbled through the door, Gina announced, 'Breakfast is served and not a moment too soon. Who are the flowers from?' She kissed Stella and Pam hello, dropping her tray on the table, and flopped onto the lounge.

Following Gina into the flat with the flowers, Stella read the card out loud, saying: 'I'm glad I took a chance on you. Congratulations. Love Mark.' Tears coated her eyes at Mark's approval of her performance.

'Con-grat-u-bloody-lations! So! How is the *woman of the moment*!?' Gina croaked, her voice husky like she'd made a career out of drinking rum and smoking cigarettes. She kicked off her boots and lay on her back, staring at the ceiling, sunglasses crookedly balancing on her face.

'I'm fabulous!' Pam exclaimed. 'I love being the mother of the moment. Of course, I'm only joking, Gina. I know you didn't intend the question for me.'

'*Of course*, I meant it for you, Pammy!' Gina joked. 'Behind every great daughter is a great mother!'

Stella took a coffee from the tray and smiled at her mother. 'Gina is right, Mum... You've always been supportive of my acting career. I genuinely appreciate how you've nurtured my creative spirit and have always believed in my ability as an actress. And Madison's, too.'

Mother and daughter exchanged glances. Pam beamed with a mix of pride at Stella's talent and a glimmer of grief about Madison and the career that neither she nor her eldest daughter would have.

'I knew you would be brilliant, darling,' Pam said, reaching over to squeeze Stella's hand. 'The only thing that could have improved your performance is if you played Stella Kowalski, not Blanche DuBois.'

Stella chose to ignore the comment; it wasn't meant with malice – it was just her mother living vicariously through her and her life-long wish to play that role. Stella flopped back on the lounge and stretched her legs out.

'You seem a bit flat for someone who is officially the talk of the town,' Gina commented.

'I couldn't have wished for a better outcome and I'm so happy but exhausted. I'm thrilled. I think I need to rest.'

What Pam and Gina didn't know was that Stella's exhaustion stemmed from not only the culmination of weeks of hard work in London, but also overcoming a decade's worth of internalised trauma and regret to see her dream realised.

Or that she was pining for Heath.

'Well! Even though I'm hungover, I plan to keep celebrating for both of us! What's *Cowboy* Heath had to say about your electrifyingly successful opening night success, Stella?' Gina asked, keeping her eyes closed. 'He must be proud.'

'For Christ's sake, don't call him Cowboy Heath.'

Gina opened her eyes and peered at Stella over her sunglasses. 'I've never seen you so emotional and sensitive about a man, Stella.' Dropping her sunnies over her eyes again, she continued, 'He *is* a cowboy – big, tough, and practical, doesn't suffer fools, and is ethical and honest. Well…at least *you* tell me he's honest.'

'He's the most honest man – human – I've met,' Stella said shortly. She hadn't spoken to Gina about how things were going with Heath and tried to change the subject. 'What time did you leave the pub last night? You were stonkered. Please tell me that you didn't go back to your hotel with one of my cast or crew members last night. The last thing I need is things to be more awkward at the theatre.'

Sensing the deflection, Gina immediately sat up, tossed her sunglasses onto the coffee table, and narrowed her bloodshot eyes at Stella. Having known one another since kindergarten, the two were always in constant conversation, decoding each other's body language with unspoken signals, messages, and words. The way Stella flinched as Gina spoke, contemplatively blinked at the ground, and bit her bottom lip were cues for Gina to back off. Stella really didn't want to hear Gina's interest in the possible demise of her and Heath's relationship, not when Gina had never had a good feeling about Heath, and for no apparent reason.

There was a long moment of silence before Gina commented, 'What time did I get in?' She wrinkled her nose as she thought. 'I can't be sure – 2? Maybe 3 – much too late. Err, no, I didn't take anyone home, unfortunately.' Gina cupped her hand over her mouth and leaned into Pam. 'Cover your ears for a moment, Pammy.' Returning her attention to Stella, she continued, 'I tried my best to lure Jimmy Marsden to my hotel room, but he wouldn't have it. He only wanted to talk about you.' Grinning, she added, 'It seems he's pretty smitten by you, Stella.'

'You've taken to calling Johnny, *Jimmy*?' Stella asked. 'Fabulous. His James Dean ego will be even more impossible than it already was.'

'You can uncover your ears now, Pammy,' Gina said, and then leaned forward to clasp Stella's hands. 'Stella, I am so proud of you. I looked up the reviews on my way over in the taxi, and they're exceptional. You have officially *arrived*, my friend!'

'Hear, hear, Gina!' Pam gushed. 'Bravo, Stella. Your father and Madison would be so proud. Alinta messaged to say congratulations; she's also emailed you, hoping you've started to use technology again. She was so distressed she couldn't take time off work to be here.'

'I have so many messages to catch up on,' Stella responded, inwardly smarting that this was the first time her mother congratulated *her* performance, having spent so much time praising herself.

'I'll ring Alinta soon. I'm just physically, mentally, and emotionally drained after last night.'

'Aside from quoting me that Tennessee Williams is a genius,' Pam said, returning to their earlier conversation, 'Alfie Knox says Stella's performance was the highlight of the production. Well, that much we can all agree on. At least I didn't have to spoon feed him that.'

'I couldn't agree with you more, Alfie boy,' Gina said. She hesitated, and then ventured, 'Hey, Stelz...'

Gina never calls me Stelz.

'What is it?' Stella asked. 'Spit it out. I know you want to tell me something... It's a good thing that *you* never took up acting.'

The three women laughed. Gina always made her feelings obvious, exposing her emotions and wearing her heart on her sleeve – usually with Stella's best interests at heart.

'Well…' Gina said slowly, 'Knowing the immense pressure you've been under with rehearsals leading up to the big opening, I didn't want to raise this before. Although, seeing the show has been received to national acclaim, and now that the pressure is off a little, I thought…well…'

'Oh, come on, Gina,' Stella said impatiently, 'stop decorating what you're about to say. Let me guess – the cast spoke badly about me after I left last night. Right? I already know they despise me. At this stage, I couldn't care less.'

'Oh, no, Stella, not at all!' Gina cried. 'On the contrary, they were impressed by your performance. Those naysayers you told me gave you a hard time are eating humble pie. Delia commented that after seeing you in full flight last night, she's converted to being a method actress – the hide of her. I suspect you'll receive apologies from several cast members today, seeking forgiveness for their dreadful behaviour.'

'Oh,' Stella said, nonplussed. 'What is it, then?'

Gina lowered her voice. 'Remember Candice? The American hairdresser Heath met in Hawaii?'

'The make-up artist,' Stella said, feeling a bit sick. 'She was a make-up artist, not a hairdresser. Why are you bringing her up?'

'The very tall one who you said is stunning,' Gina said, watching Stella closely. 'The one Heath apparently broke up with because she lived overseas. The reason Heath despises long-distance relationships. It bothered you that Heath was in regular contact with her?'

'For heaven's sake, Gina, spit it out already,' Stella snapped. 'What's your point?'

'I have a mutual friend, Fleur, who happens to know Candice,' Gina said, speaking so quickly her words ran together. 'Candice commented on one of Fleur's social media posts, and I asked Fleur about it before I came to London.'

Stella was biting her bottom lip again; this time, though, she didn't look down at the floor but rather met Gina's gaze.

'Candice lives in Hawaii.'

'Not at the moment, apparently. Fleur confirmed that Candice has been in Australia for a while and that she and Heath have caught up. I'm so sorry.'

'Oh,' Stella said faintly.

Gina hesitated, clearly debating whether to say any more, before finally saying, 'Fleur said Candice is in Australia for at least a month. I asked Fleur if Candice is there on business or pleasure, and… seems…' Her voice trailed off.

'Seems what?' Stella could barely get the words out.

With a wince, Gina revealed: 'Candice is in Australia for business *and* pleasure.'

CHAPTER 33

Candice slept in the bedroom as Heath read over a copy of the letter he'd sent to Stella.

Dear Stella,

Even if I could break up with you via text or over the phone, I would never diminish what we shared to such a crude break-up.

I thought of coming to London to speak to you in person, but I didn't want to distract you from your West End debut.

Writing a letter seemed the most proper way of communicating that I'm ending our relationship.

I'm deeply hurt and disappointed with how things have gone between us.

My trust is broken.

It doesn't mean I don't love you.

I'm getting on with my life, without you.

I am sorry for the timing of this.

I wish you the very best, always.

With love,

Heath

The letter made him miserable. As though he inexplicably needed to feel even worse, he started up a BBC interview with Stella and Johnny, rewatching it almost obsessively as the actors talked animatedly about the play's success. Waves of sadness rolled over Heath as they discussed how they'd prepared for the role. The actors talked animatedly about the play's success, discussing how they'd prepared for the role by rekindling a ten-year friendship to form an unshakeable bond, something they described as essential for situations in which immense trust was required and tested, particularly during intimate scenes. The media interviews, though undoubtedly necessary to sell tickets, felt like a slap in the face.

His phone rang as he finished watching the seven-minute interview for the third time. Except for his mother, who rang on weekends, nobody would else have the audacity to ring him at 7 am on a Sunday. He checked the screen and wasn't surprised to see it was Stella calling. He quickly put his phone on silent and allowed it to ring four times, trying to decide if he'd answer the call or let it go to voicemail. However, Stella's name and familiar profile photo popping up on his phone made him catch his breath; he answered the call.

'Hey, how are you?' Heath asked quietly. 'Just give me a second; I'm cooking eggs. I'll turn the heat off.'

'Okay.'

He raced to the bedroom and closed the door.

'Sorry about that; you caught me in the middle of a Sunday morning cook-up.'

'I miss those,' Stella said. When he didn't respond, she continued, 'What have you been up to?'

'It's been crazy at home with the new exhibition. Lots happening.' He knew he sounded stilted, that Stella could probably hear in his voice that things weren't the same anymore.

'What else have you been up to?'

'I went to visit Dad and Mum yesterday and spend some time with the family.'

'Did you stay at your parent's house last night?' Stella asked. 'I was wondering why you didn't pick up my call after opening night. I thought you would've wanted to hear how the play went.'

'Yeah, I stayed overnight,' he lied, even though he didn't need to, since as far as he was concerned, he'd ended the relationship with the letter he'd sent Stella, and thus had done nothing wrong. 'I read the reviews, though. Congratulations – it looks like the show is a major hit. Mission accomplished, hey?'

Clearly able to hear his cordial, and non-intimate, tone, Stella switched mid-call to FaceTime, catching him off guard. When he didn't accept it immediately, she rang again on FaceTime, and this time he picked up.

She hasn't read my letter, Heath surmised. *Jesus.*

Stella couldn't conceal her relief when he answered the call. 'Hey! It's so good to see your face. I didn't think you were going to answer.' She paused, frowned slightly. 'Is everything alright?'

'Look, Stella,' Heath said, his voice serious, 'clearly things aren't alright. Nothing's been okay since you left for London.'

'I know,' she said awkwardly. 'I owe you a massive apology for how suddenly I left for London and how I stayed largely out of contact. I am so sorry...'

'Stella...' Heath sighed. 'I wish you would have said this earlier.'

'I know, hon, and I'm so sorry. I've been incredibly selfish, and I regret what I've done. The decisions I've made. Still, it's pretty average that you didn't bother to take my call when I rang you after opening night.'

'Cut me some slack, Stella. I was on the way to my parents' house.'

'Early in the morning?'

'Um, yeah.' He couldn't keep the annoyance from his voice. 'Look, you're being a bit of a wet blanket. At this stage, I don't need to explain myself.'

'Okay... But you haven't returned my call,' Stella said again. 'It's been 24 hours. I just... I can't shake the feeling that something's wrong.'

'That's a bit rich,' Heath said sharply, 'considering the last time I spoke to you, you were so drunk at Johnny wanker's house that you could barely speak, falling all over him like a cheap bloody rash.'

'Jesus!' Stella pulled back from her phone, shocked by the anger in his voice. 'There's no need for that. Nothing happened, honestly. We were rehearsing and I had some drinks. Too many drinks. We got together to help break the ice so we would perform better on stage. We were just getting to know each other better.'

'Seems to have worked,' Heath muttered. Before Stella could respond, he continued, 'Stella, this whole scene has been a shit show. Honestly –' he shook his head sharply '– I can't do this. You walked out on our relationship and then went offline for the better part of a month.'

'I know it looks bad,' Stella said earnestly. 'I am so, so sorry. I stuffed up. Badly. I've been a self-consumed idiot.'

'What you did drove a wedge between us.'

'I'm back online now. I wanted to get the first performance out of the way and be authentic to the role…' Seeing this wasn't helping her case, she moved on, saying, 'Listen… There's something I want… There's something I need to tell you, which will help to make sense of why I behaved the way I –'

Heath raised his voice and snapped, 'Save me this shit show! Save whatever you've got to say for Johnny wanker!'

'What!? No!' He could hear the hurt in her voice but ignored it as she continued to speak. 'No. Stop it, Heath. No, look, Heath, I need to talk to you about something important, that happened in my past.'

'What are you even talking about? There's no point discussing the past.'

Stella didn't hear him ask if she'd read his letter as she spoke over the top of him.

'Please, let me explain. I need you to know why I quit acting –'

'Stop, Stella! What does any of this have to do with acting?' He let out a sharp bark of laughter. 'Stop bringing up the past. It's too late. There's no point flogging a dead horse. The way you cast me aside, as though I'm nothing, has told me a hell of a lot about who you are and your priorities.' Realising how loud he'd become; he lowered his voice to continue. 'Please, let's not make this any harder than it already is. You know I've made up my mind.'

Stella was so beside herself that she couldn't comprehend what Heath is saying and fixed on his voice. 'Why are you whispering?'

'It's early in the morning here. I don't want to wake the neighbours.' Heath ran a hand through his hair and shook his head, saying, 'I can't do this, Stella. Look, you're celebrating the show's success, and clearly, you've made some new friends. You don't need me. Let's see this for what it is: the end.'

'Are you ending the relationship?' Stella cried out, as tears began to creep down her cheeks. 'I can't believe you would give up on us. You see me, and I see you, remember? You're being ruthless.' Her voice was getting more frantic the more she spoke. 'There must be someone else. Tell me the truth, Heath. Are you – are you seeing someone else?'

He didn't afford her the decency of a response, his attitude as removed as a farmer castrating its livestock. 'I'm sorry, Stella,' he said flatly. 'You should have read my letter. The relationship is over.'

In tears, her voice increasingly pleading, she continued, 'This is ruthless. Look, I screwed up. I know I got my priorities wrong, but I wish you'd let me explain, because I think you'd understand a lot more if I could – God, it's horrendous doing this over the phone. Can you take a week off work and visit me in London? Please, Heath, *please*. You are the love of my life.'

'You were the love of my life, Stella. You know that.'

The shock on her face at the past tense almost made him reconsider. Then, before he could give in to a moment of weakness, before she could say anything, he heard the bedroom door open behind him. He glanced behind him to see Candice – tall, beautiful, and wearing only a long t-shirt – standing in the doorway, looking at him.

'Hey,' she called, voice husky with sleep, 'What are you doing?' and shuffled off to the bathroom.'

He quickly repositioned the phone to directly in front of his face, keeping Candice out of view, and replied, saying, 'I'm speaking to a friend, give me a second.'

For what seemed like an eternity, Heath and Stella stared at each other, silent: the apparent betrayer and grief-stricken betrayed.

Then Stella ended the call.

***

A few hours later, at his surf club, Heath cursed himself for turning up to compete in the weekend surfing competition so soon after actually breaking up with Stella and the consequent remorse. He wished he'd allowed Stella to say what she was trying to tell him – now he couldn't help but wonder what it was that she'd felt was so important. He'd just let her walk away, without explaining that he and Candice hadn't been intimate ... That they'd gone out for drinks and she stayed over, too drunk to do anything the night before. If Candice hadn't been at his apartment, he might have called Stella back to let her say her piece – the least he could do for the woman he'd been contemplating asking to marry him a month ago. The sincerity in Stella's voice weighed on his conscience – his wife-not-to-be begging for forgiveness, admitting to being inconsiderate, and vigorously denying she was unfaithful – yet he hadn't given her an inch.

No matter how often Heath wished the phone call ending their relationship had finished differently, there wasn't anything he could do at this point to erase Stella's torment. It should be enough that she'd seen a woman coming out of the bedroom in which she and Heath had nurtured their love and passion, shared secrets and dreams, and talked of an *Endless Summer* – a song they'd played on repeat since their first date.

Heath's small, unremarkable flat – its bedroom with artwork, half-burnt candles in mismatched jars, and earthy décor – was their place, and theirs alone, something Stella had articulated more than once. It wouldn't have mattered if that room were a cardboard box; the love that the two of them had exchanged in it was priceless. And now Stella believed someone else had lain in Heath's bed, her expressions of love written in oil quickly and permanently erased, as if only imagined.

Heath's generally sensible relationship with social media was overwhelmed by the impulse to post a message of some kind, one pointed directly at Stella. He wanted to upload a post laden with insinuation about not judging his choices without understanding his reasons – a sorry attempt to get Stella's attention to say there was more to the story – yet he did nothing.

Surf club captain Jed Donahue was first to rankle Heath's feathers by mentioning Stella.

'Hey, Heath,' he said as Heath arrived, 'we've got good waves today. It should be a fun heat. What's news with you? Oh, I hear your better half is plastered all over the media – she's been a big hit in the show she's in, hey? My missus says that your missus is all over the news. So, I guess you're famous by association. What have you got to say for yourself about that?'

Kicking at the sand, Heath waited until Jed stopped asking questions before trying to divert his attention. 'How many competitors are surfing today?'

'I think most of the club turned out, the waves are so good.'

A gust of wind swept Heath's hair across his face. He raised an arm to block out the harsh sun, a noticeable line forming in the middle of his forehead, barely audible he mumbled, 'It should be fun.'

Christ Almighty. Every man and his dog are going to talk to me about Stella today.

He considered faking a migraine so he could pull out of the competition and retreat to the safety of his apartment. Everything was still too raw for him to be discussing Stella with anyone. Instead, he turned his attention to trying to remain competitive in the surf, troubled emotions still bubbling at the back of his head.

A couple of people in the crowd on the beach jeered as he came back in from his heat, having muscled up to another competitor – an altercation entirely out of character for him.

'Jeez mate, calm down!' one spectator yelled. 'We're surfing for fun, you dickhead.'

Another onlooker taunted: 'Hey mate, pull your head in before someone pulls it in for you. Chill out, mate!'

Once on the beach, Heath drenched his head with a water bottle before ripping off his leg rope and storming back up the beach with his surfboard under his arm.

He checked his phone to see it was lit up with flirty messages from Candice; she might wear her thumbs out with the number of kissy lip emojis she liked to send in a single text message. Not wasting any time, she'd invited him to lunch at a swanky restaurant the next day, clearly wanting to progress their friendship into a relationship again.

What better way for him to drown his sorrows? In any event, Stella would never believe that he and Candice hadn't slept together. Might as well make it the truth.

***

The tailored electric blue suit and sky-high white heels Candice chose to wear to lunch make her look like a fancy real estate agent. At nearly six feet, the glamazonian came to eye level with Heath in heels, which he had to admit he didn't dislike.

Today, Heath planned to ignore that Candice's ego had exploded since they first met and that she spoke of herself with such high regard that even the waitstaff rolled their eyes at her behind her back.

For now, he was just enjoying the distraction.

At the back of his mind, though, he couldn't help thinking that it was really a classic rebound in a cautionary tale of an epic love story gone wrong.

***

A week later, back home in Australia, Gina's text and photo to Stella rose to feel like an ongoing assault.

Ping!

> **Cowboy Heath and Candice are wasting no time rekindling their relationship.**

Ping!

A photo landed on Stella's phone that Candice had posted to her Instagram account – courtesy of Gina, via Fleur – which featured two bowls of ramen, sans people. The caption read:

> **Bon Appetit! My lover and I are treating ourselves to a much-anticipated lunch.**

Gina had circled an incriminating comment under the caption where Heath had responded to one of Candice's celebrity girlfriends, acknowledging that he was her company at lunch…with an emoji smile of ruinous implications.

Ping!

Gina sent another text to Stella:

Cowboy Heath is a dick.

***

Two weeks later, Stella lay in bed in her pigsty hotel room in London, grateful the Sunday matinee was over and she didn't have to perform for several days. Except for a few picked-over frozen meals, the fridge was empty, while the wine bottles strewn across the apartment added to the general miserable ambiance. A bunch of flowers from Heath lay decaying in the kitchen corner; the card he sent with a single, 'Let me explain,' crumpled next to them.

That Heath had gone back to Candice was senseless in Stella's mind. More than Heath being with Candice, it was tearing Stella apart trying to understand why he'd chosen her, knowing that she lived in another country.

In her heartbroken stupor, she reasoned that Heath had reaffirmed the relationship with Candice to punish her for going offline, and for flirting with Johnny. Although this explanation didn't really make any sense, since Heath was the least vindictive person she knew.

The strident piano notes in Taylor Swift's *Exile* haunted Stella. She'd played the song repeatedly, as though willing herself into a depression; amazingly, her neighbours hadn't made a noise complaint. If the neighbours did complain, she'd first tell them of her grief and then advise them to listen to the song, certain they'd empathise with her.

Stella swapped the introductory reference of a man wrapping his arms around a woman in *Exile* with a woman wrapping her arms around a man. In her melancholy state, she could imagine Candice wrapping her arms around Heath, plastered against the familiar contours of his broad chest and cut of his waist. It was sick that she imagined this scene, subconsciously trying to magnify her confusion, denial, anger, and longing to realise her worth and move on. With the sex of the lead character swapped, the song's other references spoke to Stella's heartbreak. They were no longer one another's homeland. She was in exile in London. The understudy was Johnny to Heath's star. But Johnny had never had a patch on Heath, a big star though he might be. She knew that Heath would have gotten his knuckles dirty for Stella. Johnny wouldn't – and Stella wasn't interested in Johnny in the slightest.

The line that most resonated was about not being the other person's problem anymore: and wasn't it just the truth? Stella and her secret would never be Heath's problem now.

And nor should it be.

***

The only good thing to come of breaking up with Heath was that Stella was able to channel the misery to intensify her performance in *Streetcar*. True to her dedication as a method actress, she infused agony and abandonment into the work, along with the different stages of grief. During the play's six-week run, she'd primarily been in denial about the break-up, using that denial as a reference point for Blanche's refusal to acknowledge how much she drank. Indeed, since their separation, and since she'd been spending more time with Johnny and the other cast members – who finally had accepted her into the fold after the play's successful opening night – Stella's alcohol consumption had increased. Two of the other stages of grief – anger and depression – came naturally to the performance. There had been a good deal of transacting, too. Some mornings, she would pray to a god she didn't believe in for Heath to return. Bargaining was a straightforward representation of grief that she was able to embed in her performance. She didn't need to stretch too far to compare losing Heath to how Blanche felt losing her young husband to suicide.

The grief stage that she couldn't manage was acceptance; there was no cooperation on this account. Just as Blanche couldn't readily accept her fate of being carted off to an asylum at the end of the play, Stella was a long way from accepting that her relationship with Heath was over.

She used these raw emotions to fuel her performance and cement her place in history as delivering one of the greatest interpretations of

Blanche ever performed. Stella Longhurst had achieved what she set out to do – professionally she was a raging success.

But privately, her life was an abysmal failure.

CHAPTER 34

London, Late November 2022

As agonising as it was for her loved ones, Melanie Tate's funeral was a beautiful final rite of passage, despite the bitter winter day in London. She died a week after *Streetcar* closed, as though she had purposely held on, so her death didn't interfere with the show's run.

The way everyone stood around the casket, respectfully wearing black, protected by large, hand-crafted black umbrellas, made the scene look straight out of a gangster movie. Breaking the colourless scene, Desdemona, Melanie's young daughter, clumsily juggled a bright orange umbrella, helping to keep her diverted from the realities of the day.

The intimate gathering of family and Melanie's closest friends avoided pomp and ceremony; this would come in a week at the public memorial service scheduled for Melanie's adoring British fans. Largely regarded as one of Britain's own, even though she was Australian, tributes had flowed for the late actress in the week since her death. Celebrities and fans had taken to social media to honour her, with the general sentiment being that she was too talented and too young to die.

Honoured that she had been asked to speak at the burial, Stella was conscientious about keeping the tone light, knowing that Desdemona would feel every word, even if she couldn't yet comprehend the full tragedy of losing her mother. Victor Tate, Melanie's husband, hadn't said much since his wife's death a week earlier and had declined to speak at the interment. A banker more accustomed to dealing with figures, Victor wasn't at home with orating; that had been Melanie's strength, not his.

When called to speak, Stella walked intently to her position at the head of the casket. She lowered her voice and spoke softly and more meticulously than usual, her slower speech a sign of respect for the dead.

The piece of paper she held in her hand trembled under a rainy and windless day, her bottom lip twitching uncontrollably. Familiar emotions of grief shot, unwelcome, through her body. Death evoked emotions she'd rather ignore, arriving in sharp rounds and spontaneous jolts, reminders of her own losses – Madison. Her father.

Standing in full view of Melanie's family and friends, Stella was so anxious she could have been mistaken for having had an electric shock. Even during the worst days after the break-up with Heath, she'd never experienced these particular emotions. The death of a loved one spoke with a volume that made breaking up feel commonplace and inconsequential.

'Melanie's husband, Victor,' Stella said at last, grateful her voice wasn't shaking as badly as her hands, 'has asked me to say a few words on his behalf.' Victor had also asked two of Melanie's childhood friends to speak at the funeral although neither felt strong enough for the task.

Stella was determined to honour Victor's request to speak when he could not: with the greatest respect.

A solo bird perched high in a tree at the other end of the cemetery listened attentively as Stella swallowed, took a deep breath, and spoke Victor's words softly.

My darling Melanie,

I find it hard to speak about you in the past tense – like it's an acknowledgement that you're really gone.

You are lovely – unspeakably beautiful inside and out.

I love your authenticity, your grace, and your generosity.

Your contribution to the arts world is enormous, yet you have always remained humble.

Your contribution to your family is phenomenal, and I am so grateful, and so honoured, to be your husband.

Desdemona is so very lucky to have you as her mother.

There will only ever be you.

Sitting on her father's lap, little Desdemona squeezed his hand; her orange brolly now dropped to the ground, she leaned back against his chest and looked upwards at the tears streaming down his face. Stella was reminded of the image of three-year-old John F. Kennedy, Jr., saluting his father's casket, just days after the president's assassination.

Taking another deep breath, Stella faced the mourners and began to recite the poem Melanie had requested to be read as her eulogy.

***

Newspaper and magazine articles documenting Melanie's brilliant career and highlighting her beauty filled newsagents across the United Kingdom and Australia and flooded the internet, reminding Stella that she should've caught up with Melanie more during her time in London.

The first time the actresses caught up after that initial coffee had been when Melanie snuck into the Palais to watch a matinee performance of *Streetcar* and later found Stella backstage to offer congratulations and no end of great praise for her performance.

The last occasion had been at the five-star hospice Melanie died in, her body skeletal, skin jaundiced from a failing liver, and her mind given to hallucinations from the pain killers that would reluctantly ease her from the world. Pointlessly, Stella had taken her a silk shawl with tassels as a gift, along with a card that Melanie had struggled to read.

The card read:

I've loved our friendship, and I love you.

With deepest love,

Stella

Melanie asked Stella to spread the shawl over an occasional chair so she could admire it from her bed. Stella would wear it just weeks later to the funeral; Victor had returned the shawl to her after Melanie died.

In between thinking she saw a rainbow on the hospice wall, pulling her hospital gown up above her waist to show Stella how unhealthily thin she was, and imagining kittens drinking from bowls of milk, Melanie had moments of lucidity.

Three incidents stood out to Stella about that final visit.

The first was the sound of a drinks trolley rattling down the hospice hallway at 11 am, which delighted Melanie.

'Oh, Stella, you're in for a treat! Wait until you see what's coming.'

Seconds later, an older woman entered the room, pushing a drinks cart with spirits and miniature bottles of wine, champagne, and soda. Her silver-white hair, curled with big rollers and sitting proud on her head, looked like a halo.

The drinks delivery lady was named Angelica, clearly indicated on her nametag, but Stella thought it was particularly fitting because of the older woman's angelic aura. When not volunteering at the hospice, Stella imagined Angelica's apron replaced by comfortable slacks, a sensible blouse, and a wide-brimmed hat, purposely worn while tending to a beautifully manicured garden.

Angelica came close to Melanie's bed and gently rubbed the back of the actress' hand. 'Would you like a drink today, dear?'

'No, thank you,' Melanie replied. She looked at Stella with a smile and said, 'She asks me every day, but I've never been much of a drinker. Ironic, isn't it, that I ended up with a rare liver cancer?'

Angelica continued rubbing Melanie's hand and said, 'Everything will be well enough, don't you worry, pet.'

Melanie didn't respond.

'Hello, dear,' Angelica said, turning her attention to Stella. 'You must be one of Melanie's lovely friends.' She gestured at the trolley.

'Can I tempt you with a drink, dear? We have everything imaginable, from spirits to wine and champagne.'

Somehow Melanie mustered some strength. She rolled onto her side, tucked her knees into her chest, and said, her breath effortful and raspy, 'Stella – you can have whatever you want. They only serve the top shelf here; it's available any time, day, or night.'

Stella selected a mineral water and thanked Angelica, who moved to the next room, floating like a human sunflower; the scent of old woman perfume trailed her, leaving an unmistakable end-of-life smell to re-infest Melanie's room. With so many lives having expired in the hospice room, a chisel couldn't scrape the scent of deteriorating body cells from its walls. Along with a combination of industrial cleaning products covered over by sickly sweet air fresheners.

Melanie's illness had bought her a one-way ticket to curtains, and the consensus was that she did whatever she liked. This scene wasn't absurd because alcohol was served free of charge to someone with a failing liver – it was the steadfast acknowledgement that when your number was up, it was simply up, and you might as take what pleasures were left to you.

Regardless of her drug-induced stupor, Melanie knew this was her final curtain call; her failure to acknowledge Angelica's comment that everything would be alright confirmed as much.

With this understanding, the penultimate remarkable thing to occur during her visit to the hospice burdened Stella with responsibility so great it was almost a duty too challenging to bear.

'Stella, I can't be bothered choosing what I'll eat tomorrow,' Melanie said tiredly. 'Can you do me a favour and select what I should eat? Order whatever you wish. I'll think of you as I eat.'

Without saying a word, Stella used a pencil to help guide her through the paper menu, occasionally stopping to squint, her eyes stinging with tears, the words blurry on the page.

'Don't forget to order dessert,' Melanie said with a hint of rebellion for the sweets she'd deprived herself of over a disciplined lifetime being rigidly thin. 'I'm not missing dessert.'

Stella pretended to cough to clear her throat.

'I thought I'd start with dessert,' she said, trying to sound cheery. 'There's carrot cake, red velvet cake, and banoffee pie... Surprisingly, there's no jelly on the menu! Still, it's a pretty good menu for a hosp...' Her voice trailed off, leaving the two friends in silence.

Speechless, Stella squeezed her pinkie finger so hard that she was afraid blood might spurt from the cuticle, caught between not daring to interrupt the quietness with trivial small talk and desperately scraping the insides of her brain for something – anything – to say. No words of wisdom sprang to mind.

This was Melanie's moment. The courteous thing was for Stella to sit patiently and quietly, to let Melanie choose to speak or not; Stella's pinkie would repair from squeezing over time.

Be quiet, Stella. This is not about you. Don't fill this time with idle chit chat. Be present. Be real. Do not cry. Do not cry. Do not cry.

Stella finished selecting the meals, carefully placing a pencil tick next to a cheese platter and red velvet cake for Melanie's dinner the following day. Having already selected pancakes with strawberries for breakfast, she chose roast chicken and vegetables for lunch. She knew Melanie wouldn't eat much of the food; painkillers combined with nausea and vomiting had mostly obliterated her appetite.

Finally, Melanie said, 'I bet you selected the red velvet cake. Didn't you, Stella?'

Of course Stella had selected the red velvet cake. When they were younger, during lunch at drama classes, they would take off to the local bakery to purchase chocolate cake loaded with lashings of cream cheese, frosting their faces stained with scarlet on their return to class.

Stella released her pinkie finger and broke her contract with herself not to cry at this memory; knowing these were some of her final moments with her friend proved overbearing.

'Sorry,' she said, blotting her eyes with her sleeve. 'I wish this weren't happening to you. I'm sorry for crying.' She shook her head in disappointment at clumsily and spontaneously unloading her grief onto Melanie.

Melanie's gaze fixed on Stella; the look didn't suggest she thought her friend was pathetic or selfish for crying – it was more empathy, knowing that sometimes the living were weaker than the dying. She was Buddha-like at the hour of her death, peaceful and unnervingly serene.

'I'm going to die, and I'm going to die soon, Stella.'

Holding onto every word, Stella didn't dare speak, although she could hear the matter-of-factness in Melanie's voice, which could have been construed as callous. There was little gentle way for a person to acknowledge they were dying.

Melanie's voice was strained, although her words were clear. 'Stella, I want you to read the poem *The Dash* by Linda Ellis for my eulogy. It's a lovely piece. The dash is a metaphor, representing how a person spends their time from birth to death.' She paused, taking shallow breaths before carrying on. 'The poem contemplates how living and loving are more important than a lifetime collecting material possessions or wealth. It's a reminder for people to live their dash to the fullest. Will you please do me the honour of reading the poem at my funeral, Stella?'

Stella, who had stopped crying and was existing in an almost hypnotic state, cast an admiring gaze at Melanie. 'It will be my honour to do this for you, Melanie.'

'*The Dash* asks us to consider if there is anything we might need to change and references being real and true. Even though it might be wonderful to receive positive reviews for *Streetcar* – all the professional accolades in the world cannot replace true love.'

That Melanie should offer relationship advice to Stella on her deathbed was the third and most significant incident at their last meeting.

After Melanie finished, the women sat in comfortable silence for a long time, Melanie falling in and out of sleep. Victor and Desdemona quietly slipped back into Melanie's room as she slept.

There was no right way to end a final visit with a dying friend.

Eventually, Stella moved to Melanie's bedside, gently embraced her friend, and then gently kissed her on the cheek.

There were no more tears, and no other parting words exchanged.

CHAPTER 35

Northern New South Wales, December 2022

Wiping sleep from her eyes, Stella tried to remember which city she was in.

Since wrapping *Streetcar*, she had completed a flying tour of Ireland, Scotland Paris, Spain, and Italy before returning home to Australia, where it was summer and where one could swim in the ocean and dare to get sunburnt.

The bright white paint in her Terranora townhouse was a blinding contrast to the brown brick walls of her London flat. Lying in bed wearing pyjama shorts and a singlet top, she rolled from a prone position onto her stomach and then to her back again, bathing in the glow of sunshine streaming through her bedroom window. Spotty scaly skin dappled her arms and legs – a legacy of using heaters constantly to avoid the frigid London temperatures. She made a mental note to purchase extra moisturiser.

She was grateful to her mother and Alinta for cleaning the apartment before she arrived home, putting fresh sheets on the bed and spoiling her with welcome home flowers. The gaps on the bookshelf where framed photos of Stella and Heath had once been revealed that Pam and Alinta had hidden any photos they thought might upset her. The fridge, formerly covered with pictures of the couple, looked sterile; the photo that previously assumed prominence, and a moment etched in Stella's memory, was a snapshot of them in his lounge room. Heath delicately cupped the side of her face with his hand and kissed her cheek. When Stella had first seen the selfie, she'd hardly recognised herself; the pure rapture wasn't anything she'd ever seen in herself before.

Instead, the shiny, photo-less fridge door reminded her that she'd lost the person she loved more than anyone – or anything.

Knowing that her body clock would take several days to adjust to local time, Stella resisted the urge to make plans. She hadn't even bothered to check her messages since being in transit.

The only good thing about turning her phone off during *Streetcar* rehearsals was that she'd become less dependent on it – an unpleasant occupational hazard from her former life as a publicist.

At 10 am, she debated turning her phone on, weighing it against the risk her mother would make a visit to check on her welfare. Pam's best intentions aside, the last thing Stella felt like doing was dealing with a visit from her mother. After three months of being on an entirely different continent, halfway around the world, there was no way she'd be able to ask her mother to leave.

She chose to leave it turned off for a little longer – being at home, in her own bed, was the closest she'd been to Heath in months, the scent of him still deep-seated in the bedding, despite it being freshly washed.

With his presence still so alive, Stella only had to close her eyes to channel him, images of Heath in her apartment flooding her memory.

There was Heath, walking from her bathroom after a shower... He was rubbing wet strands of hair with a towel and sharing his frustration about a painting he was creating... His physique was jewelled with drops of water – smiling as he spoke, as Heath did even when he was under pressure.

Next, she visualised Heath in her kitchen making a curry. This time he looked directly at her, seated at the kitchen table drinking a glass of wine, and asked, 'Are you happy, Stella?'

She remembered how spontaneously she had responded to the question: 'I'm the happiest I've ever been, Heath.'

Then, Heath was fixing her kitchen cabinets. Next, he was play-fighting with her, gently pinning her and kissing the soft underside of her arms, his kind, green eyes glistening and smiling only for her.

Gosh, this is torture.

I hate this!

Desperate to distract herself from thoughts of Heath, Stella threw the sheet off, plodded to her bag, and fossicked around for her phone. She switched it on and shuffled off to the toilet as messages downloaded.

Ping! ping! ping! sounded non-stop.

Predictably, there were 13 missed calls from her mother. There were also missed messages from Ray, Alinta, Gina, Johnny, and Stella's new acting agent, who she'd secured while still living in London. The Australian agent had reached out to Stella after the positive reviews for *Streetcar* had made her a hot commodity. The agent wanted to secure her as part of their stable of actors.

Stella opened the message from Johnny first.

> **Hey, Stella Rock Star!! How is life back at home? I miss you already!!**
>
> **Moving back to Australia could be the death of your career but what would I know!!? Seriously, wishing you the best of luck performing the new show.**

Christ it's annoying how Johnny punctuates his sentences with two exclamation marks.

Nonchalantly responding to text messages, Stella went to the kitchen to make herself some breakfast. She put the kettle on, dropped a tea bag into a cup, and pulled out some bread from the freezer, appreciative that her mother had remembered to pick up her favourite bread, and loaded two slices into the toaster. It struck Stella, as she flicked off a text message to Pam that she'd ring soon, how satisfying it was to use her own toaster again.

As she took honey from the cupboard, the sound of Bernard Fanning's *Grow Around You* – the personalised ring tone she'd set for Heath – tinkled from her phone.

Luckily, the honey, which slipped from Stella's hand to the floor at the sound, was encased in plastic, not a glass jar.

'Oh my God,' Stella said aloud. '*Jesus.* Heath's ringing me. What should I do?' Rhetorical question aside, she answered the phone before Bernard Fanning had a chance to sing 'I will throw my love around you' – the words in the song's chorus.

'This is a surprise,' Stella said, moving restlessly and stepping on the jar of honey; its contents spilled onto the floor, oozing between her toes.

'Hey, welcome home.'

Stunned, she said, after an overly long pause, 'Thanks. Yes. I got home yesterday.'

Silence from the other end, and then, 'I read you turned down another play in London for a play back at home.'

Attempting to keep the excitement from her voice – Heath had kept up with her whereabouts? – she replied, 'Oh. Yeah… It sounded like a good opportunity.' Before Heath could respond, she added, 'Um… Mainly, I wanted to come home…' She cleared her voice. 'I wanted to be home for Christmas.' As she waited for him to respond, she stepped off the honey and grabbed a towel to clean off her foot.

'I'd like to catch up,' Heath said. 'Are you free later this afternoon?'

One of the many things Stella loved about Heath was that he preferred a phone call over texts and was always direct.

'Today?'

'Sorry,' Heath said. 'In the first instance, I should have asked if you actually want to catch up, and then asked if you already have plans today?'

'No!' She pulled the phone away to take a few breaths and slowly slid to the ground, her back pressed against the kitchen cabinets. 'I meant to say no, no, I don't have any plans today. And yes, it would be nice to catch up.'

'Okay. There's a band playing at the park near my place.' He cleared his throat. 'How about we meet at three o'clock at the bakery and go from there.'

'Sure…' she said, a bit stunned. 'See you soon. At the bakery.'

Hanging up, Stella unglued herself from the floor, sprinted to the bathroom to jump in the shower, and made an appointment with the hairdresser.

***

Arriving early, Stella snagged a premium park outside the front of the bakery, located at the top of Heath's street. Homey smells of bread, pastries, and coffee wafted through her car window, reminding her of when they'd eat breakfast at the bakery on weekends.

She texted Heath:

Hey! I'm here. I managed to snare the world's best park.

He immediately texted back.

I'm already here. Waiting outside the bakery.

Even though she couldn't see him yet, knowing that Heath was only a few metres away and precisely where he was sitting sent a rush of adrenaline surging through her body. She smoothed her navy and burgundy floral dress and threw a jacket over her bag in case they continued the date on to dinner.

Is this a date?

Neither had dared say.

Stella caught her breath when she saw Heath, casually dressed in a grey t-shirt, jeans, and sneakers, seated at a table behind trees in a garden bed.

She wasn't sure why she jumped out from behind the garden bed and exclaimed, 'Boo!' but was grateful it broke the ice enough to make them both laugh.

Without sunglasses to hide his eyes, Heath couldn't hide the tears welling in them as he stared at Stella. She nervously fussed with her bag and carried on too enthusiastically about how she had no trouble getting a park on the busy street.

Remaining seated, Heath wrapped his arms tightly around her and pulled her close. A light breeze floated over them, gently lifting Stella's hair to wrap around Heath's neck, their hands rubbing each another's back as their cheekbones slotted together, oblivious to everyone around them.

***

Heath and Stella sat on a blanket listening to reggae music, sipping apple ciders in the park, knees and shoulders resting against one another. Though impatient to know more about where they stood, Stella let herself join Heath in surrendering to the music, resisting yelling over the four-beat acoustic drum rhythm in case synapses of feelings expressed were misconstrued. Instead, she basked in the joy of being in his presence – the irony of Bob Marley's *Is This Love* playing, chanting a love language.

Stella leaned back to catch a glimpse of Heath as the singer expressed words about wanting to love and to treat a person right. She was reminded that sometimes when they made love in Heath's apartment, with music playing in the background, she'd make a mental note to replay a particular song later, to transport her to their lovemaking when they weren't together. Heath knew she was looking at him, and she couldn't help but play to that, drawing her torso back and turning her head to watch him.

Later, at dinner, they ordered a bowl of wedges, calamari, and salad to share. As they waited for their meals to arrive, watching each other carefully under the dim amber restaurant lighting, they could have been mistaken for a happy couple out for a dinner date.

'So, it all went according to plan, hey?' Heath said at last. 'I read the reviews – you were a huge hit – even bigger than expected.'

'Flattery will get you everywhere,' Stella jested, flicking her hair over her shoulder. 'To be honest, I think I was in the right place at the right time. From opening night, everything just clicked.'

'You got your second career wind,' Heath commented, and dolloped tartare sauce onto calamari rings. 'Do you feel like you've put all your eggs in one basket, coming back to Australia? The British seem to love you.'

Stella had missed Heath's idiomatic way of speaking, the way he spoke with an authority that suggested he invented the idioms he used. He naturally understood the power of the brevity of words, unlike Stella... She often jammed sentences with convoluted words, sometimes using a complex word with a meaning one might need a dictionary to define.

'It wasn't without its problems...' Stella admitted. 'I had a terrible time with the cast. And... Melanie dying.'

'I'm so sorry about Melanie,' Heath said. 'I thought British audiences might adopt you as a replacement for her.' Seeing that mentioning Melanie upset Stella, he rubbed her arm gently. 'Did you get to spend much time with her?'

'The last time I saw Melanie was at the hospice,' Stella said. 'I felt terrible I didn't try to see her more when she was sick. I was too caught up in performing and not failing in the role, her role… Well.' She looked down at her lap. 'I let a lot of people down.'

'Don't beat yourself up,' Heath said roughly. 'We all mishandle situations. Sometimes fear gets in the way.'

'Oh, it was – it was a surreal experience seeing her at the hospice.' Stella's eyelashes fluttered as she held back tears. 'I remember as I walked out, thinking, knowing it would be the last time I'd see her, seeing all those empty vases in a room next to the bathroom at the hospice… Crystal vases lined up and emptied of flowers because their recipients were dead.' She dashed away a tear before it could trickle down her cheek. 'Melanie's last words to me were about not getting too caught up in my career and focusing on what matters. Though I'd probably go further in my acting career if I stayed in London and agreed to play Lady Macbeth in *Macbeth*,' she admitted, then said, 'Anyway, I'm excited about performing in *The Removalists*. Do you know it? By David Williamson.' She sucked in a deep breath. 'After losing Melanie, I need to be with the people I love.'

Heath paused, then asked, 'Did you throw out the flowers I sent you for opening night…or the other ones I sent…?'

Stella ignored this question and sat up straight in her seat, her demeanour thoughtful. 'When was the last time you saw your girlfriend, Heath?'

He pulled back slightly. 'Two weeks ago. And she isn't my girlfriend.'

She remained silent for a moment before saying, with absolute conviction, 'After tonight, I'm not interested in pursuing anything if either of us has even an atom of attraction towards another person.'

Heath blinked tears away before taking Stella's hand. 'I've missed you and your crazy way with words.'

'I've missed us… But ours is now a complex story.'

A waiter nearing their table to check if they needed anything sensed the increase in intensity in their conversation and did a 180 in the opposite direction.

Picking at crumbs around the side of her plate, Stella continued, 'My brain can't fathom how we can go back… To what we had… I feel like everything we had has been erased.' She sniffed and barely resisted crying. 'It sounds straight out of a B-grade movie, what

I'm about to say, but I'll say it anyway… I can't help thinking of your body as a canvas. It was once a blank canvas and I painted a masterpiece on it, but now…every brushstroke I painted has been painted over – erased – by Candice.'

Heath closed his eyes but said nothing.

She continued, 'You said that you and Candice haven't seen each other for two weeks.'

'That's right.'

'Why did you stop seeing one another?'

Heath shifted his weight on the seat. 'That's not exactly fair. I haven't asked you about Johnny.'

A frown flickered across Stella's face. 'Do you not want to ask me about Johnny because you don't want me to ask you about Candice?'

'We stopped seeing one another because we have…' He stopped before finishing the sentence, sucked in a breath, and said, 'Nothing at all in common. And…'

Stella waited.

'You know I'm still crazy about you,' he said. 'Being with you, I was the happiest I've ever been. In every way.'

'Every way?'

'Yes,' Heath said roughly. 'I love your mind. You make me think. Make me accountable. You make me laugh! And, well – ours was the best love I've ever had.'

'But you wasted no time in moving on.'

'What did you expect?' he asked. 'You got up and left to resurrect your career and left me for dead. You treated me like shit. Be honest.'

She acknowledged this with a nod. 'All my terribleness aside, it was never my intention to hurt you or for the play to end our relationship. I thought you'd at least try to come to London.'

Sitting up straighter, Heath commented, 'How you went about things was gut wrenching… Seeing you drunk as a skunk in Johnny wannabe's apartment…'

'Nothing happened. I didn't cheat on you.' She swallowed hard. 'We were together once *after* I found out that you were with Candice, and I just… I wish I hadn't…' Her voice trailed off.

Green and blue eyes squared off at one another.

Heath said emphatically, 'Neither did I, Stella. I did not cheat on you.'

Neither said anything.

Natalie Merchant's *Jealousy* jangled about in the back of her head – a song questioning if the man's new female lover would have novels by her bedside. Stella contemplated that Candice wouldn't have had books by her bed – and if she did, she wouldn't have read them. She gave in to the irrationality of thinking this way to try to make herself feel better.

Still, they said nothing.

Heath excused himself to go to the bathroom. He eventually re-emerged with some toilet paper scrunched into the top pocket of his shirt. He eased himself back onto the seat, his movements slow and conscious, like he was protecting his bones from breaking.

After another protracted silence, his lips glued together, Heath's bloodshot eyes met Stella's. He blinked several times before speaking. 'Neither of us is innocent in what happened, Stella.' He paused for a moment and then continued. 'Of course, I was devastated about Johnny, as I'm sure you were about Candice.' He sucked in a deep breath and finally said, 'I am so sorry… But you cut me deeply…'

Stella jumped in. 'I know I handled the situation terribly, and I'm so sorry. It's just – I want you to know there's more to the story.'

As her eyes found the floor, she could feel a rash surfacing on her neck.

'*What*, Stella? Has this got to do with what you wanted to tell me on the phone?

She drew in a shaky breath and blurted out, 'I haven't been honest with you, and I hate myself for it.'

CHAPTER 36

Stella equipped herself with a bottle of red wine when she headed out to Heath's apartment – a necessary prop for their impending discussion. Dressed in light blue denim jeans and tan boots, and wearing a French tuck on her crisp white shirt, she knew she looked beautiful, aside from an unfortunate stress rash. She'd intentionally aimed to look her best, using it as a kind of armour to protect herself from Heath's reaction, if things didn't go well. That said, she knew the rash, red and unambiguous, was clear evidence of her anxiety, and Heath knew her too well to interpret it as anything else.

Feeling her heart rate beginning to tick upward, Stella pulled the car to the side of the road and took a few deep breaths as she considered cancelling the date. The conversation with Heath was going to be bad enough; doing so while covered in puffy splotches on the side of her face, neck, and partway down her chest was more suited to a nightmare. She plucked a cold water bottle from the passenger seat and rolled it across her skin, hoping it would help and knowing it was only a band-aid solution, as Heath might say.

Moments later, her phone pinged with a message from Heath.

> I've moved my car out of the garage into the visitors' spot. Park in the garage. See you soon.

See. You. Soon.

Those three anticipatory words reminded Stella that Heath was awaiting her arrival.

Having sufficiently cooled the rash, she resolved to finish what she'd started. She took a moment to fix her make-up and set off again towards Heath.

As she walked up the curved pathway to Heath's apartment, Stella couldn't help but wonder about the last time Candice walked the same path, possibly making idle chatter about the lovely tropical gardens. The pink hydrangeas, which always seemed to be standing to attention, looked wilted and dull, and she brushed the soft petals with her fingertips as she made her way to the door.

Taking a deep breath, she pressed the intercom, holding the button down longer than intended, distracted by thoughts of Candice being the last woman in Heath's apartment.

***

'You look beautiful,' Heath commented as Stella briefly hugged him and made her way to the kitchen, wasting no time in opening the bottle of wine she'd brought.

Candice's ghost was pervasive. In the 30 seconds Stella let the wine breathe, she imagined Candice twirling in the lounge room and fawning over Heath in the kitchen as he cooked. When an image of Candice in Heath's bedroom arose, Stella quashed it. The real issue tonight was for Stella to come clean about her past.

Stella poured two glasses of wine and set them on the coffee table before sitting at one end of the lounge. Heath slowly sank down on the other end, his attention focused on her. Still navigating how to be around one another, neither jumped in to say anything. So much had happened since the last time they were in this room together; they were sniffing around one another like dogs acquainting themselves at a park.

Heath's loungeroom suddenly felt small, and Stella was momentarily tempted to run out the door. Fingers trembling, she gulped her wine and accidentally spilled it down the front of her shirt. Everything she'd rehearsed in anticipation of speaking to Heath had flown out the window.

Stop being so dramatic! Take a breath, Stella. Relax! B-R-E-A-T-H-E.

Instead of taking a breath, as if to stop herself from saying the words as they come out, Stella covered her mouth with her hand, then sputtered so quickly that Heath almost strained his neck, leaning toward her, trying to understand what she'd said.

'I – I never told you why I stopped acting.'

Heath's eyes followed her hands as she pulled at the collar of her shirt. She stood up, thinking she'd dart off to the bathroom to splash water on her face, and then sat back down. The single light at the opposite end of the room felt like someone was shining it in her face, intent on interrogating her. She shifted position, crossed her legs one way and then the other, and jerked at her shirt.

She'd never told a partner that she was assaulted, and it was like there was a block in her throat, strangling the words she wanted to say.

Get up and run, Stella. You don't need to say anything! Run as fast as you can from this apartment.

She took another mouthful of wine for courage. 'I know you've been curious about why I stopped acting.'

'Of course,' Heath said, and then added, a bite to his voice, 'Although, I know it's a *very* sensitive topic.'

Tears spilled down Stella's face as she finally got the all-important words out: 'I … I was assaulted and verbally abused in an acting class.'

'What the hell?'

'By a male actor. In front of other acting students and a director. He did nothing to stop it.'

'What?' Heath sounded stunned. 'Why haven't you told me about this?'

'Shame,' Stella said thickly, dragging the back of her hand across her eyes. 'I wanted to. I did. But the shame…' She shook her head. 'The director made me play a scene where I was a prostitute and the male actor took the scene completely off script. He assaulted me under the guise of acting out the scene.'

Heath shuffled closer to her, clearly trying to make sense of what he was hearing, 'Was it like a casting couch-type incident?'

'Gosh, no! It was nothing like that. But Steve, the actor, pulled my hair, and forced my face into his crotch. I can still feel his hand…' Stella gestured towards the back of her head. 'I feel his filthy hand pushing my head whenever I think about it. For a long time, I found it difficult to be in an intimate relationship. It was different with you because I immediately trusted you.'

Heath visibly softened at her words, emotional at the idea that Stella had been able to trust him in an intimate setting, before rage overtook him. 'Is the dickhead still alive? I'll beat the living shit of him.'

'Yes, he's still alive, and so is the director. He went nowhere in his acting career. As odd as it sounds, in some ways, what Jay, the director said to me that day, and how he humiliated me in front of other actors, negatively impacted me more than what Steve did.'

'And so you stopped acting.'

'Partly.'

'Jesus. That's horrible.'

Stella took a deep breath. 'I had a panic attack when it happened and thought I was going to die. I've struggled with anxiety for years since. It ruined me.'

'That's the other part of what you've been keeping from me?'

Stella looked away as she found her next words, the pain still acute. 'I've always felt so much stigma about having anxiety, particularly because I know how confident I was before. Anxiety felt like a weakness. It's been an old, festering wound that I kept on ignoring until I finally decided to confront it by auditioning for *Streetcar*. And when I auditioned, it opened up all the old trauma I needed to heal. In many ways, auditioning and returning to acting finally addressed the pain I've been carrying with me for a decade. It took all my focus just to get myself onto the stage, which is why I couldn't focus on us.'

'It isn't your fault, the assault,' Heath said gently.

'I know this now,' Stella said, and her words escaped in a rush, so relieved to finally get the confession out. 'But when anxiety first struck me, it was a taboo subject. I've also lived with the remorse of freezing when the assault happened – like I somehow let it happen – the fact is, I couldn't move. And to top it off, I was piss weak and let them get away with it, which probably means they did it to other actors. What's that saying, about bad things happening when good people do nothing? I've been angry at myself for a long time for not speaking about the injustice of it.' She took a moment to regain her composure, and then ventured, 'Even more so, I've been upset for not being honest about my mental health.'

'What stopped you?'

Sniffing snot and wiping mascara from her face, she said, 'The first panic attack I ever had came directly on the heels of my assault. At the time, I had no idea what it was. When they kept happening, I truly believed I was going insane, and I was terrified I'd never get better.' As she pushed each word out, it felt as though she was dislodging something that had been stuck in her throat for far too long.

'My whole body would tremble and my teeth would chatter uncontrollably when I had an attack,' she explained. 'I'd hyperventilate, and I couldn't breathe, and I would be so scared I'd pass out. My mind and heart would both race. Anxiety can feel like you have another heart in your stomach – furiously pounding away. I stopped going out or socialising. The panic attacks felt like an out-of-body experience, almost like I was disassociating from myself. I was a one-winged bird. Eventually, I came across a book called *Power Over Panic* by Bronwyn Fox and realised I have high-functioning anxiety. To be able to label the condition was such a relief.'

Heath wiped a tear from Stella's face and carefully enfolded her in his arms, waiting to make sure she didn't want to pull away. 'I am so sorry that you experienced all of that, and that you felt you couldn't tell anyone. You're the most amazing person I know. And one of the best communicators I know. I never would have known. I don't think any less of you. Honestly, it just makes me think you're even more incredible.'

Stella took some long, deep breaths, soothed and comforted by Heath's understanding. 'I wish I'd told you earlier,' she said after a long moment of just letting herself be held. 'If more people spoke honestly about trauma and mental health, we'd be more compassionate.' She pulled away slightly to look up at his face. 'I'm going to need some time to let everything settle. I want it to work between us, so much, but so much has happened and I don't know where to start.'

Heath cupped her cheek with his hand as he rose to his feet. He went into the bedroom, re-emerging moments later with a canvas.

'You were right,' he said, 'the 1930s Hotel in Paris photo deserved to be painted.' He took a deep breath and turned the canvas around to face her.

'This is my love letter to you.'

CHAPTER 37

One year later

In between acting roles, Stella had positioned herself as a highly coveted public speaker and ambassador for mental health awareness, delivering keynote addresses at national conferences.

It was still easier for her to deliver a high-profile TED-type talk to hundreds of audience members than a handful of university or high school students in a small room.

Whenever she delivered a presentation – large or small – she always called upon her trusty mantra to steel her nerves.

As she stood at the side of the room at her old high school, about to address the students, she silently recited, 'confident, cool, composed Capulet' several times. Then she walked across the room to stand on the stage before the enthusiastic young drama students.

Before she commenced her presentation, she scanned the room to find Heath, spotting him seated discreetly near the back. His quiet and encouraging presence was always welcome at these talks.

'Hello everyone,' Stella said, a smile on her face as she looked out at the bright faces in the auditorium. 'My name is Stella Longhurst. I've been in a couple shows you might have heard of. I'm an actress and I have anxiety. There's an odd juxtaposition in that sentence – actress and anxiety!' She laughed, lightening the mood. 'Just because someone is deemed successful, it doesn't mean they mightn't struggle with mental health. I'm here to tell you that as dire as anxiety might feel at times, it is not a reason to live a small life or to think that you're not good enough. Or that you can't succeed as a performer.'

She paused and waited for the rustling and murmurs to die down before continuing. 'Now, I'm not saying that having anxiety doesn't create challenges, but it's a lot more commonplace than most people realise. In fact, anxiety is one of the most diagnosed mental health conditions globally.' She paused and moved to the side of the stage to commence the PowerPoint presentation. 'According to the Australian Institute of Health and Welfare, approximately two in five Australians aged 16 to 85 have experienced a mental health condition at some point during their life. Just in the past 12 months, one in five Australians has experienced a mental health condition.' She let that sink in for a moment before continuing, 'The good news is that there are many practical tools and techniques available to help you manage your anxiety.'

'Mental health conditions like anxiety and depression are often referred to as being "all in your head" or, in other words, imaginary and not a "real" disease. But there are real psychological changes that happen!'

She clicked to the next slide, an image of the brain.

'Now, I've got to give a disclaimer here: while I have years of experience wrangling with anxiety and its effects on my life, I'm not a doctor and therefore can't offer medical advice. That said, I don't recommend hiding from your anxiety. It can be a hard approach to take because anxiety, like depression and other mental health conditions, is heavily weighed down by social stigma. But hiding it, pretending it's not sitting on your shoulder, simply doesn't work in the long term. As actors, we're almost too good at morphing our real selves for the roles that we play, and it can be tempting to perform the role of yourself as a character without anxiety. This is what I did for many years. I was ashamed of myself, that I couldn't push through my anxiety. Actors are meant to be confident, right? We're supposed to be able to own every room we walk into, to exude confidence from every pore. But that's a deceptive image, one that's not representative of the actual experience of an acting career.'

She noted several students nodding at her words.

'Okay, so, I'd like to do a little exercise. You don't have to participate if you feel uncomfortable, but to help everyone feel more at ease, I'd like you all to close your eyes.' She waited a moment and then said, 'Can you put your hand up if you knew before today that most people experience anxiety at some point in their life?'

Many of the small group of students shot their hands into the air.

'Can you put your hand up if you knew that anxiety triggers a fight or flight response?'

A few hands went down as a few others went up.

'The fight or flight response is triggered when your brain reacts to a threatening situation or environment by sending adrenalin zooming through your body,' Stella explained. 'It's a physiological response that you don't have any control over because it's an automatic defence mechanism designed to keep you alive. Sometimes it can be so strong you might feel like you're going to die, but it's simply how we've evolved to keep ourselves safe from threats. In other words, while it might feel like you're having a heart attack, anxiety is not life threatening. So, moving on, could you lower your hands but keep your eyes closed. I want you to raise your hand if you know someone who suffers from anxiety.'

Several hands popped into the air, some slower and more hesitant than others.

'Okay,' Stella said. 'One more question. If you've already got your hand up, leave it up this time. Again, keeping your eyes closed, please put your hand up if, at any point in your life, you've experienced anxiety.' She watched as every student in the room raised their hand, heads cocking at the sound of the mass movement.

'Now,' she continued, 'I want you all to open your eyes and look around.'

Eyes opened and a murmur spread throughout the room as everyone took in the scene.

'As you can see,' Stella said, 'you're not alone. Every person who struggles with anxiety is surrounded by other people who know exactly what that feels like. You can put your hands down now.' She waited until the students had resettled and said, 'Some of us find it easier to deal with anxiety when it hits. Again, I'm not a doctor, but I guess you could put it down to differences in brain chemistry along with differences in access to resources.' She nodded to the brain on the slide.

'What's important to remember is that you are not alone – and there is help available. But because there's so much stigma around anxiety and other mental health disorders, it's common not to ask for help. It takes courage to open up, to discuss wanting and needing help is coping, and it's those courageous discussions that are needed to break down the stigma around mental health and traumatic experiences. I've struggled to deal with my vulnerability around these topics, and for much of my life I've felt ashamed for my struggles. Being an actress taught me how to pretend and create a mask for myself, something I'm sure many of you also have experience with. But as actors, we must be especially alert to the ways that such coping mechanisms can actually cause us further harm. The truth is the thing about shame is that it eventually has to release itself.'

As Stella looked out over her audience, she felt a sense of satisfaction akin to acting, except it healed a separate part of her. She had spent so many years letting Jay Styler and Steve Crosley control her life, the shame she'd felt at her assault overriding everything else she had ever wanted to do, making her doubt who she was. Now she had come to accept it as part of her past, part of what had made her who she was, but it no longer ruled her life. They no longer possessed any control over who she was or how she lived her life – and that, perhaps, was the greatest thing of all. Her success as an actress and public speaker was the sweetest revenge.

She stood with a smile on her face, finally at peace with herself after so many years.

Confident, cool, composed, Stella Longhurst had arrived.

Acknowledgments

Thank you to my dear family and friends for supporting me on this journey.

I would like to acknowledge the following people:

To my son, Oscar – you've always been a creative spirit. Chase what calls you, because anything's possible. It really is. I love you.

John and Marie Farrell, thank you for being parents who encouraged my creative pursuits (and for not thinking I was crazy when I rehearsed my acting lines opposite a tree in our front yard). You believed in me as a writer, Dad, so I hope you're proud up there. Thanks also to my brothers, Michael and Robert, for putting up with me as an ambitious young actress.

Makenzi Crouch, my brilliant editor, thank you for investing in this story.

Valerie Foley and Tess Merlin, thank you for casting your sharp eyes over this manuscript.

Thanks to those who read this novel's first draft and offered feedback and support: Kim, Jac, Jenny, Chris, Nicole, Dylan, and Rebbell.

Veronica, thank you for introducing me to the arts.

Geord, thank you for putting that book under my nose that day.

Most importantly, dearest readers, thank you for taking the time to read my book. I genuinely hope you enjoyed it.

Karen Farrell is a debut author from the northern beaches of Sydney, Australia.

With over 30 years of experience as a communications specialist, commissioned writer, and editor, she has built a reputation as both a masterful storyteller and a respected industry professional. Karen was the Project Editor for Simone Callahan's wellbeing book, *Growing with Grace*, published by Simon & Schuster in 2024.

A former actress, Karen brings a unique depth of insight to her writing. In her debut novel, *Stella's Next Act*, she weaves her passion for acting and her firsthand knowledge of the entertainment industry into a compelling tale of love, loss, and the pursuit of dreams. With lyrical prose and richly drawn characters, Karen invites readers into the world of actress Stella Longhurst, crafting a story that lingers long after the final page.

www.ingramcontent.com/pod-product-compliance
Lightning Source LLC
Chambersburg PA
CBHW020008140726
47904CB00018B/2001